To the lovely Sonja.
Thank you for all the
interest you have shown
whilst the book was being
published.
With love and.
Best Regards

G. Delacroix

LOVE IN THE
SHADOWS OF WAR

Guillaume Delacroix

MINERVA PRESS

MONTREUX LONDON WASHINGTON

LOVE IN THE SHADOWS OF WAR
Copyright © Guillaume Delacroix 1997

ISBN 1 86106 203 6

First published 1997 by
MINERVA PRESS
195 Knightsbridge
London SW7 1RE

Printed in Great Britain by
Antony Rowe Ltd, Chippenham, Wiltshire

LOVE IN THE
SHADOWS OF WAR

A Romantic Historical Wartime Novel

Contents

EUROPE
1939–1944

The Clouds of War

It was Friday the thirteenth. Arthur Lansdown would never go to the races on Friday the thirteenth: 'It's bad luck,' he thought.

This time, however, he made an exception because he wanted to speak to his friend, James Fenbeau, who was a racehorse trainer. Arthur wanted to impress upon him the need to evacuate to England; the clouds of war were hanging over Europe and James was by birth an Englishman.

Arthur was the British Consul in Brussels, and as such he felt responsible for warning British subjects living in Belgium about what could happen to them should they be caught by a German army of occupation. James and his family were special to him and he wanted them to benefit from his personal understanding of the present European crisis. He had to act fast because his transfer to the British Embassy in Paris had suddenly been brought forward. His fears that the Germans would invade the Low Countries in the spring of 1940 stemmed more from his personal understanding of events rather than official sources. He wanted James to act on his advice and not listen to the Belgian and French High Command, who believed themselves to be superior in strength to the Germans. As far as Arthur was concerned, only the sea would stop the Germans. If James and his family stayed in Belgium, they would be made political prisoners of war in view of their British connections by birth, marriage and descent. To him nothing was more pressing than that they should evacuate to England; it was already October 1939.

One of James Fenbeau's horses had been entered for the 2.30 race, and that was Arthur's reason for going to the races on Friday the thirteenth. It was 2 p.m. when he drove his car into the grounds of the racecourse at Groenendael. He parked his car and made his way straight to the paddock where he knew James would be; he could see him giving the jockey his final instructions. He didn't rush. He could afford to wait, the rest of the day was his. The only thing that was on his mind right now was whether he could resist the temptation to place a bet; already his eyes were picking out a favourite. His compulsion to gamble was as strong as, if not stronger than his belief that Friday the thirteenth was unlucky.

When James finished talking to the jockey he made his way to the grandstand to watch the race. As he walked past the betting shop he could not believe his eyes when he caught sight of Arthur.

"Arthur!" It was the tone of voice in which James called out his name that made him look round sheepishly: he'd been caught in the act.

"Hello James – didn't think you'd be finished so soon – I saw you talking to the jockey." Arthur failed miserably in his attempt to pre-empt James's implication.

"Am I seeing things or are you just pretending to gamble? I didn't even expect to see you here on Friday the thirteenth, let alone gambling."

"It's you I came especially to see, old friend, so if I've done wrong then you are to blame. I suppose the next thing you'll tell me is that I picked the wrong horse."

"Well if you didn't put your money on my horse, which I suspect you didn't, then there is a strong possibility that you have. And it's too late now – they're under starter's orders."

"What are you saying? The other day when you entered that horse for the race you told me that all you wanted from her was to run and get the feel of things, not win."

"I know, I know." The gesture James made indicated that it was just one of those things which happens unexpectedly. "It's the very thing I was discussing with the jockey. That filly is running well and I have a strong feeling that she wants to be up in front. I told him not to push her, but if she wants to be in front then let her. If I'd known you would be gambling on Friday the thirteenth I would have tipped you off – she's running at 100 to 1."

"Damn!" It was Arthur's safety valve – he just had to say it. Nothing gave him more pleasure than to bet on a good outsider which, occasionally, James made possible through his understanding of horses. Now he was going to miss out – it was too late.

Both were watching through their binoculars. James was right – that filly wanted to be up in front. They could see the jockey letting her run the course her own way, and when the horses came racing past the finishing post she was still in front and three lengths ahead of the second horse.

"Damn!" said Arthur again.

"I'll have to go, Arthur. I'm supposed to be in the winner's stall to receive them. You said you came especially to see me – what is it?"

"Oh, it can wait until you're finished with the formalities." It was obvious that Arthur was disappointed.

Before they parted, James pushed a piece of paper into his hand on which he had scribbled the name of a horse for the next race. He'd managed to do this whilst Arthur wasn't looking.

"Place a bet on this one in the next race – it's a certainty, but it's not 100 to 1."

The piece of paper gave Arthur a new lease of life. The sparkle returned to his eyes and Friday the thirteenth was completely forgotten.

"Meet you back here, okay?"

"Okay."

His eyes returned to the piece of paper which he held open like a treasure map. When James said it was a certainty then, unless lightning struck, he knew that he could depend upon it, but the odds were poor.

When they met again James had that confident look about him, as he rightly deserved. Arthur had the expression that said it all: "I won."

Seeing him reminded James. "Oh yes, what was it that brought you to the races especially to see me?"

"I am leaving for Paris sooner than I thought," Arthur began. "Tuesday of next week in fact. I had to see you today because I am finalising everything over the weekend and Monday is the only weekday I've got to settle my affairs in town."

"Oh no! What brought this on? Isabel and Madeleine will be disappointed." James immediately thought of his wife Isabel and Madeleine his daughter-in-law, who were already heartbroken because he had told them that a transfer was in the offing for the spring.

"That's the whole reason for my wanting to see you today," continued Arthur. "I may not have the opportunity to speak to you on the subject before we meet again. I'm convinced that, come spring, the Germans will launch an attack through the Low Countries to get into France. If that happens it will be so sudden that you and your family will be caught. I don't have to tell you what that means. You were in Belgium during the last war, constantly hiding for fear of being made a political prisoner of war, but this time you have your grandchildren to think of. Take my advice and evacuate to England before it is too late. This is not an official recommendation, but take it from one who knows and don't listen to the Belgian and French High Command. They put too much faith in the Maginot Line and the Albert Canal."

James listened to every word Arthur said. He was right about the last war – he had suffered, and the very thought of another German occupation frightened him. This time, however, his circumstances were different. During the last war he had been penniless, but now he owned property and a business which he acquired soon after the war, when his boss had signed over the deeds to him on the understanding that he would clear his debts and his name. James had taken on the challenge and made it and it was his son and grandchildren of whom he was now thinking. He intended his business to pass on to them. To evacuate to England meant that he would lose everything for which he and his son had worked so hard. The other problem on his mind was his family, who were of different nationalities, scattered all over Europe. His son George was married to Madeleine who was French, his daughter Yvonne was married to Jean who was Belgian and his wife, Isabel, was from the Netherlands. He himself had no family left in England so his family by marriage were the only ones of whom he had to think.

Arthur kept quiet. He could see that James was doing a lot of thinking and, knowing the circumstances, he realised that it would not be easy. In his opinion, however, James would lose out on property and business anyway, because, once the Germans attacked, property would either be destroyed during the fighting or confiscated by the army of occupation. He was more concerned for their lives. Some disturbing rumours were now circulating about atrocities being committed by the Gestapo during the fighting. Groenendael, where James lived, was situated in the south-east sector of Brussels where the British Expeditionary Force had been sent to defend the Brussels sector. The fighting was bound to be fierce.

It was James who finally broke the silence.

"I know you mean well, but move to England? I'm not sure that's possible. Most of the horses in my stables are owned by Baron Declercq as you know. I owe him some loyalty. He told me the other day that he has been ordered to take up a command post at the front line near Maastricht. He too spoke of a possible German attack and should this happen he asked me to evacuate his horses to his farm near Concarneau in Brittany. We could stay there until things blow over."

Arthur was looking down at his feet as he listened. How could he convince James that the German *Blitzkrieg* was something to be really feared, and that Brittany or any other place in France was not safe because, in his opinion, only the sea would stop the Germans?

"Do you really think that the Germans could break through and overrun France?" James asked the question more because he saw that Arthur was disappointed when he had said that he would follow the Baron's request rather than take his advice. This saddened him – Arthur was a good man and would always be fair to him, but he did not have the same understanding of the German strike force that Arthur had.

"I'm certain of it," replied Arthur, "but it would take me hours to explain the strategic implications and then I'm not sure that I could convince you of the danger you are facing."

James felt caught already. What was he to do? Arthur was a man who knew what he was talking about and his advice should not be taken lightly, but this was something he could not decide on his own. It concerned the whole family and the Baron.

"All right, I'll speak to George and the rest of the family. Together we'll speak to the Baron – we'll have to work something out."

"That pleases me, James, that pleases me," repeated Arthur. "Try to come up with the right decision. Evacuate from the Continent – it's a matter of life or death."

James gave one of those nodding movements with his head which indicated 'all right, point taken, but that's a hell of a thing to ask of anyone.'

He turned the conversation away from evacuation because he had to return to the van which was ready, waiting to take the horse back to the stables. George, his son, was already there.

"Listen, Arthur, I took the liberty of phoning Isabel and Madeleine to tell them that you're here and that you would be coming round for dinner. You are staying, aren't you?" The way he put it made it impossible for Arthur to say no.

"Yes, of course, I wouldn't dream of leaving without saying goodbye. Thanks."

The two parted. Arthur returned to his car to make his way to the house. The racecourse at Groenendael was situated on the main Brussels to Charleroi road and James's house was only a short distance from this main road, close to the railway station of Groenendael, about two or three kilometres from where he now was.

Madeleine was by the window overlooking the courtyard in front of the house which gave a full view of the main gate through which Arthur's car would arrive. Across the other side of the road lay the forest. She was very pensive. His visit was so unexpected and James hadn't said why he was here when he phoned because at that time he hadn't known himself, only that Arthur was there specifically to see him. Her two children, Jeannine and Pierre, were staying with their favourite school friends, the Bronowskys, until evening, when her husband George would pick them up straight from work.

It was about 5 p.m. and Arthur wouldn't be long now. Suddenly she was disturbed from her thoughts by the sound of a car. She looked through the window and saw his Chevrolet turn into the courtyard; she recognised it at once.

"Bobon! Arthur is here!"

Bobon was the name given to Isabel by her grandchildren. It was a term of endearment given to grandmothers in Belgium, so to everyone Isabel was also known as 'Bobon'.

"All right," came a reassuring reply from the kitchen. "I'm putting the kettle on."

Arthur was very fond of his tea. He knew that the family made tea the English way, not like the Belgians who used tea for medical purposes and not for pleasure.

Madeleine was at the front door even before Arthur's Chevrolet came to a stop. She was a beautiful woman in her early thirties with shapely shoulders and bosom, which were fully exposed by the fashionable dress she wore. She was a very animated person, full of enthusiasm. Because this was so special to her character she showed enthusiasm even when she didn't want to, to avoid disappointing those who expected it from her.

"Arthur, I'm so pleased to see you. Do tell me that all these rumours of war and invasion are just that – rumours." All this she said before giving poor Arthur a chance to come in.

He quickly stepped into the hall without paying the slightest attention to Madeleine's animated greeting, simply because he was so accustomed to her ways. He shook himself slightly to get rid of the few raindrops on his jacket; it had started to rain.

"I hope this rain doesn't set in for the rest of the evening. I hate driving in town with the windscreen wipers going all the time." He wore glasses with such strong lenses that they made his eyes look small – he was very short-sighted. Sometimes, to examine an article with small print, he would lift up his glasses and hold the article practically against his face in order to read it. Only when he removed his glasses was the soft expression in his dark brown eyes revealed. Women found them irresistible. He spoke French with only a trace of an English accent.

Madeleine, standing slightly on tiptoe, kissed him on both cheeks, as was the custom in Belgium.

"You poor dear," she said, dropping the premature barrage of questions fired at him earlier on. "Come in. Bobon is making you a cup of tea," she added confidentially.

"Ah, just what I need," he replied.

Then, throwing his voice in the direction of the kitchen to Isabel, he shouted "Hello Isabella," accentuating the 'a' in Isabella. Just one of his little jokes, the origin of which had long been forgotten.

"Hello Arthur. I won't be long with the tea," came the reply.

Arthur gave a playful grimace and for a split second he betrayed the expression of a little boy for whom a special delicacy was being prepared. However, he soon adopted his usual manner, that of the diplomat, the consular adviser.

He entered the room. It was a warm and embracing room, very well-furnished but with just a trace of pretentious grandeur. It was no surprise to him that Madeleine came straight to the point and asked him the reason for his visit to the racecourse on Friday the thirteenth – that was her way. He hesitated for a few seconds before answering because he knew that the news of his sudden transfer to Paris would upset her. He searched for the right words to soften the blow.

"You remember my telling you that a transfer to Paris was being discussed at the embassy?" he began. "Well, it's been confirmed." He paused.

Madeleine's face changed from a look of bubbly enthusiasm to a painful expression which he knew would culminate in a plea asking him to revoke what he had just said, for at that moment she was unable to take it in.

"No, tell me it's not true!" But his eyes lowered and he remained silent. She put her head against his shoulder as a sign of submission to the inevitable. Then came the final blow. She lifted her head and asked, "When?"

Before he could answer they were disturbed by the footsteps of Isabel entering the living room. It was his sudden move towards Isabel to greet her which convinced Madeleine that he didn't want to answer her question just yet.

'He must be going to Paris sooner than we thought,' she concluded.

Arthur took the cup from Isabel, placed it on the table and greeted her warmly with the usual kisses on both cheeks. Isabel was a small woman with a round figure and greying hair which she wore in a chignon. The hard work of her earlier years had taken their toll.

She immediately sensed the atmosphere.

"Why are you both behaving so strangely? Is there something wrong?"

The silence that followed was as awkward as it was long. Arthur didn't want to be the one to speak first because he was bringing sad news, and Madeleine was still trying to take in what he had said.

"Well?" Isabel insisted, her eyes moving between Arthur and Madeleine.

It was Madeleine who spoke first.

"Arthur's transfer to Paris has been confirmed. He's leaving sooner than we thought."

"Yes I am," he replied. His words were directed to Isabel, but it was Madeleine at whom he was looking. She turned her eyes away so as not to meet his and pretended to rearrange the cushions on the sofa. It was not hard to sense the underlying feeling between them.

"Much sooner than we thought? How soon then?" persisted Isabel.

"Tuesday of next week." He was still looking at Madeleine, who suddenly stopped fussing with the cushions.

"Tuesday! But that's only three days away!" She looked him straight in the eyes: she didn't care to hide her feelings any longer.

"Oh Arthur, we'll miss you," interrupted Isabel, in a way that took the drama out of the atmosphere.

"Don't think you've got rid of me yet," he said with a playful gesture towards her. "Paris is not a thousand miles away."

"Of course it isn't. I'll pick you up from the central station myself," added Madeleine with a pretence of enthusiasm, but she had great difficulty in hiding her grief.

A more relaxed atmosphere followed these light-hearted remarks, and Arthur felt as though a weight had been lifted from his shoulders.

"Tell me, what made you go to the racecourse on Friday the thirteenth? I've never known you to do that. You could have come straight here," enquired Madeleine.

"I wanted to talk to James privately," he replied. Then, adopting the manner of the consular adviser to which Madeleine reacted very fast, he continued, "It's a matter of grave concern for me that none of you are caught by a German army of occupation."

"You're talking as though the Germans will definitely overrun this country. Please don't frighten me like this," interrupted Madeleine, who was genuinely frightened by what he was saying. The words, 'invasion' and 'occupation' were used so often in conversation these last few weeks that it gave everyone a sense of insecurity. "Have you heard something in diplomatic circles that we don't know of?" she continued searchingly.

Arthur sensed that he had frightened Madeleine and quickly returned to his more familiar tone of voice.

"I don't know any more than what is said on the news, but I do feel that with England and France already at war with Germany the safest place for you all is England."

Isabel grew more concerned with each word he spoke. By nature she was very protective, especially towards her grandchildren.

"What about Yvonne, my daughter, and her two little boys? I can't possibly leave them. Jean is in the front line, you know." Her voice sounded both apologetic and pleading.

"But wouldn't Monsieur Van Den Bos take care of Yvonne and her two boys? After all, she is more than a housekeeper in that family and Jean is more than the chauffeur." He made this remark because he knew the circumstances of the relations between Yvonne and Monsieur Van Den Bos, who was also her employer and landlord.

"Oh yes, I dare say he would, but he has his own family to think of and he must think of them first – they are wholly dependent on him. His wife would insist on it."

Arthur came to the conclusion that his attempt to advise the family to evacuate could be fruitless, but then he had never thought it would be easy. If only he could make them see just how dangerous their position was without driving them into a state of panic. He knew that he couldn't convince Madeleine of this danger because, in her opinion, the signing of a non-aggression pact by most countries at the Treaty of Locarno in 1926, when she was a young woman, was a landmark in European history and it had been said that it would put an end to all wars. Since then she had fixed her mind on bringing up her children without being torn by the anxiety that her sons would be killed on the battlefield for some obscure cause, and she could not be dissuaded from that belief.

"Everything will be resolved, given time," she argued.

Arthur didn't want to rob her of that belief, because it would only throw her into despair. He became the listener rather than the adviser. The purpose of his visit was not to be.

So engrossed were they in their conversation that none of them heard James enter the house. George had gone straight from the stables to collect Jeannine and Pierre. James gave a sigh of relief when he entered the house and heard that the conversation was not about war and evacuation. Arthur was the first to realise that he had entered the room.

"Don't stop on my account," began James, seeing that he had been observed. "What did you think of the race? That Baron knows a thing or two about horses. We've got Barnum and Ivory and now this filly – I wouldn't be surprised if we had another winner here."

Arthur had a broad smile on his face as he listened to James talking about his favourite hobby – horses, racing.

Isabel recognised the signs.

"Come on, Madeleine, we'd better go into the kitchen and prepare dinner – this is man's talk."

George had now returned with the children. The living room door flew opened and in walked Jeannine and Pierre. They both had a look of anticipation in their eyes. Jeannine had long, dark, wavy hair which framed her face and fell below her shoulders. Although she was only fourteen, she looked very grown-up and showed signs of becoming a beautiful young woman. Pierre had fair hair which he must have inherited from his mother's side. He was very tall for his age, but he still had that boyish look. There was a difference of eighteen months between their ages; he was thirteen.

The look of anticipation was connected with Arthur's visit. They moved as fast as they could towards him. The reason was simple. Not so long ago two films had been released, Walt Disney's *Snow White and the Seven Dwarfs* and the other by Warner Bros., *The Adventures of Robin Hood*, starring Errol Flynn. Both were in Technicolor – one of the seven wonders of the modern world. Arthur had bought them each a sticker album relating to these films, for which they now collected the picture cards found in the wrappers of Belgian chocolates. He never failed to bring one or even two bars of these chocolates for each of them, and this was the reason for all the excitement.

"Uncle Arthur, I've got one third of the pictures for my album – we swap the duplicates at school. I've got three more – look!" exclaimed Pierre as he drew close to Arthur and showed him the pictures.

"And I've got two for my album of Snow White," said Jeannine, also showing him some pictures.

"Children, children!" protested Madeleine, who had returned from the kitchen into the living room. "Where are your manners? Say hello to Uncle Arthur first – all this excitement!"

But he was too delighted to take offence, for he liked to spoil them whilst they were still at this age.

"Heaven knows they grow up fast enough," Arthur would say. His own daughter was now a married woman. But he always played a little game by pretending that he didn't know what all the fuss was about. He knew that they wouldn't dare come out with the question, although it was written all over their faces.

"All right, you two," he said finally, unable to hold back any longer. "They're in my coat pocket." With that he produced four bars of chocolate containing the picture cards. He laughed. The whole episode amused him no end.

"Aren't they lucky to be children at a time when such a remarkable man as Walt Disney is alive? Pure magic, pure magic."

George had now joined the party and after the usual greetings he said, "Buying those albums was one of your greatest ideas. It keeps them occupied for hours."

The evening meal was enjoyed in very much the same way as usual. The conversation was light-hearted and there was a warm atmosphere of togetherness. Arthur had now forgotten about Friday the thirteenth, but the feeling that all this could soon come to an end hung over him.

It was a cold winter. The country lay under a deep blanket of snow. In some areas in Europe the temperature fell to -20 Celsius. The Fenbeaux were not too badly affected because in their living room they had an open fire which gave out glowing heat, but most villagers were less fortunate and suffered from the bitter cold. The early morning rides were hard for James and George when they had to take the horses for their daily exercise. As they rode along the Brussels to Charleroi road, passing under the little railway bridge leading to the training track, both man and beast were engulfed in the steam of their own breath as it condensed about them. Walking in Indian file, the stable lads were constantly breathing into their hands to keep them warm. The cold made it difficult to keep a firm grip on the reins. Most of them wore insufficient clothing to withstand the cold. They were even too cold to admire the botanical gardens through which they had to ride in order to reach the training track. Normally they would spare an admiring glance at the garden, but when they were feeling so cold they had but one thought – to get back to the stables where they knew that Isabel and Madeleine had the stove glowing in the store room, waiting with hot drinks to revive their half-frozen bodies. It was this outdoor life which gave James and George their tanned look and lined their faces with deep cracks around the mouth and forehead; George was so like his father in every way.

The store room and tack room, where saddles and bridles were hanging from the walls, had a strong smell of polished leather. Simone was always to be seen in and around the place helping with the chores. Her husband, Raymond, was the chief hand at the stables and they lived in the small but comfortable apartment above the store room. They were childless. Raymond was part of the stables: he had been there ever since James acquired it in 1918. He had been there throughout the hardship of the earlier years and was now enjoying the better days. His favourite saying was 'Let's hope it lasts' – probably because in his opinion racing was a gamble.

"So what's in the news this morning?" enquired James of Isabel, who was glancing at that day's paper.

"Oh dear. It seems that there's been more trouble in the Atlantic Ocean. The Germans are sinking merchant ships, and near Norway they sank another warship. I'm getting worried – there doesn't seem to be any sign of reconciliation between us and the Germans," she replied.

"Reconciliation!" cried Raymond as though someone had suddenly rattled his cage. "This lull in the fighting is only due to the winter. You mark my words, as soon as spring is here we'll see an escalation in this war."

"Raymond, must you always look at the black side of things?" said his wife reproachfully.

"Well, it seems a natural enough conclusion to come to," he added, determined to have the last word.

"Pay no attention to him, Isabel – he's no expert in these matters, but he knows how to get you going." She gave her husband a hard stare.

"I don't think Hitler will push this war between France and England any further than he has to," began James, looking into space like one who knows. "It's Nazism versus Communism – that's the real issue here. I don't think Hitler has any desire to enter into a conflict with the whole of Europe. Of course things could go wrong and upset all his plans. That would give him a problem, because the slightest hardship suffered by the German people could land him in a lot of trouble." Then, quoting something he must have read, he added, "'The fortunes of a man destroyed are blown away as easily as the dried leaves of autumn.'" He was still looking into space as he uttered the quotation. Then he suddenly turned to George and said, "Come on, son, let's go out for one more run – you take Barnum for a canter. Be careful, though. He doesn't like the hard ground." Turning to the stable lads who were still warming themselves, James added, "After you've warmed up, you lads get on with your work."

The stable lads sat there looking very impressed. They'd heard every word James had spoken, but the message had gone straight over their heads – it sounded impressive though.

"I'll saddle the horses for you, Monsieur James," said André, the youngest of the stable lads. With that, he bounced to his feet and opened the door for him.

"Good lad," James said as he walked out.

"Are you sure you're warm enough?" Isabel called after him.

"I shall fall asleep if I stay any longer, dearest. We'd best get this over with – we'll have plenty of time to sit and warm ourselves later."

As the two men walked out, the ice crunched under their feet.

Mady

Although Baron Declercq was now in the army, his two daughters, Dédé and Mady, maintained their regular visits to the stables owned by James Fenbeau. Each of them had received a horse as a birthday present from their father, and these were kept and cared for at the stables. Dédé was the eldest. She was fifteen years of age but looked nearer eighteen. She was a very aristocratic looking young lady, especially in her riding outfit, with her long dark hair. She was an excellent horse rider. When she sat in the saddle the horse and she became one in movement. When exercising and in full gallop, her long dark hair seemed alive as the current of air passed through it and gave it movement like that of a dolphin gliding through water.

Mady, the younger, was the same age as Pierre – by all but two months. She was still very young with an angel-like face. She had light brown hair which she wore in a pony tail, but everyone agreed that when she grew into a young woman her angel-like face would bring every young man to his knees. She was very religious, so much so that it worried her father, perhaps because some members of the family had already entered the Church. He didn't want to lose his little daughter to some religious order which denied themselves all worldly attachment.

The horses were specially trained and suited to young people. They had once belonged to the Belgian *gendarmerie*, who, for one reason or another, had dismissed them from their specialised duties, but they were obedient and remained manageable in most traffic conditions. Jeannine and Pierre took part in exercising and grooming the horses. The four went out together, two riding and the other two walking alongside. This they took in turns. Their favourite haunt was the gentle valley of the forest only a short distance from the stables where the River Ijzer flowed and formed a string of lakes across the Forêt-de-Soigne. It wound along, passing through the village of Hoeylaert and so onwards to add its waters to the River Schelde.

The valley was an ideal place for horse riding. Round the lakes were grassy areas where they could canter and gallop to their hearts' content without being afraid of getting caught by overhanging branches.

Along the valley there was also a wide footpath where they could walk the horses. It started at the embankment of the Brussels to Charleroi road and railway line and ran as far as the edge of the forest where the village of Hoeylaert began.

On a hot summer's day the lakes were an open invitation for bathing. This, however, was against forestry laws. Bathing was not allowed. A year ago Pierre and Mady had discovered that the hard way. They had been in the valley on their bicycles on an extremely hot day and the temptation had been too great. Both had stripped to their underpants and gone into the water.

It was just their bad luck that the forester was in the area. They saw him but it was too late. Hiding amongst the tall reeds of the lake, they watched him cycle by. They could not be seen but their bicycles and clothes were only partly hidden and he soon discovered them.

He did no more, but gathered their clothes together and then, in a loud voice, shouted, "All right, you daredevils! You can pick up your clothes at the Maison Communale (Town Hall). Let's see how you explain that to your mum and dad."

Rather than face their parents, Pierre and Mady had followed the forester on their bicycles wearing nothing but their wet underpants. Fortunately the ancient château which houses the Maison Communale could be reached without going through the village.

Never had the two been more frightened than when they entered the great hall of the château and came face to face with a policeman. Pierre begged and pleaded with him not to tell their parents because it meant that they would not be allowed to go out together again, and that seemed to frighten him more than anything else. Mady hadn't stopped crying since they left the lake. The whole of her little body shook with fear.

After solemnly promising that this would never happen again, they were allowed to go. So ashamed were they that the incident was to remain their secret. Sometimes they would throw each other a quick glance as they passed the lake, which reminded them of that day, and it was to become their special lake.

One day in April 1940, when the four children went out for their usual ride in the forest, there was a strange atmosphere surrounding their outing. They rode towards the embankment of the main road to start their walk along the wide footpath, but they were very subdued. It had all started at the stables where the neighbours were gathered to discuss the escalation of the war. Denmark was occupied by the Germans. King Haaken of Norway was appealing to all Norwegians to fight. Sweden had to bow to the Nazi ultimatum. All these events were being discussed. The four couldn't help overhearing, but what upset them most was what M. Questiau, who was James's closest neighbour, had said. He argued that the High Command of France, Belgium and Holland were to blame for not doing something to prevent fear spreading amongst the people.

"It was", he said, "up to them to advise the people what to expect if an invasion did take place, and what to do. It's not as though they had no idea," he added. "Some sort of lesson must have been learned from the *Blitzkrieg* so far. In Poland it was said that the refugees caused so much congestion on the roads that the Polish army was paralysed. And what of those rumours of atrocities being committed against civilians by the Gestapo? They are all intended to demoralise the civilians, and demoralise they do. Isn't that what's happening to us now?" he shouted.

On that note the four had left and it was this which had left a bitter taste and caused the bad atmosphere.

Mady, being an oversensitive creature, was the one most affected. She was frightened and the convoy of army vehicles along the main road added to her distress. It was a reminder of the oncoming war. Her thoughts went to her father who was stationed near Maastricht at the fortress of Eben Emael, which guarded the confluence of the Albert Canal and the River Meuse on the Dutch-Belgian border. The fortress was said to be impregnable, but it was bound to be the first object of enemy attack. She began to pray for his safety.

"Please take me to the little chapel, Pierre," pleaded Mady suddenly, on the brink of tears.

None asked why, because all of them knew how she felt. Pierre gave Dédé a quick glance. Being the eldest, it was for her to say yes or no. Dédé, although not affected in the same way, understood.

"All right," she said, "but don't be too long. We will go for our walk to the end of the footpath – we'll meet you back here."

To reach the chapel they had to follow the path up alongside the embankment and then cross the main road. On the other side of the road there was a bridle-path leading to the Château Prince Léopold at Bonne Odeur, the name given to the area where the château and the little chapel were located.

Whenever they were alone, they would ride double, Pierre in front and Mady behind in the saddle of her grey mare, which she called Désirée.

She held on tightly to him as she normally did when something disturbed her, her head resting on his shoulder, silent all the way. They were too young to understand, but a relationship of love was already theirs.

Pierre stood near the chapel holding Désirée by the reins while he watched Mady, who was kneeling on the steps of the chapel which was known by the name of Our Lady of the Lovely Scent (Notre Dame de Bonne Odeur). It was a small chapel with a statue of Mary and her child, and stood alone amongst the tall trees of the Forêt-de-Soigne. It had a railing in front of the entrance, but inside there were benches which could seat at least a dozen people. On special religious occasions the railing was opened and mass was said by the local priest. Through the railing one could reach a box filled with candles and people religiously left money by dropping it into the box put there for that purpose. Pierre had never seen the chapel without lighted candles and he often read the inscriptions of gratitude left by people who had found comfort or recovered from their illness, which they attributed to The Lady of the Lovely Scent.

Mady, with hands folded and eyes closed, seemed almost in touch with a religious dimension unknown to Pierre. He had seen her like this in prayer before and had even tried to share in this dimension, but whenever he prayed his mind would wander to other things and then when he came to he felt guilty.

After what seemed an eternity, she moved as though someone had instructed her to. She stretched her arm through the railing, took a candle and lit it. Turning to him she said, "Can I have some money for the candle please?"

It was not the first time that she had caught him like this. She had obviously no idea of the value of money.

"Light a candle first and then ask for the money," he mumbled to himself as he fumbled through his pockets. Luckily he found a ten *centime* piece. He was not concerned whether this was enough to pay for the candle because that was all he had.

"All right, I'll put the money in the box for you," he said. With that, he dropped the nickel coin into the box, hoping it would fall with the sound of silver.

The visit to the chapel worked wonders for Mady. Her little face was alive again because by nature she was a very happy child. She could bounce back in no time. Her sadness was not for herself but for another.

"Come on, let's walk along the path where the bluebells grow and then we can turn back and canter all the way to the railway bridge," she suggested.

"Yes, come on, let's. We can't be too long, we mustn't keep the others waiting."

The bluebells stretched like a carpet all along the side of the path leading to Boitsfort, a suburb of Brussels.

"Do you think this is why they call this place 'Bonne Odeur'?"

"I don't know. They don't seem to give off any scent, but they do look lovely."

They had looked forward to the ride and in spite of everything it had turned out to be just perfect.

Major Aue

Major Aue of the British Expeditionary Force was highly delighted when he discovered that his living quarters were in an attractive property standing in its own grounds of approximately two acres. It lay on the outskirts of Waterloo, along the Brussels to Charleroi road on the edge of the Forêt-de-Soigne, situated in the south-east sector of Brussels. His unit was one of the first to be sent over to the continent.

Being a keen horse rider, he soon discovered Groenendael with its stables in and around the area, only a short distance from his living quarters. He wasted no time in exploring the area. He met George, who invited him to the stables. The family took to him immediately – Major Aue was a very likeable person. He had dark hair and wore a neatly trimmed army type moustache which accentuated his military bearing. His way of talking sounded as though he were constantly issuing orders. Madeleine was amused by the way he made his rounds, visiting the horses.

"He looks like an officer inspecting a parade ground," she said.

This was due to his walk and manner and, of course, the uniform. He too seemed to have that natural feel for and understanding of horses.

On Thursday the 9th May, Madeleine and Isabel were very surprised to see the Major at the stables. He had only been the day before and as far as they knew he was on duty for the rest of the week. He looked very serious.

"Hello Mrs Fenbeau," greeted the Major as he stood at the front door. "Sorry to disturb you, but it is rather important. Is George or James about?"

"Major, what a surprise to see you. We thought you were on duty."

"I am, but something rather important has come up."

"Oh well, you're in luck. Both George and James are in – you'll find them near the store room."

"Thanks," said the Major and with that he hurried along.

"Oh dear," mumbled Isabel. She was speaking to herself in her native tongue, which was always a sign of worry. "Oh dear," she kept repeating.

George saw the Major hurrying towards him.

"Hello Major. I didn't expect to see you here today. Don't tell me you're also the bearer of bad news. We've already been told that the Belgian Army have cancelled all leave. M. Van Den Bos is taking Jean back to Namur. Yvonne is in a terrible state."

"I'm afraid that I am, George," replied the Major. "Norway has been evacuated – their government is in exile in London – and it would seem that the pressure is on us now. If you have any plans to evacuate those horses and yourselves to Brittany, I advise you to do it now. It may be too late already."

George had half-expected something like this to happen, but it had been going on for such a long time now that he was unable to grasp the urgency. James was standing in the doorway of the store room. He heard every word the Major said.

"Are you sure, Major?"

"Do it now, Mr Fenbeau," said the Major in his usual manner, which made it sound like an order.

"But you didn't indicate any urgency yesterday," James protested.

"This has only just come to our notice. I can't be absolutely sure," continued the Major, "but we think that the German attack will be through Holland, Belgium and Luxembourg – the 'hook attack' as it is known, devised by a certain General Schlieffen during the last war. The Ardennes and the Maginot Line present too much of an obstacle. It is now almost certain that they will make their hook attack through the lowlands and in a vast encirclement fall on Paris to try and trap us all. I came down specially to warn you. Please take my advice and move now. I can't stay, I must get back to my duties. Good day to you both and good luck."

With that, the Major gave a quick salute, turned on his heel and disappeared at the double. It had all happened so fast that they both stood paralysed by his warning. Neither had said thank you or goodbye. They watched the Major disappear through the gates and heard the noise of his army vehicle fade into the distance, leaving just the sound of the wind caressing the young leaves of the trees in the forest.

It was not until Madeleine and Isabel came running towards them that they came to.

"George, what did the Major have to say? He seemed serious. I haven't seen him like that before. Is it serious?" Madeleine was breathless when she spoke. She had worked herself up waiting for the Major to leave before she dared interrupt to find out the reason for his sudden visit. Now, with uncontrolled breathing, she hurried along to find out what it was all about. Isabel followed close behind, still speaking in her native tongue. The only audible words from her were: "Yvonne... the children... we must go to her."

George suddenly realised how indecisive his father was. It was so unlike him.

"Are you all right, Dad ?"

"What about the flat races? What shall we do about the season in Ostend?" James had a strange and faraway look in his eyes, as though nothing seemed real. The news the Major had brought affected him far more than George ever realised. The whole of his life was threatened and on the verge of collapse. He alone experienced this – it was a close repetition of what had happened to him in 1914 – history repeating itself – but this time something told him that he was going to be the loser.

"Come on, Dad, let's decide what to do. We'll get back to the races and Ostend later. Let's consider our next move. The Major made a special journey to warn us."

"Yes, of course," said James, still distant and vague.

Isabel was too worried herself to see the sudden change in her husband. Her thoughts were with Yvonne and the children.

Madeleine was still waiting for a reply to her question. "What did the Major say?" she insisted. "Why is Dad in such a state? How bad is the news?"

Seeing that his father was not answering, George replied to her question.

"The Major advised us to move the horses and ourselves to Brittany as soon as possible. He said that the army thinks the Germans will attack through the Low Countries to get into France. It seems like a repetition of the last war. He gave it some name, but I can't remember exactly what it was. Some general who worked out this plan of attack to overpower France. The danger for us is that we are in the direct line of fire, but it's only his personal advice – nothing official."

"Oh George, what are we to do?"

He decided. "Go on, Madeleine, take Mum and Dad into the house. Dad's taking this very badly – I think he's in shock. Make him lie down and give him a hot drink and keep him warm. I'm going to ring Van Dam and arrange for the vans to take us and the horses to Brittany. We'd better take the Major's advice."

Van Dam was the owner of the vans. George held on to the telephone. It rang and rang, but there was no reply. He decided to go round and see for himself.

"Don't leave me here alone," pleaded Madeleine. "I don't like the way Dad is."

"I must go. Can't you see we may be too late already? The news may have gone out and we won't be able to get anyone to take us at all."

Isabel then joined in, pleading with him not to go.

"Mum, can't you see? I must go."

With that he left.

When he arrived at Van Dam's place it was only to discover that all four vans had already left for the south.

"I'm afraid you're too late, George," said Mme Van Dam. "The businessmen from Brussels have booked every vehicle I know of. I doubt whether you'll find anything now. This has been going on since yesterday and all through the night. The strangest thing is", she continued, "that payment is made in gold, jewellery or other valuables. Our paper money seems worthless all of a sudden. Unless you can pay with gold you won't be able to get anyone to take you now."

On his return George telephoned every other contact that he and Raymond could think of, only to come up against the situation of which Mme Van Dam had warned them. Vehicles were offered to the highest bidder who could pay in gold, diamonds or other valuables.

George had nothing, other than Madeleine's jewellery, and that was not enough.

Madeleine, in the meantime, was trying to get in touch with Yvonne. Isabel insisted on finding her. Eventually they were told that Yvonne had been taken to Brussels by M. Van Den Bos, who had moved to his apartment over the shop. They were now waiting for news from Jean, who was in the front line. It was agreed that as soon as something was known Yvonne would telephone and they would all meet to decide what to do, according to the circumstances dictating the situation. This did not console Isabel, who wanted her family around her.

"We seem to be splitting up!" she cried. "We must stay together."

The only good thing which came out of that day was that James recovered and felt more like himself by the late afternoon. They decided that, since there were no vans to be had, they would have to consider leaving the horses in Groenendael. This meant finding an area where they would be free to roam, with plenty of food, water and shelter.

George knew that the Château Prince Léopold had been evacuated.

"Couldn't we leave them in the fields behind the château? There is plenty of water and shelter there, and the grass is plentiful," he said.

What he didn't know was that the British Expeditionary Force had decided to turn the château into a fortress. Barbed wire was placed in and around the fields and trenches were dug – a real death trap should the animals stampede. Without this knowledge, it was decided that, with the horses safely in the fields, the family could plan their next move. Raymond and Simone had no place to go to so they decided to stay and keep an eye on the animals, assuming that they would not be forced to evacuate.

A sleepless night followed. Isabel and Madeleine moved from room to room looking at all their belongings, not knowing what the next day would bring.

The following morning, on May the 10th, James and George made an early start at the stables. Several times they heard a rumbling sound coming from the east. At times the earth itself seemed to tremble. There wasn't a cloud in the sky so it could not be thunder: it had to be the sound of gunfire.

"The army must be on manoeuvres," remarked George casually, but neither said another word for fear that one would confirm what they were really thinking. Quietly they worked on.

It was not until James's neighbour, M. Questiau, burst into the store room that their fears were confirmed.

"Have you heard, James? The Germans have attacked! The fortress of Eben Emael has been overpowered! The Germans landed on its roof in gliders. They laid special charges of explosives and blew their way through the walls. They say it was all over in a matter of minutes."

Questiau was shaking from head to foot. He had to grab the back of a chair in order not to keel over.

"The fortress of Eben Emael? But that's supposed to be impregnable. That's where the Baron is stationed, and Jean is in that area too! Oh my God!" exclaimed James.

George stepped forward to get hold of M. Questiau, who tried to straighten up and leave.

"I'm going, George," he said. "I'm leaving for my house in St Jean-de-Mont. I don't think it is safe to stay here – it's too close. Listen to those guns! Can't you feel the earth trembling? My sister is in a terrible state."

It was easy for Questiau to say 'I'm leaving'. All he had to worry about was himself and his sister . He had never married and his sister was widowed. The two lived together in the same house. They also owned a small house at the French seaside resort of St Jean-de-Mont in La Vendée where they could stay until such time as it was safe for them to return. James, on the other hand, had responsibilities which made it all the more difficult to reach such a decision. He begged Questiau to come into the house and repeat word for word what he had heard. It was too important to miss even the smallest details.

Questiau was right. The Germans had attacked at precisely 5.20 a.m. on the 10th of May 1940. Nine German gliders of the assault section, about fifty men, had swooped silently on to the roof of the fortress of Eben Emael. They placed charges of explosives known as 'beehives' against the observation cupolas and, to the surprise of the Germans themselves, blew huge gaps in the deeply buried fortifications. They poured through the acrid smoke in pursuit of the terrified Belgians. Only the heart of the fortress held out for a few hours more.

Was it not Questiau himself who, less than a month ago, had said that the whole concept of the *Blitzkrieg* was to confuse and demoralise? Yet now that it had happened everyone was taken by surprise.

Upon hearing the frightening news, Isabel insisted that they should go and see Yvonne and the children in Brussels.

"We must stay together. We can't separate like this," she pleaded, with folded hands stretched out towards James. "There is no news from Jean – Yvonne must be in a terrible state."

James agreed that they should go to the city to see their daughter and the children. Fortunately George had taken the precaution of laying a supply of petrol in the house. Petrol was bound to be in great demand and very short supply.

So it was decided that Isabel and James would leave for Brussels to see Yvonne and the children and return that same evening. George would stay and, with the help of Raymond, try to keep some continuity in the stables.

The following day, the 11th of May, brought more bad news. The Germans were sweeping west through Belgium – there seemed to be no stopping them. During the two days that followed the whole family was absorbed in various activities. Everything in the house was turned upside down. All the doors stood wide open and all the furniture had been moved. If it should ever come to it, everything would have to be abandoned. The rooms were littered with wrapping paper and string.

With the help of Simone, Madeleine organised the storage of all household belongings and kept shouting at Jeannine and Pierre, who were running around in excitement. Far from helping or being useful, they got in everyone's way and were a real nuisance. To them everything that happened seemed a cause for laughter and rejoicing. Something extraordinary was happening and that, to them, was always exciting.

George drove into the city collecting all the rumours that were in circulation. The strangest and most contradictory rumours circulated about town. Some said that no one was to be allowed to leave while others said that everyone would be forced to go. Some said that there was to be a great battle to the east and north of Brussels where the third line of defence held by the British Expeditionary Force would resist the attack from the German *Blitzkrieg*. Others reported that the British Expeditionary Force was already preparing to withdraw into France. Others whispered that traitors had been seized; that all British civilians caught by the Germans were shot. This was a cause for great concern to the family for most of them had an identity card bearing the term 'Foreigner'. One man told everyone that the artisans were collecting weapons from the city of Brussels and, though King Léopold had said in his broadsheet that he would surrender to the Germans rather than suffer the total destruction of his city, civilians were to go armed and join the BEF in their stand against the Germans.

James was trying to contact the family of Baron Declercq. The last contact he'd had was with the Baron's son. He knew little about him except that he was a child from the Baron's first marriage. The Baron's son had agreed that James should remain at Groenendael, but that had been at a time when there was no cause for alarm. Now the situation was escalating rapidly and he wanted to tell the family Declercq that he was forced to stay in Groenendael due to the fact that no transport could be found. He knew that this would worry the Baron enormously, but under the circumstances there was very little he could do. He had tried to remove the horses by rail but that too had failed, as rail transportation had been reserved for the military. Perhaps he was unable to contact the Baron's son due to the fact that, with all this bad news, he may have acted fast and was now in the process of moving the family to the South of France or even to the farm near Concarneau in Brittany.

By the 14th of May the situation had worsened. Rotterdam was taken and the Dutch government fled to England.

Isabel had a headache brought on by the noise, turmoil and disturbing news from her home country. Nothing was known as to the whereabouts of her family. She was lying down in the living room with a cold compress on her head, but she felt guilty for being idle whilst everyone else was so busy. She continually called out to ask if she could do something to help, but Madeleine insisted that she stay where she was until she felt better.

Madeleine, who was going through her dresses and personal belongings, was now in a dream far removed from what should have been occupying her mind. 'How sad,' she thought, 'having to leave all this behind. What will the outcome be?'

She was roused from her reverie by the noise in the courtyard. It was James and George, who had returned with Raymond and the stable lads. They had taken the horses to the fields behind the Château

Prince Léopold and on arrival had discovered that the BEF had turned it into a fortress. It was all the excitement which roused Madeleine.

There being no alternative, James had left the horses in the field furthest removed from the château where there was no barbed wire, but it meant that they were restricted to a much smaller area without water. The question was, had he made the right decision? George had made up his mind that he would stay with Raymond to look after the horses, in spite of the rumours that English civilians were being shot by the Germans.

By lunchtime M. Van Den Bos was at the house. He wanted to leave for the South of France immediately. He had his own family to think of. It was only because Yvonne pleaded with him that he had come round to collect Isabel and James. Isabel was ready to go, but James begged Van Den Bos to give him until morning so that he could finalise everything at the stables before handing over completely to George.

Reluctantly M. Van Den Bos agreed but he threatened to leave without him if he was not there early in the morning. Already the roads were congested with refugees from the Low Countries who were fleeing to the west and the south.

Isabel took James's face in both hands and with tears in her eyes said, "Be sure you get there on time, James. Be sure."

Early in the afternoon, whilst all hands were absorbed in finalising the closing of the stables, the sudden drone of approaching aircraft distracted them. It came from the east. Was it friend or foe? They all looked up towards the sky and saw the planes silhouetted in the clear sky of the early month of May. None of them was able to identify what nationality the planes were, due to their lack of knowledge of insignia and silhouette.

"I know what they are!" shouted André, the youngest of the stable lads. "Those are gull-winged Junker dive-bombers of the Luftwaffe! I've seen pictures of them in my—"

"Quick!" shouted George before André finished his sentence, "They're coming in to attack! Take cover!"

George ran towards the house to find Madeleine and the children whilst the others ran into the store room to take cover under the heavy staircase. He was right. One of the Junker dive-bombers suddenly went into a dive – it seemed to be aiming for the house. The shrieking noise of the plane diving appeared to be unending. George was convinced that the plane would not come out of its vertical dive in time. This was followed by another and yet another, three planes in all. Suddenly the sound of the engine of the first plane changed as it straightened out. This was followed by an explosion that shook the earth. Instinctively they all covered their heads with their arms for protection. Then came the second and third attacks, each time getting closer to the house. On the third explosion, glass flew everywhere. Plaster and dust filled the rooms as the house shook to its very foundations. All this noise was intermingled with the repetitive sound of anti-aircraft machine guns fired by the BEF. Then, as the noise of the third explosion died away, calm returned, broken only by the distant screams of refugees near the railway station of Groenendael and the main road.

Was there going to be a follow-up to the first attack? George, who had dragged Madeleine and the children under the staircase of the house, waited for a while before venturing out. Obviously the house had not been the target; it had only seemed that way. Raymond was the first out, followed by James. When he saw George coming out of the house he shouted, "Are you all right? I wonder what the target was."

"I'm not sure. It seemed to come from the village, but that third attack must have hit something, perhaps an ammunition stack along the main road. I wonder if they will come back."

More from fear than anything else, James suddenly cried out, "The château! The horses!"

He moved as though he were possessed by a supernatural source of energy. Forgetting all the fears he may have had before, he ran to the car, then, realising that he didn't have the key, he ran into the house and so back to the car without even asking Madeleine if she was all right.

On seeing that James was going to start the car, Raymond and George ran as fast as they could. They were just in time to open the car doors and jump in. Madeleine and Simone couldn't make out what was going on.

"George, don't leave us here alone!"

But James had already started the engine and was moving out of the main gate like a madman. He took the corner too fast, mounted the kerb on the other side of the road and narrowly missed the steep slope into the forest.

"Dad, slow down!" shouted George. "You'll get us all killed."

But James took no notice. It was not until he made a right turn by the railway station that he had to slow down. Refugees were blocking the road. They were following the railway lines leading to Brussels and had taken cover amongst the trees in the forest when the planes attacked. They were now all over the place. As their car approached the little railway bridge on the main road, the situation worsened. Army vehicles were caught up in the congestion and confusion as they tried to head for the château. It became clear that the target had been the château and the ammunition stacked along the main road amongst the trees. The fire and smoke caused by the explosions were now rising high above the trees. Craters where the bombs had fallen were visible. James became so distressed that George had to take over the wheel. He did not hear the screams of the refugees all around him, nor did he see the fear in their faces. His thoughts were with the horses. Some refugees were crying; others were looking everywhere for their loved ones. Some were being cared for by the soldiers of the BEF, who appeared with first aid boxes. There were casualties among both civilians and soldiers.

One of the soldiers, a sergeant, approached their car with his hand raised: " Sorry, sir, but you can't go any further than this. The road ahead is closed."

"But I need to go on – my horses are in the fields behind the château."

"Sorry, sir, those are orders and I can't disobey orders. You must leave your car here or go back," replied the sergeant, irritated by such a request.

George realised instantly that there was no point in arguing. Human lives were more important at this moment than a request to rescue horses.

All three got out of the car and decided to go the rest of the way on foot. James was still possessed by this spur of abnormal energy. Oblivious to his surroundings, he began pushing his way through any obstacle, followed by Raymond and George, who had great difficulty in keeping up with him.

As they were making their way forward, George suddenly heard his name being called out.

"Mr Fenbeau! Mr Fenbeau! Over here!"

George looked to his left and there by the side of the road, in an army vehicle, was Major Aue, with one arm stretched out to draw George's attention.

"Major!" shouted George, his face lit up on seeing someone who might be able to help.

Raymond, who had also heard the call, grabbed James by the arm to make him stop. He hadn't heard it at all. In the meantime George had reached the Major.

"Am I glad to see you!"

"George, I thought you were well on the way to Brittany by now. Why did you stay?"

"That's a long story. Right now we could do with some help. We had to leave the horses in the fields behind the château and we need to get there as soon as possible."

"The fields behind the château?" Major Aue listened to George and realised the seriousness of what he was saying. "Oh Lord, we have orders to dig in. This place is now the target of enemy attack."

"I know, we saw that when we brought the horses round but we had to leave them. There was no alternative."

No further talk was needed. The Major understood exactly what George was asking.

"Jump in and I'll take you there."

James, who had been trotting up and down by the vehicle, suddenly roused himself to the task, shouting confused instructions to Raymond. The closer they moved to the château the fewer were the refugees, since they had run away from this area for fear of a second attack. George looked around and was surprised at the accuracy with which these new planes had dropped their bombs. The château itself had suffered no direct hit. It was the vehicles, guns and military equipment that were the targets. The refugees were victims for no other reason than that they had been in the way.

The fields were the focus of all eyes. Had the horses stayed where they had left them, or had they been frightened and injured themselves by trying to escape?

"Stop!" shouted the Major. "I can see them over there – do you see?" he said, turning to George and pointing.

"Yes, I see them, but that is not the field where we left them."

"There is something wrong," said James. "I can tell by their behaviour."

He was ready to jump out but the driver stopped him, saying, "Don't jump, sir. I can get to the horses through that gap in the fence over there."

As the vehicle moved along George kept looking at his father. He could not get over the fact that he was behaving so strangely.

'Not like him,' he repeated to himself. 'Just like that day when Major Aue brought the news and advised us to leave for France. Did he have some sort of premonition, or was he reliving something that happened to him during the last war?' He couldn't tell and thought it best not to probe, but it worried him. Added to this, his father had to be in Brussels by early morning or Van Den Bos would undoubtedly leave without him.

James's fears for the horses had turned into reality. The thoroughbreds, already tense through lack of exercise, had been driven hysterical by the explosions. They had broken loose from the lower field and found a way into the others in their desperate attempt to escape the noise of the explosions and had come to a standstill here, where they were found, exhausted, with nostrils wide open and eyes bulging with fear.

A hundred yards further along in the next field, on the other side of the barbed wire, they could see two horses half-buried in a trench. James made a quick note of the horses around them and discovered that Barnum and Ivory, two of their best horses, were missing.

"It's Barnum and Ivory!"

George had to pull his father back as he tried to find his way through the barbed wire.

"Dad, for heaven's sake, you'll tear yourself to pieces!" he shouted, as he struggled to control him.

"I must go to them!" cried James.

Raymond also came to the rescue, though the two barely managed to hold him back.

Major Aue, who was looking around, found a gap into the field where the horses were lying. He and the driver walked towards the trench and pieced together what had happened. There was a huge crater not far from the trench. Barnum and Ivory, being the two best horses, must have been well ahead of the others and jumped the barbed wire, only to meet with disaster. They must have been close to the spot where the bomb exploded and had been thrown into the trench in which they now lay.

Instinctively the Major's hand went to the side of his body where he wore his service revolver. One of the horses was still moving.

The little group in the other field were watching. They could see the Major and the driver approaching the trench. The Major removed his revolver from its holster. James became still and looked on in disbelief at the scene before him. Without even looking in the direction of the little group, Major Aue took aim, holding his revolver with both hands. He had a determined look on his face. Two shots rang out and Barnum gave one final jerk, then became quietly still even before the echo of the shots had died away.

Above the sound of the shots came James's spine-chilling cry: "Barnuuuuum!"

The other horses bolted.

The Major and the driver gave one final look around, then rejoined the little group.

Turning to George, he said, "Pity we didn't get here sooner – that horse must have suffered."

Being a professional soldier he soon took complete control of the situation, in spite of his love of horses. Looking at James, he knew that something had to be done.

"Come on, we'd best find a first aid post. Your father is in need of help."

George was holding his father with both arms, but there was no struggle, no resistance. James, a broken man, let himself be guided like a child.

The medical orderlies at the château had opened the rooms on the ground floor to be used as a field hospital. A number of casualties needing immediate attention had been brought in. The exact number of injured was not yet known.

Major Aue glanced inside the rooms. On seeing the rows of casualties lying on makeshift mattresses, he came to the conclusion that immediate attention for James was out of the question. He had no visible injuries – it was his mind which had snapped after the sudden disintegration of his business and the death of his best horses. He turned to George with a, "Hmmm," shaking his head in a negative way, as much as to say, 'No chance of getting any attention here.'

James had now recovered enough to realise that all the fuss was over him. The last thing he ever wanted was to be fussed over.

George recognised the signs and realised that once his father got to that stage, nothing would persuade him to be reasonable.

"Major, I think we'd best forget this. There are too many badly injured people here. I'd better find a way of getting my father to M. Van Den Bos in Brussels. He's leaving first thing in the morning and he has already threatened to leave without my father if he is not there on time. Mme Van Den Bos can look after him - she used to be a nurse."

"Perhaps you are right," replied the Major, taking a final look around. "I'll see if I can release the driver to take him. I'm sure you will be wanting to get back to the horses and salvage what you can. Come on, I'll take you to your car."

"Don't worry about anything, Dad." George was trying to get through to his father to persuade to leave for the city and join the family, but he was being unreasonable and wanted to stay. "I know where M. Van Den Bos is taking you - it's to his villa in Menton-Garavan. If things get bad here I'll join you there. In the meantime, I'm going to find a way of getting the horses to the farm in Brittany, which would be for the best all round, even if I have to ride them all the way. I'll take Raymond and some of the lads with me."

He promised all these things to his father, more as a way of getting him to leave. He did not have a clear idea of what he was going to do. He had no idea. They were in a situation which paralysed any clear thinking. Every hour that went by gave a different picture. Only one thing was consistent: events moved from bad to worse.

James tried to fight back, but his mind had been affected. Eventually George persuaded him to leave by giving promise after promise, which he knew very well he was in no position to keep. He watched as the army vehicle disappeared into the distance among the refugees, taking his father to the city. For that, at least, he was grateful, but a sudden feeling overtook him as though a change in time had occurred. The past, as he knew it, would be lost. Something new and different was beginning and it sent a cold shiver down his spine.

"Come on, George, let's get back to the horses."

Raymond's voice pulled him out of his trance.

"Look who's coming towards us on his bicycle - it's your son," continued Raymond, pointing to the cyclist approaching them.

"Dad!" shouted Pierre. "I've been looking for you. Mum's very worried - you left without saying where you were going!"

Pierre was on the brink of tears because his mother had told him not to leave the house for fear that he too would get lost, but he had disobeyed her.

"I know, son, but we couldn't help it. Your grandfather took off so fast we had no way of stopping him."

"Where is Granddad?" enquired Pierre, seeing that his grandfather was missing.

George felt that he could tell his son exactly what had happened – he was old enough to understand.

"Barnum and Ivory dead?" repeated Pierre, as he listened to what his father was saying.

"Go to your mother as fast as you can and tell her we are on our way. Get everything ready so that we can leave and see to the horses. We'll need bridles, saddles and ropes."

It did not take Pierre long to reach the house. He knew every little path in the forest. His mother gave a sigh of relief when she saw him turning into the courtyard. She was angry, but her anger soon subsided as she listened to what had happened.

"Oh dear, I do hope your granddad is all right. He must be a broken man," she said after her son explained the sudden disappearance of her husband.

"Go on, do as your father said and get everything ready." With that, she returned into the house.

Jeannine was in the house helping her mother and Simone with the broken glass and plaster-covered furniture. She was no longer running away in excitement because the extraordinary things which were happening were no longer exciting. On the contrary, they were frightening, destroying everything she loved.

Instead of the brimming enthusiasm Madeleine usually displayed, she was having difficulty in keeping her mind on the work she was doing. Finally, Jeannine asked her what was wrong.

"I'm not sure, darling. Everything is happening so fast. Your father will be here soon – perhaps he will be able to tell us."

She didn't insist. She could see that her mother was disturbed. Instead, she came closer for that cuddle which always says far more than a thousand words put together.

The streets of Brussels were thronged with refugees. The army driver taking James to the city was having difficulties in finding the house where he had to be. James's directions were vague, and once or twice they took a wrong turning. Finally they arrived. The driver declined the invitation to have a drink. He was anxious to rejoin his unit because contradictory orders were being issued constantly.

"Thank you just the same," said the driver as he bade farewell to James. "I hope all goes well for you and your family."

With that, he left him on the pavement in front of the shop above which Van Den Bos lived.

Isabel appeared in the doorway before he had a chance to reach the doorbell. Her eyes had obviously been glued to the window and she had seen the army vehicle pull up at the shop.

"James, what's happened to you?" she exclaimed when she saw his dejected figure standing on the pavement.

He turned to her and with glassy eyes said, "We've lost everything... everything... Barnum and Ivory are dead. George is trying to save the others." He uttered these words with the despondency of a broken man.

Isabel once again broke into her native tongue. "Lieve God! Hoe is dat tog mogelijk!"

M. and Mme Van Den Bos and Yvonne, who had also rushed down, arrived in the doorway just in time to hear the words uttered by James. Van Den Bos helped him to climb the stairs leading to the apartment.

Yvonne, who had not received any news from her husband, other than that his unit were prisoners of the Germans, couldn't hold back her tears. This angered Mme Van Den Bos who objected to all the attention being given to the Fenbeaux when her own family needed help. She triggered off an argument when some bitter words were spoken. It all stemmed from the fact that before Yvonne was married to Jean, she and M. Van Den Bos had had a love affair. She was a beautiful, fair-haired Scandinavian looking woman, and he was very attracted to her physically. Before their love affair had turned into a scandal they had seen the danger and parted. It was difficult to understand why Mme Van Den Bos tolerated the nearness of Yvonne to her house, but she was a clever woman and didn't want to lose her man. Having her so close to the family circle gave her a better chance of keeping her man – it made it difficult for them to be alone. The present situation, however, proved too much and she unleashed all the bitterness she had bottled up over the years.

James began to wish that he had stayed with his son in Groenendael in spite of the rumours about English civilians being shot by the Germans. The therapy he needed right now was peace and quiet, something he was not going to get here. His one thought, whilst harsh words and accusations were being exchanged, was that he was running out of cigarettes. He walked out without even being missed and left for the corner shop hoping that it would still be open for business as usual.

He was in no fit state to be walking alone in the streets of a city at war where people had but one thought, that of saving themselves. The streets were swollen with people pushing their way forward, some with carts pulled by horses, others dragged along by men. As he reached the corner shop, he was caught up in a stream of oncoming refugees, who pushed him into the path of a horse-drawn cart. Although the cart was moving at a slow pace, it threw him forward on to the pavement where he hit his head hard against a concrete step.

Not a soul seemed to care. The population was in the grip of a great fear. Their country was being raped, and there is nothing worse than a violation against which there is no defence. Men were seen crying because they felt powerless. What could they do? Where could they go, and by what road? The enemy was all around.

Unaided, he crawled into the doorway of a nearby house and after a while he left, completely dazed. Dragged along by the crowd, he saw nothing.

Thousands of families passed that night in churches and other shelters, an agonising night of tears and prayer. The whole city gave the impression of being a gigantic lamb fatted for the sacrifice.

The Invasion

On May the 16th all families living in Groenendael and Hoeylaert received orders to evacuate the area. This included George, Madeleine and the whole family. All scattered their own separate ways in spite of being advised to move to Brussels, which was declared an open city, and most left for France. A battle was expected between the Germans, who were breaking through, and the BEF, who had been sent over for the defence of the Brussels sector. No one could foresee just how fierce the fighting would be. During the night, however, the BEF received sudden orders to abandon their defence. The Hague and Amsterdam were now occupied and the Germans had crossed the River Meuse at several points in Belgium. King Léopold of the Belgians informed his allies that his position was hopeless. General Lord Gort, commander of the BEF, decided to retreat and give battle at a later date, but he neglected to inform the Belgian sovereign of this.

In the early hours of May the 17th, the Forêt-de-Soigne and the Bois-de-la-Cambre were deserted. One lonely figure of a man was seen walking through this deserted area. He was swaying along more as if he was walking on the deck of a ship in high seas. It was James, his hair and face caked in dried blood from the wound he had sustained on the side of his head. He must have walked most of the night and was instinctively moving towards Groenendael. How he managed to cross part of the city in the opposite direction to the flow of refugees was hard to imagine. He moved along, unable to give up and too confused to realise what he was doing. He had not even seen the solitary army truck by the side of the road.

"Hey, Bert, there's a bloke walking towards us," said one of the soldiers working on the broken-down truck. "Let's talk to him and find out if he knows anything. He may have seen some of our chaps. We could ask him which way they were heading."

"Do me a favour, Jim," replied Bert, the second soldier working underneath the truck. His remark made it obvious that in his opinion no one knew what was going on.

"Well, you don't know, he might know something. Er... I don't like the way he is walking. He's been hurt. There's blood all over his head." Jim noticed the state James was in as he drew nearer. "I tell you, Bert, he's been hurt. Just look at his head."

"How can I look at his head from where I am?" remarked Bert, with a note of annoyance, as he reached out for the spanner. "Why don't you stop playing the Good Samaritan? I could do with some help."

But Jim was already moving towards James. He was a friendly and jovial type who would have a go at anything.

"Pardon monsieur... parlays vuz Anglaize?" he began in his awful French accent.

James walked on as if he hadn't heard.

"Ere, mister, are you all right?" Jim said, concerned, as he put himself in the path of James.

James suddenly paid attention on hearing his native tongue spoken.

"Can you tell me where my son is?" uttered James with a distant and glassy look in his eyes.

"'Ere, Bert, he's an Englishman!" shouted Jim, who was taken by surprise when he heard James speak. "Maybe he's one of our spies. Look at his head – he's been hit by something. Perhaps they left him for dead."

At that point Bert crawled from underneath the truck, having done his best to get it going.

"You and your imagination," he growled as he got to his feet and dusted off his uniform.

At last James had found someone willing to help. He stopped walking, like a piece of machinery coming to a halt. He stretched out towards Jim as if pleading for help. The accident of the previous day had done quite a lot of damage to his head. He could not remember things and kept repeating, "Can you tell me where my son is?"

Jim managed to get one more piece of information out of him. His son, as far as he could make out, was on his way to Brittany, but anything else James said made little sense.

"You're moving the wrong way, mister, if your son is on his way to Brittany," said Jim, speaking to himself, not expecting any reply.

After some clever talking he managed to get Bert to agree to take James along with them in their truck.

"You'll get us both into trouble, taking a civilian along," said Bert as his final warning for letting himself be talked into taking James along.

"Think of it, Bert, you've just saved that poor chap's life. You know what the Jerries will do if they catch an Englishman in civilian clothes."

"All right, you've made your point. Let's get going," said Bert in final submission.

The three left, travelling west towards the Channel – two soldiers of the Royal Essex Regiment in search of their unit and James, whose memory had gone completely, letting himself be taken further and further away from his family.

Unbeknown to George and Madeleine, James was but a short distance from where they had taken refuge with friends, M. and Mme Blewett, who owned a small sweet shop at Boitsfort. The little shop was situated near the railway bridge where the number sixteen tram crossed on its way to the city centre. Madeleine had decided to go there because she was sure that the elderly couple, now in their eighties, would not leave their house.

When George woke up on the morning of the 17th, he was completely bewildered when he discovered that the BEF had left silently and swiftly, leaving hardly any trace.

'The Germans must be close,' he thought. His feelings were mixed. Why had they left? He and his family would be caught. Then he thought of Jean and the Baron. The Belgian Army was left in a pocket to fight alone. What would become of them? And the horses. Now that there would be no battle and no one to stop him going back, he could get to them and give them access to all the fields. Madeleine did not want him to leave at all.

"Suppose the Germans get here before you return," she said, but he insisted that he could get back in about one hour using Pierre's bicycle. He no longer had his car for it had been requisitioned by the army.

"I must get to those horses. I can open the other fields to them – they will be safe then," George said.

"We will never get to the farm in Brittany now," Madeleine cried. "Why did the English leave? Why didn't they fight? The Germans will be here soon! What will they do to us? Oh, George, I'm so frightened."

He did not answer because he had no answer except to give her a comforting hug. He too was worried. The rumours that circulated had done their worst, but he came to the conclusion that even those who evacuated right at the start would not make it either. The speed with which the Germans were moving was unbelievable. What's the difference between being caught here or a few miles into France or Brittany? Arthur was right – only the sea would stop them.

Since the start of the invasion on May the 10th, Dédé and Mady had disappeared without so much as a word.

"What could have happened to them?" asked Pierre while he and Jeannine were talking.

"I can't think what could have happened," she replied. "We saw them the day before the invasion. They knew nothing then, otherwise they would have said. They must have left in a great hurry."

"I'm going round to the house to see for myself. It's no more than five minutes over the other side of the bridge."

"You will get yourself into trouble with Maman. She doesn't want you to go too far from the shop. The Germans could be here at any time," warned Jeannine.

"She won't know. I won't be more than ten minutes or so. I just want to make sure that the house is empty."

Pierre left.

He felt as though he had to go. He missed Mady far more than he realised. It was different when she went on holidays because then he knew, but this sudden disappearance he could not accept. He felt pain at the thought that she might have been taken somewhere far away so that he could not see her again. He could not say why he felt this way – he had not yet realised that she was his first love.

He ran down the hill towards the church of Boitsfort, near where the house was situated, without even considering the risk he was taking.

Boitsfort was almost deserted. Here and there men stood in conspiratorial groups, pointing towards the east, from which direction the enemy was approaching.

His heart sank when he saw the empty house where once the dog, Bobby, would have playfully announced his arrival. All the shutters were closed, which gave the place a look of foreboding. He went no further than the front gate – he had seen enough. Mady was no longer there. He hardly gave a thought to the other members of her family. Mady was all he could think of.

He tried hard to fight the pain in his heart as he made his way back to the shop. His throat felt constricted and he held back the tears.

On his return, he and Jeannine stood by the front door of the little shop. The enemy was near.

Again they had the excited feeling. Something extraordinary was happening, but all their questions remained unanswered. This time they would have to wait until they saw for themselves. Pierre felt sure that he was going to witness an historic event: the triumphant entry of a victorious army into a conquered city, probably on the same lines as the armies of antiquity led by Caesar, Alexander the Great, Napoléon! Pierre was transported – his imagination ran wild.

His train of thought was disturbed by the sound of bicycle bells. Irritated by this sound, he looked towards the bridge whence it came. Suddenly the bridge began to swell with cyclists in grey uniforms – they came over the bridge like water breaking over a dyke.

'What could this be?' he thought.

Madeleine, who was also disturbed by the unexpected noise, came running out of the shop and pulled him by the arm.

"Come inside," she whispered. "It's the Germans."

Could Maman be right? Was this the conquering army? On bicycles? Pierre felt cheated!

"Come inside," repeated his mother with fear in her voice. Then she added, "What could have happened to your father? He's been gone over two hours. I warned him that the Germans would be here before him."

One by one the soldiers stopped and parked their bicycles outside the shop. In no time the shop was packed, inside and outside, with these tall young, proud looking men in their grey uniforms.

"Guten Tag! Gnädige Frau, Schokolade bitte," requested the soldiers, with the behaviour of tourists.

Madeleine stood paralysed behind the counter, not knowing how to cope.

"We would like to buy chocolates and sweets please, madam. Don't be afraid," said one of the soldiers who was able to speak French and had noticed the state she was in.

"Oh, chocolate and sweets... Of course," she replied, practically glued to the shelves and forgetting that she was in a sweet shop.

After listening to the reassuring laughter and conversation of these well-behaved young men, she too began to relax and, little by little, she rediscovered her own enthusiasm, but a little voice inside kept warning her – is this genuine?

"We weren't expecting anything like this," whispered Mme Blewett, who had ventured to come out and give her a helping hand. "What is this strange money they are giving us?"

"It's their own money – German marks. The young man over there who speaks French is helping to convert the amounts. He says that tomorrow this money will be in full circulation," replied Madeleine as she opened the till and showed Mme Blewett the bundles of marks that filled the drawer practically to the top.

"You will be out of stock soon at this rate," said Madeleine.

"I've got nothing to refill the shelves with," replied Mme Blewett, her eyes opening wide with worry. "Do you think they will turn on us when we run out?"

The sudden appearance in the shop of André, the youngest stable lad, brought Madeleine back to reality.

"André! What are you doing here? How did you get here? Where is M. Fenbeau?" she asked, alarmed at his sudden arrival.

"I used M. Fenbeau's bicycle to get here. He asked me to come and tell you that he is being questioned by the German soldiers at the château. It's because of his foreign identity card," replied André before giving her a chance to ask more questions.

The directness with which he delivered his message was too much for her.

"Oh, mon Dieu! They'll kill him!"

"No, I don't think so, Mme Fenbeau," continued André, realising the effect his message had on her. "The German officer said he was going to hold him until he has been instructed what to do, because German civilians have already been interned in England, and he warned M. Fenbeau that this could happen to him too. M. Fenbeau asked me to tell you that. He also told me to ask you for cigarettes – he hasn't got any. I'm to take them to him."

Madeleine recomposed herself and, talking more to herself, she said, "Oh, thank God. Perhaps there is no truth in those rumours." Then, more as an afterthought, she asked André, "How come you and your family are still in Groenendael?"

At that very moment, he was being given a bar of chocolate by one of the young soldiers who patted him on the shoulder and spoke to him in a jovial manner. He could not understand a single word he said.

"Well, we left about the same time as you did, but my mother can't walk far – her legs are very bad. We only managed to get as far as the château, where she collapsed. When we saw that the English soldiers were leaving, we went back home. Later I went to the fields to see what I could do for the horses and that's where I met M. Fenbeau. Then the Germans came."

"Mon Dieu, mon Dieu," repeated Madeleine, her eyes turned towards heaven. "What will it be next?"

She then went to work and prepared a parcel of cigarettes and chocolates for George which she gave to André.

"Tell M. Fenbeau that I shall stay here for as long as I can, then to look for me at Groenendael," was her message to her husband, not knowing what else to say. She was still ignorant of what was happening to the rest of the family.

James, meanwhile, was moving still further and further towards the Channel in the company of Jim and Bert. Their truck had slowly filled with wounded soldiers as they met up with several groups of the BEF, but regimental organisation seemed non-existent. They followed the individual units who had retreated to the coast in disarray, not knowing to where their own unit had moved. Some news reached them here and there. On May the 22nd they learned of a counterattack by the French and the English at Arras where, it was said, the Germans had taken a beating. A victory at last! Had the Germans been stopped? they wondered. But the following day, May the 23rd, they learned that the BEF was making a tactical withdrawal to Dunkirk.

"'Ere, Bert," began Jim as their truck moved along, "if we move any further west we'll get our feet wet. The Channel can't be far off."

"Good, perhaps we'll have a chance to get back home to England. I don't like it here. We seem to be doing all the running. We've been beaten good and proper. Look at us! We look more like a bunch of refugees than soldiers."

"I hate the water," continued Jim, talking at cross-purposes. "Remember how sick I was on the way over? I don't want to go through that again," he said. He twisted his face at the thought of it.

"Aw, you'll be all right," came Bert's consoling reply as he looked at Jim, with one eye on the road.

"I wonder if they will give our passenger a lift?" added Jim, pointing to James who sat silently beside them.

"I'm wondering how much longer we can keep him as a passenger. I dare say sooner or later we'll be ordered to take on more of our wounded."

No sooner had he spoken those words than a young lieutenant stopped them and requested that five of his wounded men be given space in the truck, but he did not order the civilian to be left behind. James looked far too frail. Jim had bandaged his head, and this was now soaked in blood. His wound must have reopened.

By May the 19th the German panzer divisions had driven a wedge between the French army and the BEF, and were at Calais. The BEF was trapped in a pocket with the Channel at their back.

Dunkirk was the only seaside town left open to them from where evacuation by sea could be attempted. It was also the town of concentrated enemy fire. The city centre was a shambles. It was burning and blowing up. The bombing raids had started as early as May the 20th. Dunkirk, known as the third largest port in France, was reduced to a mass of burning wreckage.

Two possibilities presented themselves in any attempt to evacuate the army: the open beaches, where small boats could reach the soldiers, and a precarious jetty known as the East Mole, extending one mile into the sea.

The truck in which they were travelling was directed to the beach at Malo-les-Bains, east of Dunkirk, there to await further orders. James was still with them. The wounded were very low in spirit, and hungry. Rations were running out.

The planes of the Royal Air Force could be seen in the sky high above cloud cover at 15,000 feet, fighting off the Luftwaffe, but this did not prevent the shelling and the low-flying Stukkas and Messerschmitts getting through and causing devastation amongst the men now crowded on the beaches.

"I don't like this at all, Bert," said Jim, as he watched the orderly lines of dejected men looking out on to an empty sea. "I can't see how they can get all of us off this beach before the Jerries get here. We'll all be prisoners, or worse."

"Perhaps the Jerries won't get here that quick," replied Bert, always ready to give an encouraging word. "Don't forget we've got some good blokes fighting our rearguard. The French will fight them off for as long as it takes."

"I wonder what the French will think of us leaving them here to fight the Jerries alone?" said Jim with a dreamy look as though his conscience was troubling him, but he quickly recovered and asked, "What do you think they will do with all our wounded?"

"I reckon they'll give us ample warning to get closer to that jetty, when they're good and ready," he replied. "Meanwhile we had better find shelter whilst this lull in the bombing continues. They're bound to get back here sooner or later."

The wounded disembarked and tried to make good use of what little shelter the beach provided. A private of the Royal Army Medical Corps did his best to make them comfortable.

Bert was right: the lull in the bombing did not last very long. Bombs began to come down thick and fast. Covering their heads the best they could, they kept low down in the sand, partly under the truck. Jim ventured a quick look from his position, and suddenly saw James wandering away from the truck. He was quite a distance away already.

"Hey, mister! Come back! You'll get hurt!" he shouted.

"Get your head down, man," ordered Bert as he pushed Jim's face into the sand while the whistle of an oncoming shell was heard.

James, who was still walking away from the truck, had reached a deep crater in the sand formed by a bomb blast when suddenly another bomb fell close by. As it exploded it threw him into the crater.

Tons of sand were thrown into the air by the explosion and as they came down, the sand filled the crater into which he had fallen. It all happened in a matter of seconds.

Jim lifted his sand-covered face, coughing and spluttering. He peered out towards the spot where he had last seen James, but saw nobody. He jumped up from his sheltered position and began frantically looking for the body, but found nothing. Falling to his knees, he began to dig in the sand. He started here, then got up and started there. Where should he dig? Where was the man he called 'Mister'?

He was still shifting sand when Bert pulled him up.

"Come on, man, pull yourself together," he ordered, holding him steady. "You'll never find him in all that sand. Where will you dig? Besides, he was probably dead by the time the sand covered him."

"Suppose he is buried alive!" shouted Jim, looking horrified at the thought that James could still be alive under the sand.

"Come on, Bert! Let's dig! Dig!"

"All right, Jimmy, let's dig, but where?" he replied, using the diminutive of Jim's name as a sign of understanding and respect for his feelings.

Both began a desperate and futile bid to shift the tons of sand with their bare hands, oblivious to what was happening around them.

Not until he was completely exhausted did Jim fall to the ground with tears flowing freely from his eyes, knowing that he was beaten. Bert's consolatory nature made him press Jim's head against his chest. He knew that words were useless.

As though forsaken by the world itself, their kneeling figures, silhouetted against the golden sands of Malo-les-Bains, could have melted the heart of any man. Yet surrounded by so much suffering it passed by unnoticed.

Once again Bert was right. As soon as a ship was sighted on the horizon, they were ordered to move as close as possible to the jetty. Cruel as it may seem, it was not the wounded who were boarded first; instead the strong and fit were ordered to walk the mile long jetty and board the ship. The country needed fighting-fit men.

Helped by the Royal Army Medical Corps, the wounded disembarked from the truck and waited. When they were offloaded, it was decided that an improvised jetty would be built by driving all the trucks side by side into the sea at low tide.

As they stood on the jetty waiting their turn to board a ship, Jim looked at the bodies of dead soldiers floating on the tide, then he looked towards the sands of Malo-les-Bains, filled with remorse.

"I brought him to this hell. I should have left him in that forest," he whispered.

"You did what you could for him," said Bert, putting his hand on Jim's shoulder. "Don't reproach yourself. What's done is done."

The Gestapo

Madeleine was still in Boitsfort with M. and Mme Blewett, waiting for news from George. Nothing was known of his whereabouts. André delivered the parcel and had also delivered her message, that much she knew, so her mind was made up to stay in Boitsfort as long as she could.

The war, as far as they were concerned, depended now on the results of the battle between the French and the Germans. The Dutch and Belgians, after a short but gallant fight, were beaten and the BEF had left the Continent by a miraculous evacuation from the beaches of Dunkirk, taking in total one third of a million men across the Channel. For France, this was a catastrophe and Anglo-French relations were broken.

On June the 6h the Germans attacked the French Army, drawn up along a line of defence on the River Somme. They broke through with the speed of lightning, as they had done from the beginning. By June the 14th they had entered Paris and on June the 17th President Lebrun empowered Marshal Pétain to obtain the best deal for France. Pétain acted promptly. Via the Spanish ambassador, he put in for an armistice and ordered the French to stop fighting.

Madeleine gave a sigh of relief. The French defeat to her meant the end of the war and they would not be made political prisoners of war, but M. Blewett collected information from other sources. Britain, now under the leadership of Winston Churchill, showed no disposition to capitulate after the fall of France. The successful evacuation of so many fighting men from the beaches of Dunkirk and the failure of the Luftwaffe to gain supremacy in the air was being turned into a great propaganda victory which earned them the admiration of the United States of America. This meant continued hostilities between Britain and Germany.

Madeleine did not understand the full meaning of all this, but what was obvious to her was that she and her family would be interned and that thousands and thousands more people would be killed. How she wished that she had paid more attention to Arthur's warning.

In early August, her fears of becoming a political prisoner of war became reality. A truck stopped outside the little shop and the Gestapo entered with their customary show of force and brutality. She was ordered to pack and accompany them. When she asked the officer in charge where they were taking her, and for how long, he replied, "Hurry, madame, we have no time for explanations here."

Abruptly she was removed from the shop, not knowing whether she had packed the right things. To where in Europe would they take her?

"Take care of them," she cried out to Mme Blewett as the truck moved away. She was afraid to say 'my children' for fear that this would alert the Gestapo. She had already made up her mind to tell them that her children had been evacuated to the South of France with the other members of her family, and that she had stayed behind with her husband to care for the horses.

The Gestapo did not waste much time in removing civilians. It was done quickly and brutally in order not to attract attention. No one dared to move or protest. Yet the news of the removal of citizens in such a manner spread through the country like wildfire and gave way to the imaginary interpretation of how the victims would be treated or meet their end. It also highlighted the enormous difference between the mass of the German people and the evil behind the Nazi regime, who controlled the Third Reich.

Mme Blewett felt more as if she was witnessing the removal of a highly dangerous criminal than a victim of circumstances.

"God be with you, Madeleine," she uttered, clasping her hands in prayer as the truck disappeared out of sight in the direction of the city centre. "God be with you."

During all this Jeannine and Pierre were hiding in the attic, as their mother had told them to. She had given them strict instructions to stay in hiding should anything like this happen, even if it meant they would be separated, because in her opinion the Gestapo would separate them in any case once they were prisoners. There were separate camps for men and women, and young people were recruited into the Hitler Youth Institutions to be brainwashed.

They could hear practically every word which was spoken and realised that Maman was being taken away. To do what she had asked of them was the most excruciating experience they had gone through so far in their short but impressionable lives. Nothing had ever touched them as much as this powerless feeling they now felt. They listened to the sound of the truck taking away from them the very reason for their existence, their Maman.

Their tears flowed. Mme Blewett tried hard to console them, but no words could heal the open wound in their hearts. Their lives were suddenly filled with fear and uncertainty, yet they felt no hate because that was something they had yet to experience. So far they had known only love.

Days passed without news, during which time they kept themselves busy by making sure that all the windows and doors were fitted with covers and blinds to observe the blackout imposed by the Gestapo. The house had to be in total darkness. One dark moonless night, a patrol of German soldiers was heard marching in the main road. They listened to the *tramp-tramp-tramp* of their boots. Suddenly there was a hammering at the front door. Had they left a chink of light at one of the windows? Frightened and bewildered, they waited. Then came the second hammering. M. Blewett got up to answer the door, forgetting that he should have turned off the lights before opening it. As he opened the door the soldier who had been hammering shouted angrily and hit him with the butt of his rifle across the neck and shoulders. He staggered back into the house as the soldier slammed the door. Mme Blewett and Jeannine rushed forward to get hold of him while Pierre, not knowing what else to do, turned out all the lights and quickly drew one of the blinds.

M. Blewett sank to the floor groaning. A blow with the butt of a rifle to a man of his advanced years could have dangerous consequences. They all stayed perfectly still, afraid to move for fear that the Germans would harm them even more. Pierre's quick reaction in turning out the lights must have satisfied the patrol. They were heard marching away. Together Jeannine and Pierre checked the house to make sure that no lights were showing outside for fear that the Germans would return.

More days passed without news. M. Blewett was not recovering from the blow to his shoulder and, to make matters worse, he could not stop worrying, and feared for the children. He could not work out how to keep them in hiding and at the same time obtain food ration coupons, which were now a vital part of their lives. Without these there would be very little food to go round. Already rationing was down to 350 grammes of bread, 360 grammes of meat and only 100 grammes of fat per week. He began to look ill and complained of pains in his chest and across his shoulders.

Mme Blewett urged him to rest and to leave all the arrangements to her. "I'll find a way to cope with the food situation, "she said.

M. Blewett promised to rest, not because he believed her but more because he had to. He felt too ill.

It was now mid-August. In spite of his condition M. Blewett, accompanied by Pierre, still kept in touch with the men who met in conspiratorial groups in the little cafés of Boitsfort. These cafés were alive with argument. Belgians mingled with French, Dutch, Polish and Jews, who lived in and around Boitsfort. In one of the cafés they frequented a well-known Belgian lawyer, Jacques Courtoy, was an occasional visitor. His knowledge of the matters of war was of great interest to them all. He was a great conversationalist. Many an hour did Pierre sit with his back turned to him, hungrily gathering every word that was spoken. He had never been one for learning, but his life was affected by events in Europe, so he listened. In this way his education progressed. He threw himself into learning with all the hunger of the starved.

When they returned home they lay open the map of the world which was kept in the house and retraced what Jacques had said. He said that the Germans were fully involved in the continuation of the war but he also added that Hitler, more than any commander at that time, understood the value of time. The war had to end before the United States of America got involved and turned it into a second world war. These words filled them with hope as they followed Jacques's predictions on the map. He said that the Germans were now concentrating on gaining control of the Mediterranean Sea, which would enable them to attack the Soviet Union by way of Armenia and Georgia. Pierre had no idea where these countries were but M. Blewett pointed them out to him. Jacques also said that the Germans would enter the USSR as liberators because it was a mosaic of subjugated people: Ukrainians, White Russians, Turkomans and others, all disenchanted with their Bolshevik masters, as previously they had been with the rule of the Tsars. By liberating these people, they would cause such an explosion that the Soviet Union would cease to exist as she was now known. But, as a warning, Jacques added that

Germany had a commander with a willingness to accept risks to further his aims and that, he said, was the unknown factor.

The warning that Jacques gave seemed to affect M. Blewett more than anything else. He saw no immediate end to this conflict, and that to a man who had accepted living each day as it came was no consolation. Pierre, however, kept looking at the map and came to the conclusion that if such a large area stopped fighting, that must be the end of the war. Then he and Jeannine would be reunited with their family. His heart filled with hope.

M. Blewett should not have been going to these gatherings. His health deteriorated. On September the 12th, when they learned of the Italian advance in Egypt and the occupation of Sidi Barrani, he told his wife that he felt very tired and had a strange gurgling sensation in his chest.

"I'll go and rest for a while, Maruska," he said to his wife, using the endearing Russian version of Marie by which he normally addressed her. "Don't let me sleep too long. I want to go round to the café to hear what Jacques has to say about the latest news on Egypt."

"I do wish you didn't go to those gatherings, dear," replied his wife. "It's too dangerous. The Gestapo might get to know." She used the Gestapo as an excuse – what worried her more was the effect these discussions had on her husband.

Jeannine and Pierre were still waiting and hoping for the return of their mother.

"How long will they keep her?" said Jeannine. "Surely once they discover that she is no threat to them they will let her come home?"

Pierre then told her what Jacques had said.

"Listen," he began, "I heard from Jacques, who knows about these things, that there is no danger of Germany invading England. They are concentrating on the Soviet Union and, according to him, this could end the war very soon."

"Oh, do you think they will let her come home soon then?"

"Well, I don't see why not."

This was how the two kept up their morale – by hoping that Maman would be returned to them soon.

It was while they were talking like this that they suddenly heard Mme Blewett cry out.

"Oh no! Oh no!"

They rushed indoors and upstairs, from where her cries came. She was kneeling by the bed holding and rocking her husband in her arms. She was sobbing profusely. "Oh no! Oh no!" she kept repeating each time her breathing allowed it.

"Please don't do this, Auntie. Don't frighten us like this. What's wrong with Uncle? Why doesn't he move?" cried Jeannine.

"He's dead... he's dead." The words seemed too much of an effort as Mme Blewett uttered them.

Neither of the children had ever seen death before. Their uncle looked asleep, except that his face was a strange colour. He had turned blue and was so still – every struggle of life seemed to have left him. Both moved close to their aunt without another word and, as though it was the thing to do, they joined her in this rocking motion, which is nature's way when grief strikes.

'Why oh why is everything happening this way?' thought Pierre, as his body rocked in rhythm with that of his aunt's. What was it that had changed their happy and beautiful home so suddenly? How could they lose everything in such a short time? Their parents, the family circle, the horses and those rides in the forest with Dédé and Mady, their schoolfriends, the Bronowskys with that large family of twelve children where they were so often invited to share evening meals of creamed potatoes because that was all the family could afford. Why had it all ended? Where was everyone? He did not understand, but he had begin to learn what it meant to live in a country where the population was in the grip of great fear.

It took a long time before a doctor came to the little shop, only to pronounce M. Blewett dead. Later in the evening Mme Blewett's younger sister was summoned to the house. She could assist in the formalities which were all too much for their aunt. She was in her eighties.

Inevitably the conversation turned to the children. With the death of her husband, Mme Blewett would find it very hard to cope. Jeannine and Pierre overheard the conversation. Although their aunt would not listen to what her sister was trying to say, they realised that she was right. They would be an added burden. On that day something else died – their childhood.

Rather than let others decide what was to become of them, both came to the conclusion that they should return to Groenendael, there to wait for the return of their parents or other members of the family.

They knew that the message which their mother had passed to their father was that she would stay at Boitsfort as long as possible, but then to look for her at Groenendael.

Without telling Auntie what they had decided, because she would only stop them, they collected all their belongings, together with Maman's handbag containing money, papers and keys, and left a note saying that they realised the impossible situation in which they had been thrown, but not to look for them nor tell anyone where they were going because this would only alert the Gestapo. They would be all right since someone from the family was bound to return from wherever they had fled.

Return to Groenendael

Pierre knew his way through the forest, the land of his boyhood. He knew every dip, every hole and every underground tunnel that remained from ancient times. Some, it was said, had been used by monks to escape religious persecution many centuries ago. It was here that he had played his imaginary battles, where he had run and hidden and eluded his imaginary foes. This time, however, it was for real.

He decided that he and his sister should enter the forest at the main square where the trams terminated their journeys from the city, in order to avoid the railway line and the main road connecting Groenendael to Boitsfort and the city centre. This would bring them out at the Château Prince Léopold where it was known that German non-commissioned officers were billeted. He kept his distance, but he wanted to see for himself. The other reason why he came this way was to call at the forester's house, whose son was one of his schoolfriends. Perhaps he could help. But by far his most compelling reason was the desire to see the little chapel. For some reason he felt that seeing it would bring Mady closer to him. How he missed Mady.

On reaching the forester's home they found it empty and deserted – no one had returned. They did meet someone they knew – the man with the shaggy little dog who once worked at the château before it was evacuated. He was an old man with grey hair who understood loneliness.

He listened to their sad story and gave them words of comfort. Then, as though he had a sudden inspiration, he said, "Wait! I have the very thing for you."

With that, he disappeared for a while and returned with a little milk chocolate coloured puppy.

"He is the last one of my puppies. Here, take him. He'll be a good friend until your daddy and mummy return. He can look after himself, so you need not worry about him. He's like his mother – she'll never starve, she's too clever," he added with a crafty chuckle.

Neither could refuse such a gift at a time when they needed love and someone to love. Having to feed an extra mouth did not even cross their minds, although this was what the old man was hinting at when he said that they would not have to worry about feeding him.

As they walked through the forest towards Groenendael, the pair regained their youthfulness. They laughed and played with their new-found friend.

"What name shall we give him?" asked Jeannine.

"Oh, that's easy," replied Pierre. "His name is Tarzan. He'll live in the forest and make friends with all the animals, just like Tarzan."

"Tarzan! What a funny name to give a little dog."

"Well, it's all I can think of."

"I know. It's because you've seen that film with Johnny Weismuller," laughed Jeannine, who was teasing him now.

As if to show his disapproval, the little dog got hold of Pierre's shoelace and began growling and tugging at it.

But the name stuck.

"Tarzan! Tarzan!" called both of them as they continued their journey through the forest.

On arrival at Groenendael, they discovered that all the houses were empty. No one had returned.

They entered the empty house, which was still covered in plaster and dust, in spite of the fact that their mother and Simone had cleaned it before they were ordered to evacuate.

The house had lost the warmth and friendliness it once had. It seemed too big and the white sheets covering the furniture gave it a ghostly effect.

"Shall we try Simone's place?" suggested Jeannine. "It's smaller and cosier."

Both went to the apartment to investigate and found it much friendlier. Strangely enough, it had suffered very little damage from the bombing.

"Perhaps Raymond and Simone will be the first to return," Jeannine said. This gave them renewed courage.

Later Pierre decided to look around in the cellar of the big house. He knew that his grandfather had always insisted on having plenty of essential food in the house because it was so remote.

'At least we won't starve or get cold,' he thought when he saw the tins of food and milk and all the fuel in the cellar.

He hurried back to Jeannine to tell her the good news and brought with him what he thought most suitable for their evening meal. All three of them were starving.

The daylight began to fade. Never before had they realised how lonely and frightening the night could be living on the edge of such a huge forest without the security of neighbours or the family circle.

The darkness of the night was accentuated by the tall trees growing so close to their house. The wild dogs were baying at the moon. Little Tarzan ran for safety, putting himself between Jeannine and Pierre, who were huddled close together in the corner of Simone's living room. Once again they were gently rocking to and fro, exactly as they had done with Auntie; this time it was a sign of deprived love.

They sat by the light of a single candle, afraid to violate the blackout, but too frightened to sit in the dark. Finally, in the early hours of the morning the candle went out and they fell asleep, still huddled in the corner of the living room wearing all their clothes, with little Tarzan, who had not even attempted to leave them.

Slowly the village of Hoeylaert returned to normal. One by one the local people arrived to repossess their houses, but Groenendael seemed empty of its inhabitants.

They kept well away from the village for fear that they would be recognised. Maman's warning to stay in hiding was stronger than their fear of being alone. Every day they waited in the house for someone to return.

One day they heard someone prowling around among the deserted houses. Perhaps it was a burglar. They kept quiet – even Tarzan did not break the silence.

The incident prompted Pierre to look for a hiding place. He knew of a cave which could be reached through the underground tunnels from ancient times. He took with him blankets, food and milk, candles and matches, just in case they had to run and hide.

One day in October, when the leaves began to turn and the forest took on its autumn colours, they decided to go to the house of their schoolfriends with the large family. The loneliness of their present existence began to tell. They needed love and affection – without it life was empty.

The house was situated in the Avenue de Bruxelles in Bonne Odeur, the same area where the Château Prince Léopold and the little chapel were located. They could reach it by walking through the forest, then along a small lonely footpath which brought them out at the avenue. The last three hundred metres or so had to be along the avenue itself. That could not be avoided. They waited until the road was deserted, then silently they crept towards the house.

Pierre's face lit up when he heard the sound of voices coming from the house.

"They're at home," he said, turning to Jeannine, who was following closely behind carrying Tarzan.

"Let's take the side entrance before anyone sees us."

The two gave the family such a shock by appearing unannounced in the little courtyard behind the house.

" It's Jeannine and Pierre!" shouted the eldest girl, who was the first to see them.

In no time the entire family was there, rejoicing in the reunion of their schoolfriends. There was Nadia, who was in the same class as Jeannine, Jules, who was Pierre's classmate, the eldest, Jeanne, Pauline, the second eldest, Paul, Robert, Jacqueline, Ann, Bernadette, then the twins Albert and Germaine, and the baby of them all, Julienne. Twelve children in all.

"Come in and tell us all about yourselves," said Mme Bronowska as she took both of them in her arms and led them into the living room, followed by the entire family.

The two children told them everything which had happened since their last visit, except that they believed their grandparents and Aunt Yvonne to be safe in the south of France with M. and Mme Van Den Bos.

So excited were they that neither of them had noticed the change in the Bronowsky family. Having recovered from his excitement, Pierre suddenly noticed. It was so obvious that he could not understand why he had not seen it immediately. On each of their garments was sewn a crudely cut, bright yellow Star of David.

"What are these?" he enquired, pointing at the stars.

Mme Bronowska suddenly lowered her eyes as though she were about to say something of which she was ashamed or afraid.

"Perhaps it would be better if no one saw you in this house," she said. "We are Jews. We've been told to wear these at all times, ever since it was announced on the radio that laws protecting Jews have been dropped. You should not be here." She kept her eyes lowered all the time she was speaking. "You will be in greater danger than you are now if they find you here."

One by one the children sought refuge behind their mother, not daring to look Jeannine and Pierre straight in the eyes. A strange silence fell.

"But, Mme Bronowska," protested Pierre, "we know nothing of this. I'm still Pierre. Jeannine and I have not changed. Who are 'they'?"

As though she suddenly realised what she had done, the woman stretched out her arms to them and said: "Oh darlings, I am so sorry, but we live in such fear. We wear these stars as though we are lepers. Please forgive us. Of course you haven't changed."

A weight was lifted throughout the house and, once again, the atmosphere of their happy yesterdays returned. Little Tarzan was now the main attraction with the whole family.

M. Bronowsky was out in search of food for his large family but great-grandmother Bronowska was there, still wearing her familiar headscarf. She was a remarkable old lady, originally from Russia, the Ukraine. She was very old, with eyes which were so gentle that you could see the years of wisdom radiating from them. Exactly how old she was no one knew, but it was said that she had been a little girl living in Moscow in the days when Napoléon entered it in 1812. She could still remember Moscow burning. That made her at least one hundred and thirty-six years old – hard to believe, but Pierre had no reason to doubt it. She was the greatest storyteller, in spite of the fact that she used many Russian words. Her facial expressions and gesticulations made her stories the most fascinating of any ever told to them.

As usual they were invited to stay and share the evening meal. This time, however, instead of the normal creamed potatoes, it was rutabaga, a type of root normally fed to cows. Potatoes had now become a luxury for the family.

They sat at the long table lined with wooden benches, as they had done so often before, and ate the simple meal as though it were fit for a king.

After dinner great-grandmother Bronowska began her story for that evening.

It was the story of the little girl who lived with her parents in the vast wastes of snowbound Russia, and was taken dangerously ill. Somehow the story had a very deep meaning that evening. Nadia looked down to the Star of David sewn onto her dress as she listened to the happy ending, where the little girl's father, faced with great dangers, managed to bring the doctor just in time to save her life. Would her own real life story have a happy ending too? Would the Star of David protect her?

It was getting late. Jeannine and Pierre had to leave. Mme Bronowska once again warned them of the danger if they should be caught in this house of Jews. They promised to be careful and left. Pausing in the dark avenue, they drew their coats about them, for there was dampness in the October wind.

The following day, early in the morning, they were taken by surprise when they heard the sound of trucks in the road outside the house. They looked through the window of Simone's living room and, to their horror, saw two German soldiers marching across the courtyard towards the big house.

"It's the Germans!"

With hearts pounding, they ran towards the door, almost forgetting to pick up their coats. They left the apartment by the side entrance and silently crept along the back of the stables, followed closely by Tarzan, who did not even attempt to make a sound. Perhaps it was something the old man had taught him.

When they reached the far end of the property, they stopped to look back. The Germans had now guided two trucks into the courtyard.

"They've gone inside the house," whispered Pierre. "They must be looking for us."

"But why the trucks?" his sister asked. "What could they want with the trucks?"

As they sat and looked, they could see three soldiers moving from the house to the trucks carrying pictures, mirrors, chairs, clothing and more.

"They are taking out all of the furniture and putting it into the trucks," said Pierre with a look of amazement in his eyes.

Two more soldiers began walking along the stables, opening and shutting every door and moving towards them.

"Let's get out of here before they see us. We'll go to the cave," said Pierre, still whispering.

Silently they crawled towards the fence and through a gap that he had purposely made ever since the incident of the burglar. Once on the other side, they made their way into the forest to look for the opening of the old tunnel which would lead them to the cave. It was situated about a quarter of a mile from the Château-de-Groenendael, on the other side of the Brussels to Charleroi road.

A small underground stream ran through the tunnel. Pierre had to guide Jeannine every step of the way by the light of an old lantern, which had been hidden there by himself and other schoolfriends who played in the tunnel during their imaginary games. Tarzan was following, quiet as a mouse. Jeannine's eyes were darting everywhere. She was frightened of spiders and this seemed like the place where she was likely to meet the biggest.

"What's the meaning of all this, Pierre?" asked Jeannine who, up to now, had kept silent for fear of being heard. "Why are they removing all the furniture? Do you think they were looking for us?"

"No, I don't think so – not any more – but I can't imagine why they took everything out of the house."

Pierre could not have known but what was happening was that the Germans were confiscating all the furniture and anything useful from houses belonging to British subjects who had been interned. Eventually these houses would be used as living quarters for their own officers.

Frightened and bewildered, the two children decided to stay in the cave and wait until dawn before returning to the house. Being in the cave they lost all sense of time. Neither had ever spent a night in an underground cave. So great was the silence that they could hear the noise made by their own bodies. Pierre thought that he could hear the sea surging against the rocks and Jeannine was experiencing some kind of meditation by following the rhythm of her own breathing. The silence was made more frightening by the shadows created in the flickering light of the candles.

"Make some noise, Pierre," she cried out. "I can't stand this silence."

Little Tarzan sensed their fear. His back arched and his tail was turned inwards between his back legs. His body was shaking. Forgetting their own fears, they became more concerned for their little friend and tried to console him. This enabled them to adjust to the silence and the strange sound that they could hear now and then.

"Oh, Pierre, I'm so frightened. Please hold me close and don't let the candle burn out." Jeannine pressed herself against him while he wrapped the blankets around her. Little Tarzan quickly jumped in the middle – he was not going to be left out.

"Do you think we could pray to Ste Marie?" she said.

"We could do that – it might help."

"We don't normally pray when things go well. Do you think it wrong that we should do so now?"

"I don't think that Jesus and Ste Marie are like that. They have more understanding. They would not hold it against us just because we don't pray when happiness is all around us."

The two began to pray.

"Pierre!"

"Yes, Boubou." Pierre used Jeannine's pet name by which Maman so often called her when she needed comforting.

"Could you sing that little tune that Maman used to sing? It would make me feel she is near. You do it so well."

Pierre then began to hum the haunting little tune that was Maman's favourite. He held Jeannine close in his arms whilst gently rocking her. She listened and felt the warmth of his body underneath the blankets and cradled little Tarzan, who lay there completely reassured. She became very calm, almost convinced that Maman was near, then she fell asleep whilst Pierre kept his vigil, watching over the candle. He was determined to stay awake.

When they thought that morning had come they decided to leave and investigate, only to discover that it was still dark. They had to return to the cave. On their second attempt Pierre saw a brightness in the eastern sky and they left. When they reached the house, they stopped to listen. Outwardly it all seemed the same. When they approached the front door they could see that the lock had been broken, and when they opened the door and entered they could see that everything had been removed, including the carpets.

"The cellar! What about the cellar?" cried Pierre, looking at Jeannine, who immediately realised what he was thinking.

In the light of a candle, which had not been removed from its usual place, both descended the dark staircase, only to find that everything had been taken out. There was not enough food left to feed a mouse.

Next they went to Simone's apartment. There too everything had been taken. They had nothing to eat, nowhere to sleep and no clothes other than those they wore. All they had left was Maman's handbag, which Jeannine had automatically picked up with her coat.

What were they to do?

'The cave,' thought Pierre. At least they had blankets, some tinned food and milk.

But what of the nights? Those awful silent nights in the cave. After spending two consecutive nights there, he came to the conclusion that they could not stand it any longer. Remembering one of Bobon's sayings, he made a decision.

'Lightning never strikes in the same place twice,' she always said. Perhaps it would be safe to return to the apartment, for at least there was a stove in the store room where they could keep warm and there was no shortage of wood in the forest. The thought of warmth overcame their fear.

Karl

Winter came early that year. November was cold and brought snow. If only Madeleine could have seen her children now – alone, waiting and looking very pale and ill. Her warning to stay in hiding had worked up to now, but it looked as though help was needed.

Living on chestnuts, walnuts and berries that Pierre found in the forest, they were able to make the few tins of meat and milk last, but the end of their supply had come and Groenendael was still deserted. Only the village of Hoeylaert had returned to near normal. To make matters worse, they both contracted an infection. It was an infection that thrives on filth and dirt and, without proper sanitation, it took a grip on them. One morning when they woke up they had huge blisters between their skin layers, containing a light brown liquid. Their blood seemed to be turning into water.

Cold, hungry and weak, Pierre came to the conclusion that he had to make a decision and make it soon. Then came the coldest November night so far. That night he did not think they would survive. He looked at Jeannine, who was too weak to even complain. She didn't seem to wake up properly. In the morning he wrapped her in all the blankets they possessed and decided that he would go to the Château Prince Léopold to give himself up. The thought of surrendering to the Germans seemed more fitting to him than pleading for help in the village like beggars and then leaving it to others to denounce them.

"I'm going to get help," he said. "Stay here until I get back."

Jeannine looked at him and nodded approvingly.

He set off towards the château, wearing the only clothes he had. What had once been a pleasant and short journey was now a long, exhausting trek into the unknown. He was frightened. What would he say when he got there? How would the Germans receive him? Those were the thoughts that ran through his head.

He kept walking. The snow was driving into his face as he fought against the wind. When he reached the Brussels to Charleroi road he felt as though he could go no further. The cold took away all his strength and his limbs refused to move. The summer clothes he wore were no protection against the icy wind and sub-zero temperatures. Overcome by a sudden fear that he might pass out, he cried "Mady! Please take me to the little chapel."

He uttered these words without knowing why, except that he needed a source of energy from somewhere. The words just came out. He remembered Mady's sudden cry for help that day when they were out riding when she too had felt this need to be taken to the chapel.

Still leaning into the icy wind, he thought of her in prayer on the steps of the little chapel of Our Lady of the Lovely Scent. He recalled the way she had looked that day in a strange dimension of prayer. He too began to pray. "Blessed Mary, mother of God, pray for us poor sinners." Then his mind returned to his present struggle and, as usual, he felt guilty.

Strangely enough, when his mind returned to the journey that lay ahead, he could not have explained to anyone how he had travelled such a long distance in what seemed a few minutes of crying out for help. Leaning against a tree, he found himself within striking distance of the château, with the little chapel on his left.

He had difficulty in focusing although the chapel stood out clearly. Suddenly a hand came to rest on his shoulder, making him jump. He looked round and there, in front of him, stood a German soldier.

'An officer,' he thought, judging by the splendid uniform he wore.

"Are you all right?" asked the soldier. He spoke French with a strong German accent. He was a tall, young and proud-looking soldier, with the smart uniform of a non-commissioned officer. He wore his greatcoat with the buttons undone, exposing his grey uniform underneath. His hair was blond and he had light blue eyes. At first Pierre thought that his eyes looked cold but then, on looking again, they did not strike him as being the eyes of a cruel man. On the contrary, he suddenly saw a warmth in them that came from within.

Pierre did not answer. He just looked at this striking figure which had suddenly appeared from nowhere, but he did a great deal of thinking. He had come to give himself up and to get help. Maybe this was the way, to let himself be guided by the young soldier.

The soldier, on seeing that the boy was half-frozen, threw his greatcoat over the young man's shoulders and then led him towards the main entrance of the château. When they entered the big hall Pierre, who had seen the hall before, was surprised to see that it had been reshaped with wooden partitions forming long corridors and many doors. One of the doors opened and another non-commissioned officer stood before them.

"Karl, what are you doing with that half-frozen young man? Have you caught him doing something wrong?" asked the NCO who had just appeared.

"Is the medical orderly around?" asked Karl, without answering the NCO's question.

The latter gave Pierre a second glance and seemed to understand.

"Yes, I saw him only a short while ago. I'll go and get him," he replied.

Until now, Pierre had not said a word. He could not understand what was being said, but he sensed that something was being organised by the officer.

"My sister needs help. I must go to her first," he said, pulling back from Karl.

Although Pierre spoke fast, Karl understood every word he had said. It had crossed his mind that this young man could not, or would not, talk.

"Wait a second," said Karl to the other NCO. "The young man says that he has a sister who needs help too. I will take him there first – I'll be back."

"Are you sure you are doing the right thing? We shouldn't fraternise with civilians. You have seen the orders," said the NCO He frowned deeply because he was aware of Karl's rebellious nature.

Karl was not even listening. He had already left with Pierre and was walking towards a vehicle, for which he seemed to have the key.

Sitting silently next to Karl as the vehicle moved along, Pierre could not resist a glance at this young German soldier.

'Is this the enemy?' he thought. 'Should I accept the help that he is offering? Why is he doing it?'

Pierre had begun to learn about hate during these last few months and pride was the by-product of his hate.

At that point Karl's head turned and their eyes met. In that split second his look seemed to say, 'I know what you are thinking and I don't have the answers either. Like you, I am caught in this war. Perhaps in my place you would do the same.'

Karl's head turned back to the road and his driving. Silently they continued their journey until they reached the little railway bridge. From there, Pierre directed Karl to the house.

As the vehicle came to a stop in the courtyard, he turned to Karl and said, "Let me go in first. It will only frighten her to see you."

Karl had no intention of doing otherwise.

Jeannine was still in the same place Pierre had left her, lying on the straw, wrapped in blankets. She was awake and patiently waiting for his return.

"I brought help," was the first thing he said to her.

A smile came to her face as she heard his words, but then she saw Karl. She drew back on seeing him, her eyes filled with fear.

"No," said Pierre, "he is here to help."

"Oh Pierre, we are in the hands of the Germans. There is no turning back now. What will they do to us?"

Karl was looking around, surprised at the empty room where the young girl was lying on straw, wrapped in blankets. He heard every word she said and his light blue eyes were cold, his expression, hurt.

"He speaks French," said Pierre.

She looked at Karl as though she was sure that he would take revenge for what she had just said.

But he was hurt for other reasons. His common sense told him that here, in the midst of their poverty, he was the enemy. It was his people who had done this to them and he did not expect to be received with open arms, although his intentions were to help. He came close to her and, in his strong German accent, said, "I can't help being a German, but you need help. I promise no harm will come to you."

She looked into those light blue eyes and saw the guilt this young soldier felt on seeing their plight. Her expression changed and could almost have been mistaken for the beginning of a smile. In response, Karl's eyes melted as his face broke into a reassuring smile.

"Come, I will take you downstairs to the car," he said as he picked her up into his arms.

Although Jeannine was tall, there was no weight to her. She was no longer afraid and put both her arms around the young soldier, resting her head on his shoulder. He smelt clean and fresh and he measured every step carefully. She glanced at his face, at those strong features and did not see him as the enemy.

"Can you take my little dog too?" she said as they both looked at Tarzan, already sitting in the driver's seat.

The NCO, who had warned Karl about fraternising with civilians, was right. He had landed himself in trouble.

When the brother and sister were examined, the army doctor immediately diagnosed that they were suffering from a contagious infection. They were put into isolation at the château, to wait for an ambulance to take them to a Belgian hospital, where they would be treated.

Karl was also put into isolation until the incubation period was considered to be over, and he would then have to face his punishment for exposing the camp to this infection.

Jeannine and Pierre did not feel too unhappy under the circumstances, because they were warm and being fed the same food that was served to the NCOs, who were on full rations. So far everyone had been very sympathetic and helpful. They could not help noticing the enormous difference between the normal German soldiers and their ruling counterpart, the Gestapo.

It was not until late the following morning when the ambulance arrived to remove them to the hospital situated in the Bois-de-la-Cambre. The hospital was run by a religious order which devoted its members' lives to caring for the poor and the sick.

As they were led inside the hospital corridors leading to the wards, Pierre felt himself being transported into history by the atmosphere of the old building, which dated back many years. 'Here you had to obey. You were no longer an individual,' he thought.

It was no surprise to him that, on arrival at the ward, he was led into a side room with a vacant bed and ordered to strip. He did as he was told and sat on the edge of the bed, waiting.

The nuns ran this institution on the same disciplined lines as those of their own religious order. They moved silently through the corridors as they carried out their duties.

The door of his room suddenly opened and in walked two nuns. Pierre was concerned at his nakedness and looked on silently as the nuns prepared a bath with hot water. His hands had never been such an embarrassment to him – he had no idea where to put them.

As he stood there, the door opened again and in walked a third nun carrying a brush and a bottle. Her headdress, which reminded him of a swan's wings, covered most of her face. It was not until she looked straight at him that he noticed her features.

"No," he uttered in disbelief, but he immediately realised his mistake. Her angelic face, or what he could see of it, was so like Mady's that for one split second he had thought that he recognised her.

The nun had seen his sudden reaction, but her training to deny herself all attachment with the outside world made her keep silent and undisturbed. Pierre did not have this training. He trembled. Her sudden appearance had unnerved him because, for some reason, he had always feared the strength of Mady's religious tendencies.

He was led to the bath, into which one of the nuns had poured the contents of the bottle. The nuns began to scrub his body, which was covered in blisters. They seemed too painful to receive such severe treatment, but he didn't make a sound. His mental pain made him immune to the physical suffering.

After his bath he was put to bed. The more severe areas of his body were soothed with ointment and bandaged. He lay there wondering about Jeannine his sister. How was she taking this treatment?

He knew that she was in the east block and that her ward was situated on the same floor at the far end of the long corridor, but he also knew that he would not be allowed to see her. He could hear the voices of men in the main ward next to his isolation room, and wondered when he would be transferred there. It was not through lack of attention that he wanted to be transferred. His day was full of events – the treatment, bandaging, medication, bed-making, meals and coffee breaks. All made the day pass quickly.

Around 9 p.m. he sensed a definite change throughout the entire building. The night shift had come on duty.

Silence descended on the hospital. His breathing slowed down as he tried to work out the origin of every sound that reached him.

After a while he could hear the rustle of a nun's robe approaching his door, which had been left open. In walked a nun carrying a tray with medication.

Pierre's eyes opened wide as they beheld the same angelic face of the nun who had been in his room earlier in the day. 'They must be working all the hours that God gives them,' he thought.

On seeing her, his heart began to beat faster, but this time he did not make a sound.

"I brought you a sleeping draught," said the nun in a whisper. "You may find it difficult to sleep on your first night here."

"Thank you," he replied, also in a whisper, his eyes following her every move.

One thing he had already noticed was that all the nuns spoke with the greatest economy of words. Everything they said was to do with the needs and care of the sick.

Silently she moved around adjusting this and that, waiting for him to finish swallowing his sleeping draught. His eyes lowered as he became aware that he was following her every move. Had she noticed that he was disturbed at seeing her? He began to wonder, and felt a certain guilt. As soon as he had finished the last drop of medicine, she collected the glass and said, "Good night. Try to rest now."

"Good night," he replied with a lump in his throat, which had lodged itself there because of his emotions.

He lay on the bed in his solitary room waiting for the sleeping draught to take effect. His mind retraced the events which had led up to this day. Seven months had passed since that day when his grandfather had driven away. It did not seem possible that, in such a short time, he and Jeannine had lost everything, having to rely on the charitable services of the institution of this hospital. It suddenly struck him how poor they were. All they possessed were the clothes in which they stood, and these he had now outgrown.

He looked around his room to see if there was a mirror, but there was none. He got out of bed and looked at his reflection in the glass door and could see that he had grown even more and his face had matured drastically. The war had forced him to grow up fast.

He returned to bed and, with the help of the sleeping draught, relived the past. Those happy, carefree days riding in the forest with Mady, her head on his shoulder, silent, while Désirée was allowed to wander at will through the beautiful Forêt-de-Soigne.

It must have been getting late, close to the early hours of the morning. He was still sitting in bed, awake, letting his mind dwell on the past.

Once again he was disturbed by the rustle of robes approaching the door. The nun stood in the doorway for a while then, on seeing he was still awake, she entered his room.

"Can't you sleep?" whispered the nun as she came close to him.

He was awake, but the sleeping draught had a very calming effect on him. He was not aware that his eyes were moist, having been enveloped in the past. Sadly and sleepily he looked at the nun – she did remind him of Mady.

He may have been slow in replying, but his observation was not slow. For a second he could read her inner thoughts and expected her to respond to his mood, but her eyes suddenly turned away.

"No, I can't sleep yet," he replied eventually.

"I'll see if I can get the night sister to prescribe you another draught. Lie down properly in your bed. It will make it easier to sleep." The nun helped him to get further into his bed whilst readjusting his pillows and blanket.

It was not long before she returned carrying another glass.

"Here, take this. It should make you sleep," she whispered as she held his head to let him drink from the glass.

Her eyes met his again, but this time they revealed nothing.

"I don't want to see you awake when I come back later," said the nun, giving him a comforting smile.

He could have closed his eyes and fallen asleep, except for one thing Mady had once said in connection with certain religious orders. If a nun weakened in her feelings towards worldly attachments, she had to confess this to the mother superior in front of all the other sisters, during one of their evening prayers.

'Is that the reason this nun's eyes had suddenly turned away? Perhaps she is unhappy in her monastic existence,' he thought.

Pierre was not thinking clearly any more. The effect of the sleeping draught made him fantasise.

Then, slowly, he slipped into a deep sleep.

Pierre lost count of the days he spent alone in his room. From time to time he received news about Jeannine, whom he had not seen since the day they were brought in.

Then, late one afternoon, the ward sister walked in and said, "Come on, young man, you're being moved into the main ward. Your solitary confinement is over."

"Oh good." He was not expecting this at all. He had already resigned himself to spending another night alone.

"Will I be allowed to visit my sister? Has she been transferred to the ward too?"

"One thing at a time, Pierre. Let's get you settled first, then we will see."

He had very little to transfer. He was wearing pyjamas issued by the hospital, so all he had to collect from his locker were his miserable clothes and the toothbrush and toothpaste given to him by the medical orderly at the Château Prince Léopold.

He followed the sister into the ward. All the patients looked at him.

At first he felt as though he were an intruder but then, when they smiled, he felt himself the centre of attention, bringing a change to their institutionalised existence, of which he himself was already a victim.

The sister walked about halfway into the ward and then stopped to guide him to an empty bed.

'Oh God. I do hope no one died in this bed.' The thought suddenly crossed his mind, but the sister soon changed that by introducing him as the youngest member of the ward.

"Don't forget to ask about my sister." He made it sound desperately important because he knew that to postpone it would mean a long delay.

"All right, all right," replied the ward sister, who could not help smiling at his craftiness. "I will see to it right away."

As she walked towards the east block his eyes followed her to make sure that nothing would distract her along the way.

It seemed ages before she reappeared and began walking back towards him.

From a distance he could not make out her expression, but then one never could. He had to wait until she stopped right in front of him and then, and only then did she smile and say, "In half an hour it will be all right for you to go and see her. She will be waiting."

"Thank you. Half an hour," said Pierre as he frantically looked around the ward for a clock.

"Don't worry. I will give you a shout," said the sister.

Never had half an hour seemed so long. He kept looking in the direction of the door.

"It's only fifteen minutes since the sister left here, son. I'll give you a call when the half hour is up," said the patient in the bed to his left.

Pierre's face had a painful expression. "Only fifteen minutes?"

Even before the half hour was up, the ward sister returned to collect him.

"Come on, it's time," she called out as she turned around, fully convinced that he would be at her heels in no time. As they walked the length of the corridor he felt as if he were walking in a time tunnel.

"Pierre! Pierre!" The call came from a young woman standing inside the doorway of the ward in the east block. She wore a white scarf around her head in such a way that her hair was completely covered, only her face showing. He was taken aback. It suddenly struck him that Jeannine's long curly hair, which normally framed her face, was her crowning glory. Without it she looked very different.

"Oh Pierre," cried Jeannine as she threw herself into his arms. "They scrubbed me with a brush! It was horrible! I felt so ashamed," she sobbed and could not speak another word.

"There, there, Boubou. Don't cry, it's all over now. Shhh."

She looked at her brother through her tears. There was something different about him, but she could not make out what it was. Suddenly she knew – he no longer had that boyish look. She hadn't paid any attention to this before, but now that she hadn't seen him for a while she noticed that he looked very grown up.

"Oh Pierre," she repeated, and threw herself back into his arms. She felt warm and safe as his words caressed her wounded pride.

"Shhhh. There's nothing to be ashamed of. These people have seen much worse." His comforting words made her stay locked in his arms.

The ward sister looked on with her hands folded inside her sleeves which she used as muffs. Her expression was serene. She did not betray any emotion.

"Nothing will hurt you any more, young lady," she said. "Not as long as you have each other."

Pierre, who was used to listening carefully, pondered on what she had just said. There was a hidden message in that remark.

The following day they were allowed to walk in the hospital grounds. They came upon the hospital chapel where the nuns prayed whenever time allowed. The open door seemed to beckon them inside. At first Pierre did not want to stay because he recognised that same religious dimension which he associated with Mady and which frightened him. At the same time he felt that this was a place where he would find renewed strength – strength upon which these nuns had to draw throughout the day in order to cope with their work of looking after the sick and the dying.

In the afternoon he suggested that they visit the inner garden of the hospital, so as to avoid visiting hour which they found very disturbing. They never had any visitors. The other reason he suggested going there was to see the tree where dozens and dozens of little birds made their home. He had observed this tree through the window of his solitary room where, early in the morning, it became alive with the song of these birds. On a given signal they all flew away, only to return in the evening and settle once again in the tree with the same commotion. Then suddenly all would go quiet until the following morning.

'How beautiful life is,' he thought, but how strange that he should feel like this when his own life was so disrupted.

The weather had turned a little milder and they sat in the garden observing the silence. Suddenly he heard his name being called by one of the nuns.

"Pierre! Where are you?"

"Here we are!"

"Come along quickly. You have a visitor. Hurry now! We had no idea where you were."

They looked at each other and with one single voice said, "Maman!" Their feet suddenly had wings.

"Quickly. Go to the ward," continued the nun as she walked away in the opposite direction.

"Maman! It's Maman!" cried Jeannine as she raced behind him.

Pierre arrived at the ward breathless, expecting to see... he was not sure whom. He stopped dead when he saw a soldier. It was the same striking figure of the soldier whom he had seen at the château when he was in such desperate need of help. He felt Jeannine's hand grab his as she too became silent.

Karl stood in front of them with those cold light blue eyes. He looked apprehensive. Then Jeannine broke the silence.

"Karl, you came to see us!" She drew close to him and, pulling him down, kissed him on both cheeks. His eyes melted once again as soon as she gave him that token of affection. He had no problem over the rights or wrongs of his visit. Pierre, on the other hand, was more cautious. Karl was a German and it was the Germans who had destroyed his entire life. But he was only just beginning to learn about hate and his hate was directed towards the Gestapo, who seemed to be a totally different race.

Jeannine looked first at him, then at Karl. Their feelings were different from hers, she could tell.

Pierre then did what she had hoped he would do. He stretched out his hand and said, "I don't think I thanked you, for helping us that day. Did you get into trouble?"

"Come to think of it, you didn't, and I was nearly demoted," replied Karl as he grabbed Pierre's hand and pulled him closer, to put his other arm around his shoulders. A burst of laughter followed this remark, more because of the way he had said it.

"Listen, you two, I've brought you some very good news. First of all your little dog Tarzan is all right. He is staying at the château."

"Oh Karl!" interrupted Jeannine. "Little Tarzan! Oh thank you."

"But more importantly," he continued, becoming very serious, "you are no longer alone. One of your grandmothers has returned. I was told to tell you that it was the one living in the cottage on top of the hill."

"Meterke," said both as they looked at one another.

'Meter' in Flemish means godmother. The 'ke' at the end of the name was an endearing addition to the name.

"Do you know whether our uncle and aunt are with her? We were told that they all left together."

"That I don't know," replied Karl. "I only heard this from the headmaster of the village school in Hoeylaert, M. Pettit. Apparently your grandmother has been making enquiries about you all."

"M. Pettit found you?" asked Pierre, all confused.

"No," replied Karl. "I found him. While I was in my room waiting, I began to wonder what would happen to you two once you left the hospital. One of the villagers told me about M. Pettit. He seems well thought of in the village, so I went to see him and that's how I found out about your grandmother. He is also getting in touch with the Swiss Consulate in Brussels who could probably act on your behalf to help with money and a place to live. He's not wasting any time."

Pierre was taken by surprise as he listened to him.

"You did all that for us? But why? You could get into trouble."

"I felt bored sitting alone in my room." It was Karl's dry sense of humour that made them burst out laughing again.

"The ward sister told me that you could be leaving this hospital any day now," continued Karl as his face took on a serious expression again. "I asked if it would be all right if I came to collect you on Saturday. I've got a forty-eight hour pass."

"That's another five days," said Jeannine.

"I know, but under the circumstances they will keep you here until then. You don't mind, do you?"

"No, we don't mind," replied Pierre. "I can't explain why but we feel rather sorry to have to leave. Everything here is so organised that it gives you a feeling of security."

"You mean you're getting soft."

Karl's remark brought another outburst of laughter. Neither of them had any problem in accepting him as a friend. He could make them laugh and that was the best medicine anyone could bring. He was like someone sent down from heaven to help.

"Come on, Karl, we can't just stand here. We'll show you around the hospital grounds. We've seen some beautiful things," said Jeannine as she pulled him in the opposite direction of the ward.

"Are you sure that's allowed?"

"No, " replied Pierre, "but we are underage and you will be the one they will punish. Come on, we'll show you the dungeons."

This time it was Karl's turn to laugh. Pierre had just paid him back with some of his own medicine.

It was well past visiting hour when Karl left. They escorted him to the end of the corridor. At the top of the staircase he paused with his greatcoat draped over his shoulders. He looked at them and, with a gesture of the hand as if to make a point, he turned round towards the staircase and said, "Saturday – don't forget. I'll be here first thing in the morning to take you to your grandmother's cottage."

"Karl, wait." Jeannine ran towards him, threw her arms around him and, looking gratefully into his eyes, said, *Danke shön*, Karl."

"*Auf wiedersehn*, Jeannine," he replied, squeezing her hand gently.

Pierre looked on and sensed that his sister liked Karl far more than she would ever admit.

"*Auf wiedersehn*, Karl," whispered Jeannine in a parrot-like fashion, lifting her hand in a goodbye wave as he disappeared down the stairs.

Then she turned to Pierre all excited and said, "Oh, isn't it wonderful? We will see Meterke on Saturday!" and promptly did a pirouette in the middle of the corridor.

Meterke had never been a very demonstrative person. When they arrived at the cottage with Karl and their little dog, she greeted them as though they had only been separated for a short time and as though nothing of great importance had happened in between. Both knew differently though. Underneath that seemingly indifferent attitude Meterke was more helpful and caring than any other member of the family. Auntie Jane, on the other hand, was shedding buckets of tears – she did not try to hide her emotions.

It was through M. Pettit that Meterke had learned of Karl, the German soldier who had shown concern for Jeannine and Pierre, and it was no surprise to her that it was he who brought them to her cottage. She showed no resentment towards him. She had lived through the last war and to her they were all Europeans. Brother fighting brother – all because Europe had been divided in such a greedy and cruel way after the last war.

"But why they have to fight to the death over it? That I do not understand," she would say.

Once the initial impact of their reunion was over and Karl had been properly introduced, Pierre wanted to know exactly what had happened to them since that day they had evacuated to France. He wanted to hear of their account as refugees in France, and work out what it was which delayed the other members of their family, assuming that they were all still alive.

So Meterke told Pierre how on June the 10th, together with millions of other refugees, they had followed the movement of the French Government who abandoned Paris because the Germans were getting so close, first to seek refuge in Tours and then in Bordeaux. Once in Bordeaux, rumours circulated that they would all be evacuated *en masse* to Algeria, there to begin guerrilla warfare against the Germans.

"Here the line was drawn," said Meterke. "This incredible idea could only result in the invasion of North Africa by the Germans and we would all perish. It was with a sigh of relief that we learned that Marshal Pétain was empowered to form a new ministry, which then ended the fighting. On our return journey", she continued, "we learned that the fighting had not stopped completely. It was being continued from Britain. When we reached Nancy, Albert, together with hundreds of other men, was taken into forced labour for the duration of the war. We had no idea what to do," she added, "but when it became clear that Albert could be held in forced labour indefinitely, I decided to bring Jane to the cottage. She is expecting her baby soon and Hoeylaert seemed a much friendlier place to be in. Nancy is crawling with the Gestapo." She looked down, her eyes resting on her hands, which were folded on her bosom, and sank into deep thought.

Then she suddenly exclaimed, "So here we are, darlings," and with those words ended the story of their flight into France. "Thank God we found M. Petitt! He has been so helpful, but so far you two are the only ones we have heard of. Heaven alone knows where your father and mother have been taken to."

She leaned back in her chair and, lowering her eyes once again, became very pensive. She was eighty years of age and Pierre wondered whence that little old lady had mustered all the energy to make such a long journey and still care for others. Her body seemed so frail and her face was so wrinkled that all femininity had gone from it. Pierre looked at the old-fashioned sepia-tinted portrait of her younger self hanging on the wall and could not believe that life could be so cruel as to turn that beautiful young face into one with so many wrinkles. How he loved that dear old little face, and how he wanted to tell her so, but she would only scorn him for being so sentimental.

Jeannine could see that Karl became increasingly embarrassed as the conversation generated hate towards the Germans. He remained silent.

"Karl, please forgive us. We don't mean anything against you personally," she said, concerned.

"Don't apologise," he said. "I do understand how you all feel. Perhaps if I tell you that in Germany the Gestapo are also feared, you might understand better. Many of our own people have been killed by them because of their political beliefs – my father was one of them."

On hearing these words, Jane lost all feelings of distrust towards him and ventured to ask, "Karl, do you think that Albert is in any danger?"

"No, I don't think so," he replied. "He's been taken into forced labour, that is bad enough, but I was referring to people who were killed for their political beliefs. He's in no danger as long as he toes the line. Dead he is of no use to them."

"But he can be so stubborn at times," added Jane as she brought her hands to her mouth and bit her fingertips at the thought that Albert would do something foolish.

"We must all bide our time for the right moment. Perhaps he will realise that," said Karl.

Pierre, who was listening while Karl spoke, reflected deeply. It seemed an unusual remark to make for a German and he wondered whether Karl implied something which reminded him of what Jacques Courtoy had said. Could it be that he, together with many other Germans, was opposed to the autocracy of their Nazi masters, just as Jacques had characterised the Soviets as being disenchanted with their Bolshevik rulers so that they would welcome a liberator?

Karl changed the conversation to a lighter note, clearly indicating that he did not wish to elaborate any further on this issue, and Pierre thought it best not to pursue his thoughts.

As a result of M. Pettit's intervention on behalf of Jeannine and Pierre, the Swiss Consulate in Brussels took steps to provide sufficient funds to cover the cost of food and fuel and to ensure that they had a place in which to live. The house and stables in Groenendael had now been taken over by the occupying army.

Auntie Jane decided to stay with Meterke in the cottage, so her house in the Avenue de Bruxelles became vacant. Jeannine and Pierre could stay there and all expenses incurred would be settled by the consulate.

On the surface it seemed an ideal solution, except for two things. First of all, although Meterke would help whenever it was possible, it was obvious that they would have to fend for themselves in order to get extra food and fuel. Rations were hardly sufficient to feed growing youngsters, so they would have to find ways of supplementing them. Attending school was out of the question, under the circumstances, and the local council agreed. Secondly, they had to make a monthly visit to the Maison Communale to sign a register, a clear indication that the Gestapo were keeping an eye on them. Jeannine was fast approaching the age when she would either be sent to a concentration camp or be recruited into the Hitler Youth Organisation. How that was to be decided, Pierre had no idea, but he was already thinking of finding a way to avoid this happening.

The constant feeling of hunger gnawing at their stomachs prompted him to do something about it. Using his uncle's bicycle, he paid a visit to a farm situated a few kilometres along the road leading to La Hulpe. It was known by the name of La Ferme Rose because all the walls were painted pink. He knew the farm because he had visited it with his grandfather, who had been interested in a piece of land of about thirty acres on which he wanted to start a stud farm, one of his pet dreams. Pierre hoped that the farmer would remember him and, perhaps, use him for odd jobs on the farm. The farmer remembered him and was very sympathetic. He decided to give him the job of looking after the animals in the farmyard, mostly the feathered kind. His payment would be milk, eggs and other food. Pierre was delighted, and the smell of the courtyard reminded him of home and the stables. The food, in payment for his labour, was of more value to him than money.

One by one the inhabitants of Groenendael returned. Just before Christmas, Jeannine and Pierre learned that M. and Mme Van Den Bos, together with Bobon and Aunt Yvonne, had returned to the apartment in Brussels, but that their grandfather was not with them. Isabel was ill with worry – all enquiries as to James's whereabouts so far had failed. His disappearance had served one good purpose, in as much as Mme Van Den Bos felt responsible for James's departure from the apartment that evening in May and because of this a closer bond had formed between the two families. They learned all this through their uncle Jean, who had been released from the prison camp once King Léopold capitulated to the Germans. He paid them a visit, driving his newly acquired three ton truck, fitted with two large gas cylinders fastened to the roof to drive the engine. How he came by it was to remain a secret but, as Meterke said, "In war there are those who lose and those who gain. Jean deserves it – he has always been a hard worker and I admire that in a man."

The news that their grandfather was still missing did not alarm the two young people too much because so many people were still missing, and slowly but surely they usually returned, each with their individual story of how they had made out as refugees. All had suffered and all were delayed by the uncertainty of the ongoing war but, as in any human drama, it was obvious that some would not make it.

Moving to Jane's house in the Avenue de Bruxelles altered their circumstances. They were able to make the occasional visit to their schoolfriends and spent many delightful evenings there. Mme Bronowska was still very worried in case they were seen, but the desire to be together was stronger than their fear of being spotted.

Karl also made regular visits and took great precautions not to be seen entering or leaving the house for fear that Jeannine and Pierre would be branded as collaborators, a word of which he had to explain the meaning and implications to Pierre. They met in places where people did not know them. Sometimes they met near the Château Prince Léopold. They waited near the little chapel, keeping well out of sight until they could hear the tramping of boots, as Karl's work party returned from the fields with shouldered garden forks and spades, marching to the sound of their favourite tune. Karl also took them to the Ardennes, that beautiful area in Belgium known as 'Little Switzerland', where they enjoyed each other's company without fear of being recognised, always accompanied by their little dog Tarzan.

Those happy days were not to last very long. Karl had applied to become a pilot in the Luftwaffe and his application came through. He received orders to report to the training centre – where, he did not say. Jeannine was beside herself. She had come to like him in a way that only one so young can. Karl's promise that he would do all in his power to make the occasional visit to see her was the only thing which made it bearable for her.

A few days later, as Pierre was leaving to go to the farm, he saw a German army truck parked outside his schoolfriends' house. From it came cries of fear and panic. As he approached, the truck began to move and when it passed him he saw the entire Bronowsky family huddled together inside like cattle, together with other people, all wearing the yellow Star of David. Mme Bronowska stood upright, stone-faced, looking silently into infinity, her children about her screaming.

"No!" cried Pierre, as he ran to try and reach the driver of the truck. "What are you doing? Stop!"

But the truck gained speed. He clung to the side and was dragged along. He lost his grip and fell to the ground. As the truck moved away, he could still see Mme Bronowska and hear her children screaming, "Mummy, don't let them do this to us!"

He picked himself up and ran towards the truck shouting, "Stop!" over and over again. But his cries were all in vain. Helplessly Pierre looked on as the truck disappeared out of sight. His face darkened as another part of him died, and his hate grew.

In spite of what had happened that morning, he had little choice but to go to the farm. They needed the milk and what little food he could get. All day long he had to fight off the tears. On his return, late that afternoon, he and Jeannine went to their friends' house to see for themselves. They stood silently in the small courtyard.

"Shhhh!" he said suddenly. "What's that noise?"

Jeannine looked at him. "I didn't hear anything."

Both kept very quiet and listened intently. There it was again and this time Jeannine heard it too. It came from the wash house which ran alongside the house. Slowly Pierre's hand went to the door handle to see if it would turn. The lock gave way and he pushed open the door. There they saw Nadia huddled in a corner amongst a pile of washing, her eyes open wide. She was shaking from head to foot, but not a sound came from her mouth. She had obviously been left behind during the confusion when the Gestapo were rounding up the family and her mother must have kept silent about her absence.

"Nadia, it's us. Don't be frightened."

Still shaking and wide-eyed, Nadia let herself be taken from her hiding place, but she was unable to speak for she was too frightened and bewildered. Pierre took hold of her and told her to put both her arms around his neck and hold on tight. He picked her up and carried her off to their house.

That evening he decided that neither he nor his sister would let themselves be taken – somehow he had to find a way. The words of the ward sister echoed in his ears: 'Nothing will hurt you, not as long as you have each other.'

During the weeks that followed Pierre spent his leisure time in the valley of the forest by the lakes. There he could relive those happy days when he and Mady were together. He found it easier there to plan their escape from the danger of being put into a concentration camp. His mind was made up. He, Jeannine and Nadia would go into hiding. He decided to go to the little cafés in Boitsfort and seek the advice of Jacques Courtoy.

It was not until June that his visit to the café coincided with that of Jacques's. Pierre did not waste any time when he saw him.

"Do you remember me, sir?" he said as he greeted him.

"Of course I do, Pierre, but you have grown more mature since I saw you last." Jacques even remembered Pierre's name. "I learned about your uncle's death some days after it happened and you disappeared about the same time."

"He wasn't really my uncle, sir, but we always looked on M. and Mme Blewitt as our aunt and uncle." He then told Jacques how they had survived since that day when they went into hiding at Groenendael.

Jacques listened to the almost unbelievable account that Pierre gave him and understood why the boy had matured in such a short space of time.

"You have an uncle living in Groenendael, haven't you? His name is Jean," said Jacques suddenly.

"Yes, I have, sir, but how did you know?"

Jacques gave a faint smile and nodded his head, as if to say, 'I've put two and two together and come up with the right answer.'

"No, really, sir, how did you know?"

"Perhaps my connections with your uncle are best left unsaid. I'd prefer that no one knew."

He looked around as he spoke and Pierre sensed that the relationship between his uncle and Jacques was connected with those conspiratorial meetings in the little cafés. He did likewise. He too looked around the café and Jacques saw that he understood.

"From what you told me, I do agree that you and your sister will end up by being removed by the Gestapo," Jacques continued almost in a whisper. "This war is moving in a most unpredictable way. Come back in one week from now, about the same time. I'll be here. In the meantime do not try to contact your uncle - leave that to me. I'll say goodbye to you now. There's no need for you to leave immediately if you want to listen to the latest news of the war." Upon those words Jacques got up and joined the group of men, who could not disguise the fact that they wanted him to join them.

Pierre once again sat with his back turned towards Jacques, gathering every word that was spoken. Jacques began by saying that the rumours of the alleged danger of war between Germany and the Soviet Union were now set for resolution on June the 22nd. The other significant event was that the Congress of the United States of America had passed the Land-Lease Act on March the 11th.

"What is the meaning of this Land-Lease Act?" enquired the men now gathered around Jacques.

"The Land-Lease, gentlemen, is an legislative act to promote the defence of the United States. It gives powers to the president of the USA to designate, as a beneficiary, any country in the world which is prepared to fight Hitlerism and his allies, and supply them with whatever munitions they need. It is, in a way, a declaration of war."

"You don't sound particularly pleased with this news," observed one of the men. "Isn't that good?"

Jacques sighed deeply and added, "The way I see it, gentlemen, is that if Hitler wins this war, we in Europe will be dominated by Hitlerism stretching from the Ural Mountains to the Atlantic Ocean. But if America, the USSR and Britain succeed in destroying Germany then, gentlemen, we in Europe will be dominated by Communism stretching from the Pacific Ocean to the Atlantic." Jacques paused for a while and looked at the silent and puzzled faces around him.

"Now, listen to me, my friends," he continued as he leant forward on his chair, a sign that he was going to take them all into his confidence. "If I can see those dangers then you can bet your life that others see it too. There is no moral or political advantage in substituting Stalin for Hitler. No, my friends. Let me tell you what the aim of the Allies will be in the continuation of the war. First they will help the USSR to withstand defeat. This has now been made possible by the Land-Lease Act. Then they will bring about revolution within Germany against Hitlerism. We can all of us differentiate between the Nazi regime and the mass of the German people. Our most profitable ally is the extensive anti-Hitler faction in Germany. The way I see it is that the Allies will channel all their energy into bringing about this revolution. They will not destroy Germany but instead use her as a buffer against the USSR, because they are the only fighting force in Europe capable of holding back Communism and we, gentlemen, will be called upon to take part in this anti-Hitler movement, so we must prepare ourselves. Help is coming."

Pierre, who was not looking directly at Jacques and, therefore, could not study his expression while he spoke, was surprised when one of the men found it necessary to ask him, "What is it that troubles you about all this, M. Courtoy?"

"Well, since you asked, sir," replied Jacques, "it is President Roosevelt's and Mr Churchill's blind hatred – to exterminate the Germans is their sole aim, and that worries me. They've already made that quite clear. This hatred could distract them from the task demanded of them, that of winning peace which would be profitable to both their countries."

"Do you think that such learned men could be so blind as to let this happen?" asked the man who had put the question.

"Hmm. Many mistakes have been made in wars through sheer blind hatred," retorted Jacques. "The last war, for instance, just to give one example. But we must be positive in our thinking, gentlemen, and prepare ourselves to assist in the movement towards the destruction of Hitlerism from within Germany. It's the only solution for a return to our freedom."

Pierre had heard enough and left for home. He had a long way to cycle through the forest and he did not want to be on the road after curfew. His hopes that by next spring the war would take a turn for the better were now high. It was for the next nine or ten months that he had to plan. Perhaps Jacques would have the answer by next week. 'How deep is the conspiracy between Jacques and Uncle Jean?' wondered Pierre as he cycled along.

When he got home he told Jeannine and Nadia everything he had learned. He held Nadia's hand as he spoke. The poor girl had not made a sound since that day when she was found amongst the pile of washing at her home. It worried him enormously, but he was too frightened to take her to a doctor for fear that she would be denounced. 'Perhaps by showing her kindness and understanding, her speech will return,' thought Pierre.

Nadia, although not speaking, understood everything that was being said. She looked at Pierre with adoring eyes. She was of an age when her affections ran deep, but he was too concerned with what he had to do, too involved with finding a way out and too in love with Mady to notice Nadia's affection for him. Jeannine could see and knew that one day Nadia would be hurt. That day would be when she learnt that he loved Mady.

Pierre kept his appointment at the little café in Boitsfort. He had not tried to contact his uncle, as Jacques had asked. Now he learned that his uncle, together with M. Van Den Bos, was involved in an underground movement aimed at keeping Jews and other political victims hidden from the Gestapo, and to smuggle them to a place of safety via a perilous route through the Ardennes, the Black Forest and the Alps into a neutral country.

Jacques advised Pierre to continue reporting to the Maison Communale and to sign the register but, at the first sign of danger, he was to go immediately to the house of M. Van Den Bos, who would give them refuge and make the necessary arrangements for their escape into Spain or Switzerland. Pierre agreed, knowing that he would not have to wait long for that day. It could not come too soon for him.

When he arrived home, Meterke was there. She too brought some good news. In her usual undemonstrative way she told them that M. Pettit had managed to locate their parents.

"Pierre! Maman and Papa are safe! Perhaps we can go and see Maman," exclaimed Jeannine, unable to hold back her excitement.

"Hush, child, let me do the talking, don't interrupt," said Meterke in a way that put Jeannine in her place.

"She is right," continued Meterke, addressing herself to Pierre but keeping a severe eye on Jeannine. "M. Pettit is trying to organise a visit so that you two can go and see her. He has already been told that she can receive visitors. She is being held prisoner at a château in Dongelber, only a few miles from Wavre. Your father is in a camp near the Polish frontier, Stalag Five, I think he called it. He too is well and safe."

The news that they could probably be reunited with Maman, plus the fact that they could be taken to a place of safety by their uncle Jean and M. Van Den Bos, was more than they had dared to hope for. Nadia, caught in her silent world, did not share their happiness. Where were her family? She felt more and more as though a dark curtain had been drawn, and that this curtain would never ever reveal its dreadful secret. They held back their excitement so as not to hurt Nadia any more than was necessary. Pierre held her close in his arms, but that only increased her feelings towards him, of which he seemed unaware.

Pierre stood at the railway station at Wavre. He and Jeannine were waiting for the local train that would take them to the château at Dongelber, where Maman was held prisoner. M. Pettit had finally managed to arrange a meeting between them. He looked towards the east, his eyes following the single railway track that snaked its way through the wooded parkland and fields stretching out before him.

'A real country scene,' he thought, and at the other end of the railway line lay a reunion with Maman, whom they had not seen for over twelve months now. What would they find at this prison château at Dongelber? Jeannine stood silent beside him, also letting her mind wander along the same lines.

It was early in the morning. They had taken the train from Groenendael to Wavre, where they had to change. Here they had to wait more than two hours for the local train which would take them to Jodonge. From here they would walk to Dongelber. Wavre, where they had changed trains, was normally a busy town, but it seemed deserted. Here and there some local people were seen hurrying along to their place of work, but other than that there was hardly any movement.

"I wonder if everywhere else is as quiet as this," remarked Jeannine.

"It's still early," he replied. "It might get busier later on."

But Pierre felt uneasy and began to wonder whether perhaps something had happened in the town that might have angered the occupying army. An act of sabotage by the Resistance movement? Who knows? Suddenly the sound of trucks turning the corner into the square where they were waiting was heard. The way the trucks sped along and then suddenly came to a halt was a sure indication that something was wrong. One by one the soldiers disembarked from the trucks, rifles at the ready. One soldier looked in their direction and began walking towards them.

"Pierre," murmured Jeannine. She was frightened.

"Stay perfectly still," he ordered, but he too felt his heart beating faster.

"Papieren bitte," ordered the soldier as he approached them.

Both understood. The soldier was asking for their identity cards and travel documents. Silently Pierre produced their identity cards, a yellow card with a bright red stripe diagonally across it bearing the word 'foreigner'.

The soldier opened the cards and then exclaimed, "Ach, Englander!" as though he had made a strike. "Kommen Sie."

Jeannine grabbed Pierre's arm.

"Not a word," he ordered again.

Both followed the soldier, who led them across the square to a building from which a German flag was flying. It was unmistakably occupied by the Gestapo. Once inside they were asked to wait. Two soldiers and a man from the Gestapo in civilian clothes entered the room.

Turning to Pierre the Gestapo officer ordered, "Kommen Sie!"

Jeannine was made to wait.

"Pierre!" she cried as she saw that he was being led away. He turned round and looked at her with penetrating eyes. She sat down again, silent.

Pierre was led through a door into the inner courtyard of the building with the two soldiers walking either side of him, the man from the Gestapo in front, leading them. As they crossed the courtyard, he saw two freshly dug holes in the ground. 'Graves?' he thought. Pierre was frozen into immobility like an animal under threat. The two soldiers got hold of him and forced him to walk on. The man from the Gestapo looked round – he had a sickly smile on his face. The psychological effect that the two holes in the ground had on Pierre pleased him. They were there for that purpose.

Once on the other side of the inner courtyard, Pierre was pushed through a door into an office in which there was the largest mahogany desk he had ever seen. Behind it sat an officer wearing the black uniform of the Gestapo. He had obviously been watching Pierre as he was led through the courtyard and had observed his reaction to the freshly dug holes. Pierre was a true Scorpio, the birth sign under which he was born, and he immediately summed up the officer's character.

'Here is a dangerous man with murderous eyes,' he thought. 'One who suspects everyone. Totally dedicated to the task of ruling by fear.' Pierre's legs were still shaking and he decided that he would answer truthfully all the questions which were asked – he had nothing to hide.

Glancing at the children's identity cards which lay on the desk in front of him, the officer then looked at Pierre's physical appearance.

"You are fourteen years old?" he asked, as though he found that hard to believe. Pierre looked more like seventeen or eighteen.

"Yes, sir, I was fourteen last November," he replied.

"Is that girl with you your sister?"

"Yes sir. We are on our way to visit our mother, who is interned at the château at Dongelber. I have the official letter here, sir, confirming our visit."

The officer took the letter he held out.

"You were born in this country?"

"Yes sir."

"What do you know of the sabotage committed here last night?"

"Sabotage, sir? We arrived here this morning from Groenendael station, sir. We don't know the town at all. We were waiting for the local train to take us to Jodonge."

The officer continued to interrogate Pierre. The questions were direct and calculated and all the time he was making notes. They went on and on until, suddenly, the man stopped. He picked up the telephone and commanded that an orderly come in. He gave the orderly a page from his notepad and told him to check what was written on it. The orderly took the paper, clicked his heels hard and left. A while later, during which time not a word was spoken between the officer and Pierre, the orderly returned and confirmed that everything on his notepaper checked out correctly.

"Well, Pierre Fenbeau, it would seem that all your answers are truthful, so you and your sister are free to proceed with your journey. I shall personally give you a 'Laissez Passer' so that you do not encounter any difficulties during your journey."

The officer looked at Pierre. His facial expression had changed completely.

"What will you do about your education now that your parents are no longer at home?" asked the officer. Pierre sensed that the education of the young was of some interest to this man.

"Our education has been interrupted since the start of the war, sir, but we were told that when we reach the age of fifteen we will be given the choice of either joining our parents at their place of internment or entering Hitler's youth organisation."

He was very careful with his choice of words for fear that mentioning 'concentration camp' or 'prison' might provoke this man.

"Ah, you will enjoy the comradeship of the youth organisation. I too was a member when I was your age – the best time of my life," the officer added. "Would you really like that, Pierre?" continued the officer with an almost paternal interest.

"Yes sir," he replied. "Ever since the day when the officer told me that this offer would be made to me, I told him that I wished to be considered as one of their most devoted members."

He held his fingers crossed all the time he spoke.

The officer put his arm around his shoulders, and with a satisfied smile on his face, said, "I'll have you escorted back to your sister. Here is your 'Laissez Passer'."

He gave the boy the signed document.

When they parted the officer clicked his heels hard and gave the salute, "Heil Hitler!" Pierre couldn't click his heels because he was wearing soft shoes, but he returned the salute as though his arm were mounted on springs. As he turned away, he made sure not to be caught giving a sigh of relief.

Jeannine was still sitting in the same chair waiting. When she saw Pierre escorted by the orderly she got up and was about to say something, but then she saw Pierre's penetrating gaze and remained silent. Once outside, they made their way back to the railway station and he told her about his ordeal. What he didn't talk about was the fear he had felt on seeing the two graves in the courtyard, because for the first time in his life it had planted the seed of doubt as to how brave he would be in the face of death, a feeling on which so far he had not been tested. He was too young to understand that in a powerless situation all men experience fear, but the seed of doubt would undoubtedly grow in him unless it was killed off by an act which he himself considered brave.

The Château de Dongelber was an impressive-looking building which stood in its own grounds. Judging by the tall shrubs and trees it was obvious that it had once been a beautiful garden, but now it looked neglected and wild. In the front garden were broken-down swings and roundabouts – it had been the home of a family. These were the thoughts which ran through Pierre's mind while he looked around. He and Jeannine looked at the tall iron fence surrounding the property. Then they caught sight of a guard who stood in front of a wooden hut. Pierre showed him the letter authorising their visit. The guard guided them to the main entrance of the château, after carefully locking the main gate.

Behind the windows of the château they could see the women prisoners who stood looking at the visitors. One of them was Maman – but which one? The children couldn't tell for they all looked alike – the same hairstyle, the same clothes. Which one was Maman?

Finally they reached the main entrance; it opened from within. A woman prison officer beckoned them to enter and follow her into a huge hall. If the hall had once been impressive, there was certainly no sign of it now. It was an empty space stripped of all its ornaments and art treasures.

Suddenly one of the women rushed forward.

"Jeannine! Pierre!" cried the woman.

There was a split second of disbelief in both their faces as they looked at the woman, but then they saw beyond the hairstyle and the clothes and there before them was Maman's beautiful face. Madeleine's surprise at seeing her children so grown up had been experience earlier on, when she saw them through the window. Now she no longer showed her surprise.

They hugged and clung together, unable to let go. The only intelligible words that came from them were, "Maman, Maman!"

"Boubou, Pierre – my children!"

There were tears and laughter. Not a single word that was spoken made any sense, but the hugging said it all. Hungrily they tried to fill their hearts with all the love that had been lost over those twelve months of separation. The other women prisoners looked on; some were crying, but they were tears of joy. Jeannine and Pierre were the only visitors.

Then came the questions, and they talked. Madeleine told them of her ordeal since that day when she had been taken from the little sweet shop at Boitsfort. She seemed to have spent most of the time travelling in trucks and trains, moving from one place of internment to another until she was brought here to Dongelber. Then she listened with fear in her eyes as they told her what they had gone through since the day when Uncle Blewett was hit with the butt of a rifle, until this very day when Pierre was interrogated by the Gestapo in Wavre.

"Oh darlings, do you think it wise to let yourselves be taken along that dangerous route of escape with Uncle Jean?" she said, afraid that some harm would come to them.

"We have no choice, Maman. What alternative have we got? The only way for us to stay together is to escape."

Madeleine lowered her eyes as a sign of acceptance.

All the women prisoners gathered around Pierre. They wanted to hear from him the things he had learned from Jacques Courtoy. His was the only news they had received from outside, other than the propaganda pushed out by the Germans. Pierre's optimism that by next spring the war would take a turn for the better gave them hope and courage.

The two hour visit they were allowed passed so fast that they could only say half the things they wanted to. The news they brought about their father was the only news Madeleine had received so far of her husband. All of a sudden it was time to say goodbye. They warned Maman not to make any attempt to communicate with them, because they would no longer stay at Groenendael, and for them to write from another country through the Red Cross would only endanger her own life.

No words could describe the pain felt by Madeleine as she clung to that final hug from her children. She felt as though she were saying goodbye for the last time. She watched them as they walked away from her towards the main gate, and shed the tears she had held back whilst they were with her. She realised that the pleasure of seeing her children grow up would not be hers: the war had forced them to grow up fast.

Jeannine and Pierre were sitting in the local train taking them back to Wavre. The carriage was rocking from side to side as it moved along the snake-like railway track that wound its way through the countryside. They listened silently to the familiar sound which came at regular intervals as the set of wheels rolled over each gap in the track.

Still dazed by the traumatic experience of seeing Maman in that prison château, they had almost forgotten that she had pushed a parcel into their hands just before they left.

"Here, take this, it's some food," she had whispered.

But they were too emotionally involved to pay any attention at that time. Jeannine's eyes were now fixed on the parcel without really looking, as she sat on the wooden bench of the carriage. Her mind was still on Maman. Then she suddenly remembered.

"Did Maman say food?"

"Yes, I think she did," replied Pierre, as though he were being pulled out of a dream.

Their hands tore at the parcel. In it were hard biscuits, bars of chocolate, tea, coffee, powdered milk and egg and more – all wrapped in paper which read 'Canadian Red Cross Food Parcel'.

"Chocolate!" cried both, as though the other food were of no importance. They could hardly remember the taste of it. It was with great difficulty that Jeannine controlled her desire to eat one bar after another, but then the thought that Maman had done without in order to give it to them gave her strength.

"No, we must save it and make it last," she said.

Pierre looked at her, almost cursing her strength in resisting temptation.

Nadia was alone in the house, patiently waiting for their return. She had gone through a frightening experience late in the afternoon, when a German soldier had knocked at the front door. Pierre had given her strict instructions not to answer the door to anyone. Quietly she listened to the knocking without answering the door, but it had made her very nervous.

Since no one answered the door, the soldier had pushed through a piece of paper on which was a message addressed to Pierre. Nadia handed it to him when they returned. She was frightened, and she wrote down what had happened.

"You did well not to answer the door," Pierre said, "but it's all right – he's Karl's friend. Karl writes to us through him and we meet now and again near the little chapel."

Then, turning to Jeannine, he said, "The message reads *Meet you tomorrow around six o'clock near the chapel, usual place*. It must be important for him to come calling like that. Perhaps Karl is coming soon."

"Oh, wouldn't that be wonderful?" exclaimed Jeannine, as she put her arms around Nadia, who stood there tense and nervous.

She had not enjoyed being alone in the house for the best part of the day, and she had never met Karl. Jeannine definitely showed that same bubbly enthusiasm which Maman had.

The following day, when Pierre had returned from the farm, they made their way to the château to meet Karl's friend. They hid near the little chapel where they were to meet him, and had only been there for a short while when they saw him coming out of the château. They moved deeper into the forest so as not to be seen by others.

Karl's friend was a man in his thirties. He had a fatherly appearance and his eyes always seemed to be laughing. As he approached them, Jeannine had an ominous feeling that something was wrong; it was his bearing, as though he shouldered a heavy burden.

"You got my note then," he said as he greeted them. There was no laughter in his eyes as he spoke.

"Is there something wrong with Karl?" Jeannine couldn't hold back. "He can't come, that's it, isn't it?"

Karl's friend looked her sadly in the eyes, as his hand reached to his inner pocket from which he pulled out an envelope.

"I received a letter from Karl's mother," he began, as he opened the envelope. He was searching for words.

"From Karl's mother?" Jeannine's eyes opened wide with fear at those words.

"Yes, she sent me this letter and in it she included another, addressed to you both."

He opened the letter and began to read. He knew that they could speak German, but they couldn't read it.

Dear Jeannine and Pierre, began the letter, *It is through my son Karl that I have learned about you, the two young people who live alone and in fear near the forest at Groenendael.* The letter went on and they listened, but then came the last paragraph which read:

It is with great sorrow that I have to tell you that Karl's plane was shot down over the Sahara Desert whilst he was on a reconnaissance mission.

Both stood paralysed as Karl's friend continued to read.

You were so close to him whilst he was stationed at Groenendael ...perhaps one day, when this war is over, we could meet. There was not one letter in which he didn't mention the two of you. I would so much like to meet you both for my son spoke so lovingly about you. I leave you my address.

The letter written by a broken-hearted mother and the news it brought of Karl's death tore at Jeannine's heart so violently that the whole of her body began to shake, and she fainted. When she came to a few seconds later, she gave out such a plaintive cry: "Noooooo! Not Karl!"

Instantly the forest became alive with the flapping of wings and the sound of the wildlife that lived high up in the treetops. It gave the impression that the whole of the Forêt-de-Soigne had received the news of Karl's death.

With the help of Karl's friend, Pierre managed to get Jeannine as far as the little chapel. There they had to part.

"Will you be all right if I leave you now?" enquired Karl's friend.

"Yes, we'll just stay here for a while. We'll be all right. Thank you."

He left after stroking Jeannine's head with his hand; he too was heart-broken. She was clinging to the railing of the chapel of Our Lady of the Lovely Scent. The tears were flowing from her eyes and she was unable to utter a word. Both she and Pierre were now holding on to the railing, Pierre with the letter from Karl's mother screwed up in his hand.

Neither could have said how long they had been there slumped against the railing when they suddenly heard the sound of marching boots in the distance, exactly as it had been when they waited for Karl's work party to return from the fields with shouldered spades and forks, singing their marching song. But that was impossible, for it was far too late in the evening. They lifted up their heads with a look of surprise. Jeannine was standing now, listening and breathing in the fresh air that was brought inside on a gentle breeze. The branches of the surrounding trees began to move with the breeze, but it was more than fresh air. With it came a scent, a 'lovely scent' which neither Jeannine nor Pierre recognised. For a while they stood silent, and a comfortable feeling overcame them.

Then, almost in a whisper, Jeannine said, "Karl's happy."

"What did you say?" Pierre asked.

"Karl wants us to know that he's happy," she said, turning to Pierre and looking him straight in the eyes. Her expression had changed. She no longer had that desperate look. It was as though she had received a message telling her that all was well.

"We can go home now," she added, and she turned to start the journey home.

Pierre looked around as she began to walk away. He had a bewildered look on his face, not fully understanding what had happened. The gentle breeze had died away and with it the lovely scent.

"Come on, Pierre," she called out. "We must get back before curfew."

'Is it that late already?' he thought, as her call pulled him out of his bewilderment.

When they were home he listened to Jeannine who was telling Nadia about the letter. She was sad and crying while she spoke, but then she confided in Nadia and told her of the strange experience she had had at the chapel of Our Lady of the Lovely Scent. As he listened Pierre felt himself strangely drawn towards the sideboard of the living room. He opened one of the drawers and reached out for the heavy silver ring which Karl had given him. Pierre looked at it dreamily, then slipped it over the middle finger of his left hand with a gesture that implied 'for ever'. It struck him that the understanding he had of the world in which they lived was so minute in comparison with the many mysteries it held. He knew that he would never speak of that day to anyone for fear of being ridiculed, and also because it was of a very personal nature, but he would never forget or dismiss it from his mind.

The Resistance

Pierre's ordeal at Wavre and his interrogation by the Gestapo officer made him go straight to M. Van Den Bos to ask his advice as to whether this was not the time to go into hiding, more so because of Nadia. If she were caught her fate would undoubtedly be that of all the other Jews who had disappeared so mysteriously. Some very disturbing rumours were circulating from Poland regarding the fate of the Jewish people. It was said that one part of Warsaw had been sealed off in which thousands upon thousands of Jews were forced to live with hardly any civil rights. Only one train crossed this area non-stop, from which very little was learned, but what was learned was heart-breaking.

The move was swift once Van Den Bos agreed that the time had come. This decision, however, implied that there was no turning back. Once in hiding they would have to stay in hiding. To return to the Maison Communale after a period of absence would lead to interrogation and certain death. It was also a time when the escape route was increasingly dangerous. The Resistance groups in the occupied countries were stepping up their acts of sabotage; the German war machine was no longer seen as invincible. This filled the hearts of the men of the Resistance with hope, and gave them the courage to wear down their oppressors. In turn it angered the German army of occupation and made them determined to stamp out the groups of saboteurs. They were hunted down like wild animals.

M. Van Den Bos's property was ideally situated at Le Pitoresque and served as a hiding place from which the Resistance could operate. Unbeknown to Pierre, Jacques Courtoy was M. Van Den Bos's closest neighbour. He lived in a beautiful villa shaped like the upper deck of a ship, with its curved window overlooking a gentle valley through which the Chaussée La Hulpe ran. The two men carried on their work in town as normal, M. Van Den Bos in his internationally known shop, Le Palais des Cottillons, and Jacques Courtoy, the lawyer, practising law at the Palais de Justice in Brussels. This was their cover up, but these men were constantly living on a knife edge.

When Jeannine and Pierre arrived at the villa, they were surprised to discover that their two cousins, Léon and François, who lived in Antwerp, were also there.

"Léon! François!" exclaimed Pierre on seeing them. "We had no idea you were here. Are you visiting?"

Léon smiled in amusement on hearing these words.

"I wish we were, cousin," he replied, but Pierre had to wait for a more detailed explanation until the proper greetings were over.

Kisses for the women on both cheeks from the men, and then a firm handshake for himself all took time. Léon was a young man of eighteen. He was very athletic and this could be seen in his movements, whereas François, who was now twenty, was much slower physically. François was the brainy one. He had already embarked on a career in diplomatic circles. But when the two brothers were together, Léon always did most of the talking and that gave a different impression.

"We're here for the same reason as you are," continued Léon after the greetings were over.

"You're in hiding too? But why? You have no connection with England."

Pierre, because of his own circumstances, thought that it was only the English and Jews who were in danger from the occupying German army.

"It's not only the English who are in danger," explained Léon. "There are a few Belgian fascist collaborators who are preparing our country for integration into the Reich. The Wallonia and Flanders battalions are sending Belgians to die with the German Army on the Eastern Front, and civilians are sent into forced labour to work in factories all over Germany."

As Léon continued explaining, it all fell into place for Pierre. Of course he should have realised this because of what Meterke had said about his Uncle Albert, who had been taken as forced labour together with hundreds of other men. But the fact that Belgians were sent to die on the Eastern Front, that was news indeed to him.

"Are you going to be taken along this route of escape too?" he asked eagerly.

"No, we're staying here. François and I are members of the Légion Nationale – we take part in the Resistance movement. The Légion is linked to the Belgian Government in exile in London. François is in touch with them. We're organising the escape of Jews and other endangered citizens like yourselves. There is also a group called 'Group G'," Léon continued. "They are engineering graduates from the University of Brussels who are masterminding an elaborate campaign of sabotage against Hitler's industrial war machine. Some of them are here in hiding. If you stay long enough you'll meet them. It's all happening here, Pierre," he added with a smile.

François hadn't said much, but he gave the impression that he had, through his nodding and occasional "hmm, hmm" sounds.

Pierre was impressed. Behind this peaceful and tranquil setting of M. Van Den Bos's villa, located amongst that curtain of dense green forest, lay a world of intrigue and conspiracy. It gave him the feeling that he had done the right thing by moving here.

By evening M. Van Den Bos and Jacques Courtoy had returned from the city, and the conversation turned to the pros and cons of the children's decision to go into hiding. It was agreed that it should be so. Nadia was sitting with Mme Van Den Bos who had once been a nurse, and showed concern at Nadia's condition.

"I think only another emotional shock can bring back her voice – something similar to what happened when the Gestapo took her family. There's nothing we can do just now – we can only wait and hope," she said.

Nadia, other than the fact that she didn't speak, behaved normally. She carried a pad and pencil on which she wrote as a means to communicate. Sometimes she would go very quiet; that was when her thoughts went to her family who seemed to have disappeared from the face of the earth. She missed them so terribly, especially her baby sister, Julienne. Pierre was her idol. Whenever he was near she would be close to him, clinging on to his every word. He still believed that by showing her love and understanding her voice would return one day. But somehow he was blind to the fact that she was growing into a beautiful young woman, and that she was waiting to be noticed by him. She was the same age as Jeannine, just fifteen.

The men who met at the villa were in deep discussion about the latest events in the continuation of the war. It was now September 1941. The Germans had invaded Russia on Sunday June the 22nd, but it was not through Georgia and Armenia as Jacques had predicted. The Germans and Italians had failed in their attempt to conquer the Mediterranean Sea and turn it into an Italian lake, as was their intention. Furthermore they were entering Russia not as liberators but as conquerors. The German soldiers of the front line, who advanced through the Soviet Union and were welcomed as liberators by the Russian people, were soon followed by special units who killed all before them.

"This is Hitler's greatest mistake," began Jacques. "It can only be explained by his blind hatred of the Russian people whom he considers sub-human. What he seems to overlook is that he is throwing the Russian masses into the arms of their hated Bolshevik masters; rather the devil they know than the one who violates their country," he added, and began to explain how the Allies should proceed.

"Now that the Russians are reunited under their Bolshevik masters, it is imperative that the Allies exterminate Hitlerism and simultaneously prevent its replacement by Stalinism. They can't afford to crush the German fighting force completely because Europe will need this fighting force to serve as a buffer against Communism, otherwise the war will be lost politically to the Western world." He spoke with a deep understanding of the danger to Europe as a whole if Germany was crushed completely.

"In my opinion the Allies will enter into close co-operation with the extensive anti-Nazi faction in Germany to foment revolution within the Reich. And we in the Resistance will be called upon to assist in this task. Let us brace ourselves, friends – there is a light at the end of the tunnel."

The men in the room were full of confidence, a feeling which came from having someone like Jacques as a leader. He was a man of vision. His understanding of events was second to none. As a strategist he was brilliant. What he said made sense and could be understood by all. If the Allies could bring about victory the way Jacques saw it, then their return to freedom was assured, because, whatever happened in the Soviet Union afterwards, the Western allies would be strategically well placed. The sacrifices demanded of them now seemed not so intolerable, and they celebrated by opening a cask of beer.

Pierre hadn't been invited to sit in with the group. He was considered too young, but he was listening and the whole of his body tingled as he too shared their confidence. When evening came the sleeping arrangements were discussed. In the attic they had camp beds and blankets, where the men would sleep.

M. Van Den Bos and Jacques Courtoy maintained a normal family life. Nadia and Jeannine were given a room which they could share, and would live in as family.

Days passed where nothing happened. Pierre became restless. The leaves of the forest would soon begin to turn and winter would be upon them. He knew that during the winter months the escape route was closed to them because of their age.

He passed some of his time by reading the comic strip escapism of Hergé's *Tintin*, which lay scattered about in the attic. The comic strips portrayed Tintin as a young private detective, whose adventures took him to many lands and across many seas, stories in which Pierre could lose himself.

One day a stranger was brought in. He was a Jew. Immediately arrangements were under way for their escape. It happened so fast that it took Pierre by surprise. They were issued with warm clothing, forged identity cards and travel documents. He watched Jean as he transferred an official German seal from a document on to their travel papers in a most extraordinary way. He cut a potato in half, placed it over the seal of a German document, and waited for a while until some of the ink of the seal had been soaked up by the juice. He then transferred it on to their papers, where it left a near perfect imprint of the seal.

"Don't try and rub it," he said when he saw Pierre examining the imprint. "It might come off."

"Ingenious," remarked Pierre.

'At last we're on our way to freedom,' he thought. The travel documents were made out to read that Pierre had been ordered by the government to work in Germany. His age on the document put him at seventeen years old. Their first port of call was Dinan in the Ardennes, where further instructions would be given to them.

Léon and François would escort them as far as Dinan. There they would be handed over to another group who would take them further along the line.

They were travelling in Jean's truck; he was taking them on the first leg of the journey. Nadia sat next to Pierre and looked at him occasionally out of the corner of her eyes. She was well pleased with herself, because the alibi she was told to give, should they be stopped en route, was that she was travelling with her boyfriend, Pierre, as far as Dinan. There she would turn back after saying goodbye. Jeannine was to say the same and pretend that Léon was her boyfriend. Nadia had a little crease in the corner of her mouth which betrayed a smile. She didn't want to look Pierre in the eyes – that would give away her true feelings for him. What she wanted most was for him to notice her. Then, and only then, would she look for a way to let him know just how she felt about him. She had never seen Pierre with a member of the opposite sex of his own age, and so she believed that there was no one for whom he cared. She was ignorant of the fact that he knew Mady. Neither Jeannine nor Pierre ever spoke much about Dédé and Mady to her, other than that they were the daughters of a baron whose horses were kept at the stables, and that they used to come and visit the horses. She was looking down at her notepad almost wishing that someone would stop them and ask for her alibi. Her imagination took over, and with an imaginary pencil she wrote the following words: *I am travelling with my fiancé as far as Dinan.* Her mental fantasy had already jumped from boyfriend to fiancé, and the little crease in the corner of her mouth widened.

The stranger, the Jew, was also travelling with them. He kept aloof and very silent. Pierre sensed that he was a hunted man, and the less they knew about him the better, just in case they were captured.

When they arrived at Dinan the orders had been altered. The arrangements were cancelled due to a series of acts of sabotage further along the route. It was too dangerous for them to proceed. The Germans had stepped up their search to uncover the groups of saboteurs. The identity papers they carried would pass an ordinary checkpoint, but they would not pass the scrutiny of the experienced Gestapo. There was no alternative for them but to turn back and try again at a later date. Only the Jew was travelling on because his position was such that he had no choice, regardless of the risks.

Pierre's disappointment was beyond words. It had to be pointed out to him that it was not only he who was in danger and that he had to think of the others too. Eventually the six turned back.

Nadia had seen his disappointment. She came close to him and held her pad in front of his eyes, on which she had written: *Are you all right?*

He smiled at her and nodded affirmatively. A simple gesture like that made all the difference. Nadia normally wore her hair pinned up, but when she showed him the notepad her hair hung loose and natural about her face. She looked very beautiful and feminine with her long, light golden hair. He noticed the change. At first he behaved normally as he touched her hair, but then he became awkward and clumsy as he realised that he was looking at her in a different way. His awkwardness grew worse with every movement he made and he became embarrassed. Nadia, on the other hand, had been waiting for something like this to happen and his behaviour was what she had hoped for.

"We must go – the others will be looking for us," he said, blushing.

Nadia couldn't answer, but she got hold of his hand, and, with a smile that said it all, guided him; she was in full control of the situation. Happiness shone from her eyes.

December 1941 brought great changes in the war. The United States of America were well and truly dragged into the European conflict. On December the 17th the Japanese Navy attacked Pearl Harbor, and on the 11th Germany declared war on the United States which, in turn, declared war on Germany.

Jacques Courtoy's words echoed to and fro in Pierre's head. "America's entry into the war has turned it into a second World War. There is no one left to arbitrate – let's hope that the Allies learned from their mistakes of the Great War." Those were his words. Exactly what it meant was not clear to Pierre, but the change it brought to the Belgian and French Resistance was noticeable: they were now being instructed from abroad. Instead of a group of men who were mainly engaged in hiding citizens resisting capture by the Gestapo and restoring King Léopold to his throne, they were being directed and shaped into a more sophisticated fighting force by the Belgian Government in exile in Britain. Jacques's prediction – that they would be called upon to assist in the uprising of the German masses against Hitlerism – looked as though it was coming true. The other change was that this development overshadowed the arrangements for their escape.

Jeannine felt most unhappy about this. She felt as though she were being treated more as a servant in the household of M. and Mme Van Den Bos rather than a member of the family. She began to feel bitter towards Tante Yvonne who was the main cause of her unhappiness. Isabel tried hard to smooth things over, but since the disappearance of James she had changed enormously through worry. She had lost all zest for life and was ageing at an alarming rate.

One day when they sat talking together, Jeannine opened her heart to Pierre, and told him how she felt.

"Tante Yvonne sits back like a lady and lets me do all the work, just because Jean is doing so well with that truck of his. I want to leave here, Pierre. Do you think we will be taken away soon?"

"We'll have to wait until the winter is over. Don't lose heart, Boubou – it's just a question of time."

He didn't tell her of the doubts which lay in his heart too. That night he lay awake on his bed in the attic thinking that tomorrow he would have a word with Jacques. He didn't want to be treated like a boy: he wanted to know what was going on instead of having to listen to the men's conversation from a distance.

As he lay thinking, the sound of sirens suddenly startled him. None of them took much notice any more, because to them the sirens were just a warning of Allied planes flying over. He glanced quickly at Léon and François who were the only ones with him in the attic. They lay fast asleep; neither stirred. When the sirens stopped, he listened to the sound of the approaching planes flying over the area, and tried to guess their numbers; at least twenty-four was his guess. The anti-aircraft guns went into action. He knew the pattern of the sound of these guns by heart: three short consecutive shots, followed by three muffled sounds high up in the sky as the shells exploded.

'Poor devils,' he thought. 'They are taking a beating tonight.' Then the sound of planes died away and the anti-aircraft guns stopped firing.

No sooner had the noise died down than he heard a strange sound in the sky. It was approaching the villa, and sounded like a meteor coming towards them.

"Léon, François! Wake up!" he shouted as he jumped out of bed. He ran towards the door which gave access to the flat roof. Looking at the sky, he saw it lit up by a ball of fire. It was heading straight for the villa, then suddenly it veered slightly towards the left, and as it passed he saw that it was a plane with all four engines on fire. The flames trailing behind gave it the appearance of a comet. François and Léon arrived on the roof just in time to see it pass.

"It's crashing into the trees!" shouted Léon. "Let's get to it before the Germans do!"

This time Pierre decided that was he not going to be left behind. He collected his clothes and ran downstairs ahead of the others. Once downstairs, they saw Jean, half-dressed and making for the truck. All three followed him. Uninvited, Pierre jumped in the passenger seat where he quickly finished dressing, whilst Léon and François jumped in the back of the truck.

"Where do you think it crashed?" asked Jean, looking at him.

"I'm sure it came down near that wide footpath leading to the forest about half a kilometre before you get to the farm, La Ferme Rose. I had a good view from the roof as it crashed."

Jean stepped on the accelerator and followed his directions. None of them had ever experienced such a bumpy ride as he turned his truck into the footpath; it was not meant to be used by vehicles at high speed. Pierre had pinpointed the crash correctly. They could see a clearing cut through the trees of the forest, caused by the crash, almost parallel to the path. A huge fire lit up the area. The flames came from the burning plane and the trees were set on fire by it. It looked as if the place had been lit up by a thousand torches.

Swiftly they jumped out of the truck to look for survivors. Pierre was convinced that their journey had been in vain, that no one could have survived this inferno, he thought. Nevertheless he followed the example of the others and ran towards the wreckage. As they came closer they had to fight their way through fallen branches torn down by the crash. He was pushing his way forward in spite of the heat when suddenly he saw a man's boot through the fallen branches.

"I've found one of them!" he shouted, but when he touched the boot it fell out of the branches, and still in it were the remains of a human leg.

"Arrrch!" He turned away his head and as he did so he promptly brought up the entire contents of his stomach.

"Where is he? Is he still alive ?" It was Jean's voice.

"No, forget it. It's only a boot."

Too late – Jean was already looking at it. He too heaved at the sight.

"Are you all right, son?"

"Yes, I'm all right. Let's look some more. Do you think anyone could have survived this ?"

"Over here!" The call came from Léon who had approached the clearing from a different angle. "Over here!" he repeated.

It was unbelievable, but Léon had found one of the crew members alive and in one piece.

"How many of you were on board when you crashed?" Jean and Pierre heard him ask the question just as they arrived.

"They all jumped," uttered the crew member, his face twisted in pain. "Only the captain and myself – we didn't make it. Find the captain," he pleaded.

François, who had just arrived, touched Léon's shoulder and shook his head in the negative.

"I found him. He's dead – his body is torn to pieces," he whispered. He was pale and shaking all over. What he had seen was indescribable.

"Let's get out of here before the Jerries find us," ordered Jean, as he realised that there was no point in searching any further.

Locking their arms underneath the co-pilot's body, they carried him to the truck. Once inside the truck, Léon and François did their best to act as shock absorbers for the injured man during the bumpy ride.

Jean was looking at Pierre who sat beside him in the cabin. He had a grin on his face.

"You're the navigator from now on, son – that was no guesswork leading us to the crash. Spot on!"

Their faces were blackened by the smoke from the burning plane. Pierre was looking in Jean's direction, but in the dark all he could see was a perfect set of white teeth. He had never seen teeth stand out so perfectly in the dark.

"Look ahead! You're pulling to the right," he shouted as he saw the truck heading away from the path.

Jean continued to grin as his concentration returned to his driving – he seemed to thrive on danger.

"Yes, you'll do just fine, just fine," he said, as he strained his eyes to penetrate the darkness of the night. "Just tell me which way to go, son. We have to stay clear of the main road – the Jerries are bound to be there."

"OK, keep driving. I'll tell you when and where to turn as we get there."

"Yes, sir, you'll do just fine," Jean repeated as he carried on laughing with both his arms practically wrapped around the steering wheel.

Pierre reflected on what Jean was saying about the Germans being on the main roads.

"What do we do if we do run into the Germans?" he asked, looking straight ahead into the darkness. He was obviously thinking about the consequences if they were caught.

Jean didn't reply. Instead his left hand went down the side of his seat from where he pulled out a machine-gun and passed it to Pierre. His hand then went down the seat again, and he produced a box with two spare clips of bullets and half a dozen hand grenades.

"That's a Bren gun," he said. "It's useless for accurate shooting, but at close quarters it's deadly – it sprays the bullets. You press it close into the side of your body and pull the trigger. It has a tremendous pull towards the right when you fire it so it's best to point it slightly to the left of your target and use short bursts. That thing there is the safety catch," he said, pointing. "You release it as soon as you see them. You don't let them take you alive. In guerrilla warfare there is no such thing as the Geneva Convention – that's for soldiers in uniform."

Jean had just educated him in Resistance fighting and he made no bones about it. In the circumstances he didn't have the time for niceties.

Pierre had listened to every word, still looking straight ahead into the dark. He felt the blood draining from his head as Jean spoke. He had a sinking feeling which suddenly took over his entire body and he was fighting not to pass out.

"We're approaching the main road. Cross the road and take the path slightly to the left and re-enter the forest on the other side." Pierre's voice didn't seem to belong to him as he gave these instructions, but it had taken his mind off the dreadful warning Jean had given him. His words echoed in his head: 'You don't let them take you alive.'

Jean was silent now, listening for sounds on the main road. He looked carefully left, then right. All was quiet. He crossed the road, took the path on the other side as Pierre had indicated and continued to follow his directions. Pierre gave a deep sigh of relief as they drove on, the colour returning to his cheeks. He felt safer now that they were on the other side of the main road. From here he knew how to reach the villa without crossing any roads. He couldn't stop his brain from imagining a situation where they would run into a German patrol. What would he do? He couldn't accept having to turn a gun on himself: that would take more guts than he had and, besides, he would need a pistol, which he didn't have. His eyes caught sight of the hand grenades. It made him think. 'Yes,' he thought, 'to pull the pin from a grenade, then let go if there was no other alternative.' That, in a state of panic and fear, he could perhaps do. His eyes again turned to the box next to Jean, and he felt the need to acquire at least one of those grenades. He was determined to ask Jean later if he could have one, and if he asked why he would explain that it was for his peace of mind. Jean would understand.

On arrival at the villa Mme Van Den Bos did what she could for the co-pilot. He would have to be moved to a better hiding place where a doctor and nurse could attend to his injuries. He had several broken bones and some very nasty flesh wounds, but as far as she could tell he had no internal injuries. His recovery, however, would take weeks.

The crash had happened in the early hours of Saturday morning. Mme Van Den Bos was anxious to leave the villa. The Germans were bound to make a house-to-house search if they didn't find any survivors. They were certain to take hostages in order to get to the truth. If questioned later she would tell them that they had all stayed at the apartment in Brussels during the weekend. The men moved to the underground cave that Pierre had told them about, and they would hide there for as long as they had to.

The war was now entering its third year. Food became scarce. The situation in Belgium was so acute that by March 1942 the death penalty for forging ration cards was introduced. Fortunately Jean, with his many contacts in the trucking business, was able to find food for them. Most things could be bought on the black market, but it took a great deal of money and most villagers were unable to pay the exorbitant prices. Meterke and Tante Jane, who had given birth to a little girl, were amongst those villagers who went hungry. Jeannine and Pierre made the occasional journey under cover of darkness to see them, in spite of Meterke's warning.

"It's too dangerous," she said. "Someone might recognise you. There could be a German sympathiser in the village – you never know," but a light shone from her eyes each time she saw them.

It was in March, when the food shortage was at its worst, that the brother and sister took the risk of seeing them. The occasion was a special one. It was Meterke's birthday. Both had made a supreme effort to save some of their food to give to her. They were able to do this with the help of Jean, who gave them some extras and also managed to get tins of powdered milk for Jane's baby. Meterke was one of those women who could produce a tasty meal with what others would throw away as scraps. When she and Jane looked at the food parcel which Jeannine put on the table in front of them, with the three tins of powdered milk, Jane was so filled with emotion that she couldn't even cry; that would come later. Meterke, for once, was speechless. The emotion aroused at the sight of food in those who have known the pains of hunger over a long period of time cannot be put into words, it has to be experienced. Jane held the tins of milk in her arms as one cradles a baby.

"For my baby!" over and over she cried. "For my baby!"

Then came the deluge of tears. She turned her eyes upwards to heaven, as though the tins were a gift from the Good Lord himself. Meterke, who was normally so undemonstrative, had to lift the hem of her apron in order to wipe away the tears that had filled her eyes. But she soon regained her composure, and began looking around to find ways and means of supplementing the food that the two young people had brought. She wanted to make a meal which would do justice to this special occasion and, at the same time, save enough of the food for the days ahead. On the stove stood a jug of soup that Jane collected each day from the soup kitchen at the Maison Communale. This had been set up by the community to help the starving villagers. The jug stood ready to be reheated on the stove, and the contents would have served as their evening meal.

Meterke soon went to work. With the soup, some of the food they had brought, plus other fresh vegetables she had managed to find, she prepared a stew that would have done anyone proud. The smell of cooking which filled her house that evening brought back memories of the days of plenty. Her birthday turned into one which would never be forgotten.

"One of these days", said Pierre, "I'll bring you a loaf of white bread all to yourself."

"Oh Pierre, you are an incorrigible romantic," said Meterke, and she had to pick up the hem of her apron once again to dab the tears from her eyes.

'How strange', she thought, 'that amongst all this poverty and danger, our happiness is so immeasurable. Will there ever be a day when we could feel happier?'

As spring approached, the Resistance stepped up their activities. Hitler's prestige at the beginning of 1942 was very different from that in 1941. His fatally mistaken policy – to antagonise the subjugated Russian people under Soviet rule – had robbed him of the aid of an internal revolution within the USSR. He was now on the defensive, aiming to take possession of the Caucasian oil fields, because without it the Reich would collapse. His other priority was to occupy Leningrad and Moscow in order to cut off Soviet communications.

Dr Göbbels's comment at this prospect was: "Possibly this may mean a hundred years' war in the east – but that need not worry us."

Such a prospect, however, worried the occupied countries. On April the 15th, the French Resistance attacked German headquarters at Arras with hand grenades, and on Wednesday the 29th the Belgian Resistance destroyed Tenderloo Chemical Works, killing more than two hundred and fifty people.

These acts of sabotage did not go unpunished. Disturbing news reached Jacques shortly after the event, which caused much anxiety amongst the men. As a reprisal the Germans began to execute innocent Belgian citizens. Already twenty-five to thirty had been killed, and it was said that the same number would be executed each month unless these acts of sabotage ceased.

Jacques pulled M. Van Den Bos to one side, and openly admitted to him that he was worried.

"This war will go on, and so will the killing," he said, glancing sideways to make sure that no one was listening. "That joint declaration which was signed by the United States of America and the twenty-four other nations including Russia, stating that complete victory over their enemies is essential for liberty, independence and religious freedom, worries me, Charles." Jacques was addressing him by his first name. "I can't imagine Germany surrendering – they'll be willing to risk their very existence rather than lose face by an unconditional surrender. That broadcast made by Churchill last year, when he said that they will never parley, never negotiate, give whatever help to Russia to destroy the Germans, can only result in Hitler being replaced by Stalin, and I don't know which is worse. I tell you, Charles, our leaders lack a sense of history – war to them is a lethal game rather than an instrument of policy. One thing has always been clear in all military studies, and that is that the true aim of war is peace and not victory. The Allies are committing the self-same blunder that Hitler made. They fail to distinguish between the pro and anti-Nazi regime – exactly the same as Hitler, who failed to distinguish between pro and anti-Stalinist peoples. Why is it that they can't see that the answer lies in destroying Hitler, not the German fighting forces, in order to maintain the balance of power? This blunder will prolong the war by years, I'm sure of it, and in spite of ultimate victory peace will be lost and make this war an absurdity."

As Jacques finished speaking, they heard a noise from behind a door nearby which stood half-open. Charles quickly glanced inside the room to see who was missing. Max, Jean-Paul and Hilaire, who were the engineering graduates from the University of Brussels, were all missing. Could it be that one of them had been listening – or perhaps all three?

"Oh, it's probably nothing."

"Maybe you're right, but I'd rather the men didn't hear me talk like this – especially now with all these killings. They feel responsible and down-hearted. It's best we keep such thoughts to ourselves. Come on, let's go back into the room."

Pierre didn't want to be left out of the action, and he was now accepted as a useful member of the Resistance. Jacques was not very happy about this. In his opinion Pierre was too young.

"It's a great sacrifice to make for one so young," he argued with Van Den Bos. "Think of what it will do to him when the war is over – he'll be expecting some recognition and reward. He already has a chip on his shoulder."

"We need every able-bodied man we can get, Jacques. Physically he is up to it, and he knows the area better than anyone else. It's the present that we're all concerned with in order for us to have a future."

Jacques gave a deep sigh.

"I suppose you're right – but I still think it's wrong."

Pierre, on the other hand, was happier now that he was involved. He felt himself part of the set-up, but Jeannine felt trapped in her present situation. Nadia made the most of things. Like Pierre, she decided to get involved. The clothes she wore and the way she did her hair made her look more like a young boy than a young woman. All she wanted was to be near Pierre: everyone could see that she had chosen him as her man. He, however, was too in love with Mady to even notice. He couldn't forget Mady. He had already been several times to her house in Boitsfort in the hope that one day she would return. He had left instructions with one of his friends, who lived nearby, to be informed of the first sign of life in her house.

One day in June of 1942, Pierre's friend came to see him. He had made the journey especially to tell him that Mady and her family were in Boitsfort visiting.

"She wants to see you, but don't go calling at the house – that will only cause problems – she asked me to warn you of this. Her father was killed on the first day of the war at the fortress of Eben Emael, and things are very different in their house now. She suggested that you meet her by the lake in the forest – you'd know which one, she said."

"You saw her? You actually saw her?" Pierre couldn't believe what he was being told. "Tell her to meet me tomorrow by the lake at ten o'clock – do you think she can make it?"

"Yes, she said for you to name the time and day. I see you're not wasting any time."

"What did she look like?"

"I'm not going to answer that, but let me tell you this – you'll be pleasantly surprised."

"She's back at last." Pierre folded his hands as though he were thanking the good Lord above. "You say her father was killed? She must feel terrible: she loved him so. Maybe that's why she doesn't want me to go calling. I had better do as she says."

The following day he was early and the first person up and about in the valley of the forest. By the lake he let his bicycle fall to the ground. He looked out in the direction from which Mady would come. He had a good view from where he stood and could see as far as the embankment of the Brussels to Charleroi road. His eyes were glued to the furthest point of the wide footpath. There was a gentle breeze playing with the leaves and branches of the tall trees. He listened to that comforting sound which brought back happy memories, his eyes still glued to that furthest point. He didn't want to miss the sight of Mady approaching. Then it happened. He saw a cyclist at the far end of the footpath. Was it her? What would she be wearing? Would she still have her ponytail? Had she grown much since he last saw her? Had her feelings changed towards him during all this time? He couldn't stop himself from asking all these questions.

The cyclist drew nearer and nearer. Pierre stood upright, motionless, with his long fair hair blowing in the breeze. Would she recognise him? He had changed drastically and he knew it. The clothes he wore made him look like a tramp. When she came close, she put one foot on the ground, hopping along to bring her bicycle to a stop. She had to look twice when she saw him. He too looked surprised: her angel-like face hadn't changed, but she had grown into a beautiful young lady. People had always said that when she grew into a young lady her angel-like face would bring every young man to her feet, and it had turned out to be true. She looked beautiful. Her hair, bleached by the Mediterranean sun, flowed freely to well below her shoulders. He stood speechless. She too let her bicycle fall to the ground by the lake.

"Pierre, is it really you?" She stood motionless for a few seconds, but then, in her usual manner, threw herself hard against him in an embrace.

'Oh yes,' he thought, 'this is Mady'. The Mady he knew so well – no one would throw themselves so hard in a loving embrace. It was as if time had stood still. Three years of forced separation hadn't diminished their feelings.

Looking at him, and taking his face in both hands, she said, "You've changed so much! What has this war done to you?"

"You too have changed. What happened to your ponytail?"

"Do you like me like this?" she asked, but she knew the answer. She had seen it in his eyes when he looked at her.

He felt that he had betrayed his feelings, so he didn't give a straight answer; instead he made a noise like "Hmmm." But the way she had asked the question gave him a warm feeling. It was so feminine, he thought. She was beautiful, yet she wanted to hear him say so.

Then, so as not to disappoint her, he said, "You're more beautiful than I dared hope."

She gave a little sound that could only be made by a young woman caressed by the very words she wanted to hear. They stood for a while letting themselves be ruled by their hearts.

Then she looked at him and said, "Did you know that my father was killed at the beginning of the war?" Her eyes immediately filled with tears as she spoke.

He held her for a while before answering.

"I heard only yesterday when I was told that you were here."

Neither spoke; it would only have resulted in tears.

"Who's looking after you now?"

"Mother is, but my stepbrother is the head of the family." Without hiding her feelings, she added, "He's hard and cruel. We don't like him – we hardly know him. We never saw much of him when Papa was alive; it's only now that he's there all the time. He seems to hate us. He aims to rule our lives, Pierre – that's why I said for you not to come calling at the house."

He saw something in Mady that he had never seen in her before: dislike for another human being. He felt an instant hatred for the man whom he had never seen.

They sat by the lake telling each other what had happened to them since the day when the war had changed all their lives so abruptly. Jeannine had guessed right when she said that the disappearance of Dédé and Mady must have been very sudden. Mady told him that it was in the middle of the night that her stepbrother had taken them from their home in Boitsfort to evacuate to the south of France. Then she described their journey through France as refugees. He told her of his own ordeal.

They talked for hours. It was a warm day, only a breeze prevented it from getting too hot. Mady glanced towards the lake, the very same lake where they had been caught bathing by the forester all those years ago. Then she looked at Pierre out of the corner of her eyes. She gave him a daring look and on her mouth was a little smile, as much as to ask 'Shall we?'

"Oh no!" He knew exactly what she was thinking.

But her expression didn't change. She kept that same little smile and daring look.

Such a playful gesture was more than he could take. He stood up, looked around and listened for a while. There was only the forest with the sounds of its natural habitat of wildlife. He began to take off his clothes, just as he had done when they were children. Seeing that he responded, Mady, with a girlish giggle, followed his example.

When they had stripped to their underwear, he looked at Mady who stood beside him. She had grown into a beautiful young woman, and it made him stare.

"Why do you look at me so?" she said, but her expression remained soft.

It was the first time that he felt a desire which he had never experienced before, and it was this that made him stare. She could have made a remark which would have turned this magic moment into something unclean. But she hadn't; instead she had asked, 'Why do you look at me so?'

He didn't speak. He came close to her and made a move as though he wanted to kiss her on the cheek, but then his lips searched for hers and they kissed for the first time. They were two young people, pure and innocent. To him Mady wore a halo: to him the purity of Mady was a barrier, and there was a gulf that he didn't want to cross. They touched and gazed at one another. She denied him nothing, but he demanded nothing. The first kiss they had exchanged was also the last. Bathed in happiness, they stayed together, then almost in a whisper, she said, "Last in the water is a coward."

Both had that feeling that they wanted to run, jump, do anything as long as they were together – their youth made it impossible to be too serious for any length of time. For reasons which he didn't quite understand himself, Pierre let Mady reach the water first, by pretending to stumble; it was his protective feeling towards her which made him do that.

At first the water felt cold, but they soon got used to it. They didn't swim, they moved to and fro in the water, their bodies aching to touch and caress, and there was not a soul about to mar this magic moment. But could it last? Were they not two different people since those days of long ago, when they went out riding together? Soon Mady, the daughter of a baron, would return to her 'villa' in the south of France, whereas Pierre, in hiding and impoverished, would seek out his 'gîte' in the Forêt-de-Soigne.

That evening on his return he looked for Jeannine. He felt as though he had to tell her everything or burst. She listened as he told her of his day out with Mady. She wanted to hear every detail; it was so like the old days listening to him. She couldn't help laughing because he spoke so fast and was so excited.

Whilst they were talking Jeannine looked over his shoulder and saw Nadia standing in the doorway. She was standing there as though struck by lightning. Jeannine immediately realised what was happening. She had always known that Nadia would be hurt the day she found out that Pierre was in love with Mady. How long had she been standing there? How much had she learned?

As soon as Nadia realised that she had been seen, she ran away.

"Nadia, don't go!" shouted Jeannine.

"What's going on?" Pierre was confused. He hadn't seen Nadia because his back was to the doorway.

"Nadia heard every word you said. Don't you understand?"

"Understand?"

"Oh Pierre! Sometimes you can be so exasperating."

Suddenly he realised what she was trying to say. Nadia's every gesture, every move, every smile she had shown him since the day when they were thrown together pointed to it: Nadia was in love with him. Even now he couldn't say whether he had always known or whether he had just closed his eyes to it because of his love for Mady. At least he had the good sense to stay where he was – he could only make matters worse by trying to follow her.

Jeannine looked everywhere she could think of, but she knew that ever since Nadia had shown an interest in the Resistance she had discovered hiding places known only to her and Pierre. It would be impossible to find her if she didn't want to be found.

Nadia could hear her friend calling, but she wanted to be alone. She couldn't face anyone. Her grief was beyond anything she had ever felt before. Her world had been eclipsed, and she wanted to die. The tears flowed from her eyes, but not a sound came from her lips. She had heard enough to realise that Pierre was in love with a girl called Mady.

For two days and two nights she was missing. Pierre was beside himself. He felt responsible, but what could he do? He was so in love with Mady. Yet Nadia was special to him too. He was confused. How could he tell her that she too meant a great deal to him? In love there is no second place.

Pierre had told Nadia about his hiding places and she had learned well. If she didn't want to be found, then she wouldn't be. Only the will to return to life would make her come out of hiding.

It was in the evening of the second day that Nadia let Pierre find her. He knew it and didn't say a word. He walked up to her and, instead of trying to explain, took her into his arms as he had done so often before. Nadia responded. Here was where she would rather be, in his arms, even though he was in love with another.

A grief such as the one she had experienced was hard to hide. Max and Jean-Paul, who were always together, were quick to see the change in her.

"Has he blotted his copybook then?" It was Max who was the first to ask her.

"Never mind, love. One of us will take his place."

Nadia straightened up and, with a deliberate theatrical move, placed herself at Pierre's side: she wanted to make believe that nothing had changed and that he was still her man. Inwardly though something had died in her: life no longer had the same meaning. The light no longer shone from her eyes as it had before.

For young men to be in hiding was no fun. There was no socialising and no girls. Léon, François and Pierre began to go out and mingle with the villagers of Hoeylaert. If they behaved normally there was no reason for anyone to suspect anything. Their identity papers were in order, although they were forged. But there was always the danger of being caught up in a situation beyond their control.

One evening in November of 1942, they were out walking. They passed the café situated on the Brussels to Charleroi road, not all that far from the Château Prince Léopold, where the German NCOs were still billeted.

"I could do with a nice glass of beer," muttered Léon, smacking his lips as he looked towards the café.

"Well, why not?" François replied. " I can see people in the café – we would not be the only ones. Come on, let's have a beer."

"That's what I like in a man – decisiveness." Léon was already walking towards the café without waiting for a democratic vote. Pierre was totally in favour – he had always enjoyed those evenings in the little cafés at Boitsfort with Uncle Blewett.

The café was an old converted house with wooden beams and low ceiling. It had a restful atmosphere and fitted perfectly amongst the curtain of dense green forest. As they entered, the locals greeted them with the usual, "Messieurs."

"Messieurs," replied all three.

When the barman came to their table, Léon turned to Pierre and said, "What will you have?"

He knew what François would order, but with Pierre he wasn't sure. Did he even drink?

"I'll have a Gueuse Lambic, thanks."

Léon looked at him with raised eyebrows. Gueuse Lambic was a strong bitter beer served in a tall glass with a plunger, and sugar for those who needed it. Pierre just winked in acknowledgement, whilst François's spectacles fell to the end of his nose and his mouth opened.

"Well, he's done this before," he said, turning to Léon.

While they were waiting for their beers to be served, they looked around and commented on the pictures on the walls, the old furniture scattered around and such things. They had only been there for a short while when suddenly they were distracted by a group of soldiers entering the café, about seven or eight of them.

"Those are Italian soldiers who are billeted at the racecourse at Groenendael," said Léon, as he leaned forward towards François and Pierre. "This could be interesting," he added.

"In what way?" asked Pierre as he too leaned forward.

"Well, you know Italians. The conversation is bound to be colourful. François speaks Italian – he'll translate."

Pierre sat back in his chair with a sigh of relief. His interpretation of Léon's remark had made him expect trouble.

Once inside, the Italian soldiers made their way to a corner table in such a way that it was obvious they'd been there before. Their conversation was subdued and ceased entirely when the barman came to take their order. They were all in their thirties, serious men.

"What are they saying?"

François began to translate. "They're talking about the war in the desert – North Africa, the battle of El-Alamein. Rommel is in full retreat – he's lost his German divisions and the bulk of his army is now largely the demoralised Italians."

"We already know that," interrupted Pierre.

"Shhhhh. Let's listen."

François continued to translate. "They've heard of an Anglo-American landing in French North Africa... They include French units... Their commander is an American, Dwight Eisenhower. These guys are also demoralised," added François. "The soldier who is doing all the talking says that he thinks that once the Allies get control of North Africa, they will invade Italy."

At that point several of the Italians began to talk, showing a good deal of excitement.

"What are they saying?"

"It's their families they are thinking of. They all feel uneasy about being so far away from home in a hostile country. They say even the Germans are turning against them."

The Italians had hardly touched their beers when the door opened once again. In walked five German NCOs from the Château Prince Léopold. They were laughing and joking while they entered. One of them was a loud-mouthed and aggressive looking type. Their laughter stopped once they caught sight of the Italians sitting in the corner. The entire room went quiet.

The German NCOs made their way to the bar where they stayed. One could feel the hate radiating from the two groups. The silence was like a loaded gun waiting for a spark to set it off. The loud-mouthed NCO's eyes fixed in the direction of the Italian group, then, unable to control himself any longer, he supplied that spark.

"Italian dogs!" he shouted, turning his back on the group in a provocative manner.

The Italian soldier who had been doing most of the talking sprang to his feet and in one move stood behind him, his bayonet drawn. The NCO turned round and stood paralysed. The move had been fast and brutal. But although brutally quick the soldier's movements remained controlled, as if the man, in spite of showing determination, hesitated to go as far as murder.

One by one the Italians got to their feet and left the café, satisfied that they had taught their German counterparts a lesson in guts: they no longer had that air of superiority.

Once they had left, the loud-mouthed NCO turned his attention to the other occupants of the café. His ego had been deflated and he was looking for easier prey.

"I suppose you Belgians think it funny," he said, addressing Léon.

Léon understood and spoke German. François's gesture to him was a warning not to let the NCO rile him, but Léon was in no mood to be bullied. He stood up to face his aggressor. The NCO's mouth curved into a grin: he had found a vulnerable victim.

"Who are you?" he demanded. "Why aren't you working in Germany?"

"I'm a Belgian in my own country – who are you?" snarled Léon at his aggressor, a question of pure form. The NCO had no intention of defending himself – it was his people who were the conquerors, and it was he who would be doing the questioning.

"So I'm right," continued the NCO, his grin widening. "You're hiding amongst these villagers?"

"There is no place I can live protected from the tyranny you have brought." Léon was unable to restrain himself. "If you hadn't transformed my country into a prison, there would be no need for me to hide at all."

François realised that the words spoken in anger by Léon would endanger their lives. He jumped up and placed himself between him and his aggressor.

"You have no cause to pick on him. Our papers are in order," he shouted, looking the NCO straight in the eyes.

For a while both men stood facing each other.

"Come on, Hermann – the man's right. You're looking for a fight," said one of the NCOs, as he got hold of his friend's arm. "We came here to have a drink and talk, remember?"

On hearing this the loud-mouthed NCO let himself be guided, as if it brought him back to reality and the real purpose of their coming here in the first place.

Another NCO turned to Léon, and said, "You must excuse our friend. He's not himself today. He had news from home – his house was hit by a bomb, his wife and daughter..." The NCO didn't finish the sentence, but his expression said it for him.

Léon's temper cooled down for he suddenly had mixed feelings towards the man. He sat down and silently finished his beer. All three realised just how close they had come to being arrested, which could have jeopardised the entire underground movement led by Jacques Courtoy and M. Van Den Bos. It was something of which they would not speak to the others.

The Italians in the café were right about the landings in French North Africa. The battles of El-Alamein and Tunis ended the first victorious Allied campaign, which had lasted for two and a half years. The invasion of Italy would soon be underway.

When Jacques learned of the Anglo-American invasion of Sicily on July the 10th 1943, he called a meeting to discuss this important event with the men of the Resistance. It was now certain that the Allies would be the victors of this war, unless they were careless enough to miss their opportunity. It became a matter of finding the fastest way to bring about peace and so reduce further loss of lives.

Jacques was leaning over a map which lay in front of him on a table. He was using his finger as a tracer.

"The Allies will rapidly move up the leg of Italy and force Field-Marshal Kesselring to withdraw beyond the River Po," he began. "Strategy dictates that they should also land in the Trieste area, which would then force Kesselring to abandon Italy altogether. That will open the road for the Allies to proceed to Vienna, Budapest and Prague. They could then concentrate on bringing about the downfall of Hitler whilst he is still engaged in the USSR. If they were to declare that there would be no indiscriminate penalising of the German people, they could bring about a revolution, and if they could achieve that they would become the arbiters of the peace."

Up to now the room had been quiet, and only Jacques's voice could be heard. With that last remark some exclamations broke out and there were smiling faces all around. Unfortunately the events which followed during the months ahead altered the feelings of every man who had been present in the room.

At the very moment that Italy was on the point of collapse, a series of political changes turned Allied advantage into disadvantage. On July the 24th Mussolini was overthrown, and ten days later Italian envoys arrived in London to discuss terms of surrender.

Because of the 'proclamation' of 'unconditional surrender', made by President Roosevelt and Mr Churchill at their meeting at Casablanca, it was feared that by turning back on this a vote of no confidence by the American people would endanger Roosevelt's re-election to the presidency, and the terms of surrender took well over a month.

During this delay Hitler poured reinforcements into Italy and the advantage was missed. Then Stalin, who was not slow to capitalise on this unconditional surrender fiasco, was pressing for a second front to be opened in the west, namely the French coast. He wanted the Allies to be as far away from Vienna as possible, because he was aware of its strategic importance. The Allies didn't want to upset him and so abandoned the Italian engagement. Somehow they failed to realise the political and strategic importance of an advance on Vienna. They were too confident that at the end of the war it would be an Allied, not a Soviet victory, and that it would be they and not the Soviets who would exercise the greatest influence.

The decision to drop the advance on Vienna did not strengthen the morale of the men in the Resistance: it embittered their feelings. Young men need hope, otherwise human weakness takes over. They felt that unconditional surrender meant it would give every German the courage of despair, that it would strengthen Hitler's position as Germany's only hope and that the masses would support him. What was also obvious to them was that an invasion through northern France, Belgium, Luxembourg, Holland and Germany would be both exhausting and destructive. It would lengthen the war, and, worst of all, it would enable Stalin to be first in Vienna. It was their belief that at the first opportunity Stalin would advance to the waters of the North Sea and the Atlantic Ocean. To them this was the worst thing which could happen. All Continental nations were terrified of a Soviet victory.

Max and Jean-Paul, the two inseparables from 'Group G' were walking around looking very despondent. So was Hilaire, the loner, also from 'Group G'. It was now August 1943 and the Allied

landings in France were expected to start in the early spring of 1944.
The three lads decided to confront Jacques and express their doubts as
to whether they should go on fighting in order to bring about the
destruction of the German forces.

"With all due respect, Jacques, can you give us one good reason
why we should give our continued support to the Allies to crush the
whole of Germany, knowing that this will eventually bring Europe
under Stalinist rule?"

It was Max who had put the question.

"Yes. Can you tell us that, Jacques?" echoed Jean-Paul. "It was
different in the beginning. We didn't know then that the British and
the Americans were following an idealistic war policy. They believe
that the alliance formed with the Soviet Union under the stress of war
will also continue in peace. We agree with the Spanish who are
warning the Allies that the Soviets intend to penetrate deeply into
Germany, and that they will profit by German engineering, specialised
workers and technicians and become a threat to the whole world. The
Stalinist dictatorship is vile!"

There Jean-Paul paused, interrupted by Hilaire who added,
"We've also learned that President Roosevelt is aware that the Soviets
will be masters in Europe, and his attitude to that is 'So what?' He
sees Stalin as a nationalist, almost a pro-democrat. We know
differently."

Jacques didn't take offence at these remarks. They were all valid
and he understood their fears. The prospect of totalitarian Stalinist
rule being extended over the Continent was enough to make any
European sit up, and if it was left to choice he wasn't sure which way
the vote would go. He pondered his reply carefully.

"I understand how you feel, my friends," he began, "but
remember this – when we saw Hitler make his blunder through sheer
hate, we were only too pleased that he did so. Now we realise that
our own side is also motivated by sheer blind hatred. The statement
Mr Churchill made, that to kill as many Huns as possible is their sole
aim, proves that they are overtaken by their emotions, but then, no
one ever said they were perfect, only that they are better than the
other regimes. The idea that we should stop fighting or change sides
is unthinkable. We are an occupied country and we need to be
liberated. Only the Allies can give us back our freedom – their hatred

and their decision to invade by way of France alters nothing. Our aim is to help them get to Vienna, Budapest and Prague first."

The three young men were listening carefully to what he was saying.

"I suppose you're right – you always are," replied Max with his eyes lowered. "It's just that we find it hard to believe such learned men could be motivated by anything other than what is the best interest of their own countries. You can count on us, Jacques, have no fear."

"I never doubted that, Max. Now let me tell you what our objective will be once the Allies do land in France. We are going to destroy Hitler's underground communication lines linking the German HQ at Arras to Brussels, Antwerp and other cities. We'll do this at a number of intervals. As soon as they repair it we will destroy it again further along. This will force them to send radio messages which will then be picked up by the Allied signals intelligence, enabling them to monitor all military messages, and we will carry the Allies through Europe faster than Stalin can reach Vienna."

"*Sacre bleu! C'est la fin des Boches!*" exclaimed both Max and Jean-Paul in their usual overenthusiastic manner. This they followed with a hand slapping ritual.

Jacques couldn't help smiling, but he was looking at Hilaire who was exceptionally quiet.

'That boy has a problem,' he thought.

Bad news no longer came as a surprise to Pierre, but when he learned that somehow Mady's stepbrother had found out she was spending the occasional day with him at Groenendael and that he had made it his business to find out about his background, it drove him to despair. His family, although well-off before the war, was now completely ruined. Even so they had never been a family of any influential importance, and to the young Baron status meant a great deal. His immediate reaction was to forbid Mady to ever see Pierre again. It was beneath her station to meet Pierre, and, to make absolutely sure, he made arrangements for her removal to the South of France.

When Pierre learned this through his friend, he threw caution to the wind and decided to go and see them, in spite of Mady's warning not to come calling. He could not just sit back and let her be taken away without some word from her on which to build his hopes for the future. But Pierre was in the wrong frame of mind to be drawn into such a situation. The hatred within him had grown out of all proportion and that hate was now more or less directed against everything.

"What right has he not to want to receive me into his family?" he cried aloud. Jacques was right when he said that Pierre had a chip on his shoulder and that he would be looking for some recognition for his part in the struggle for freedom. Others could see it from the young Baron's point of view. Pierre was without education and without a future. His grandfather was missing, his father had been in a concentration camp since 1940 and, if he did return from this, would most likely be scarred for life. The family business was ruined, and the intimacy that had existed between Baron Declercq and James Fenbeau meant nothing to the young Baron.

Pierre had a different point of view. He was now convinced that when the Germans were defeated the struggle for freedom would continue throughout the whole of Europe. They would be fighting Communism instead of Hitlerism. As far as he was concerned that was probably to his advantage, because if their country did come under Communist rule both families would be equal. Neither would have anything, and he felt that, of the two, he was better equipped for survival. To be in hiding was now a way of life to him and Mady would be better off with him.

Needless to say, Mady's stepbrother would not have shared this view. He was probably more of the opinion that it would be the Allies, and not the Russians, who would have the greatest influence after the war and so he would always remain Monsieur le Baron Declercq, and Mady would do as he wished: marry into a family worthy of this title. That was a good enough reason for him not to want Mady to see Pierre ever again.

Pierre's unannounced visit to the house of the Baron was considered in bad taste. In addition, he made one or two fatal mistakes in his approach. The first was to speak to the Baron as an equal. On seeing how Pierre was dressed, the Baron took one step back as if to avoid the plague. Pierre's bearing suggested that the clothes he wore were those thrust upon him through circumstance rather than by upbringing, but this did not stop the Baron from staring at him as if he had just crawled out of the gutter.

His second mistake was to speak to the Baron as if he had no right to remove Mady to the South of France and to prevent her from seeing him.

"Hmm... I find that rich," exclaimed the Baron. "To even dare imply that I have no right to send my sister to France! There is no reason I should tell you why I am sending her away, but since you have the audacity to bring up the subject, let me tell you that I shall make it my duty to prevent her from ever seeing you again, until such time as she comes of age. By then I am sure you will have found someone of your own kind. You are all the same when it comes to a good thing: believing that you could ever be accepted into this household!"

Whilst the Baron was piling insult upon insult, and he did have a way with words, Pierre was moving slowly towards him. Mady, who was standing at the top of the staircase listening, could see Pierre's face darkening. She saw him slowly advance towards her stepbrother. Then he made his third and biggest mistake. He got hold of the Baron in a vice-like grip around the neck and shoulders and said in a low voice, "Monsieur, I advise you at this moment not to utter one more word of insult, or interfere with Mady and me."

The Baron fought back as if convinced that he could free himself from the grip Pierre had on him, but the young man just tightened his grip.

"You are choking me," cried the Baron finally.

All this time Mady was still looking on from the top of the staircase. Somehow she had sensed that Pierre was going to do just that. It was the way he looked at her stepbrother and the way he slowly advanced towards him which had convinced her of it. Such violence was probably the worst thing Pierre could have done in her presence. She was too gentle and pure to accept it.

"Pierre, what have you done?" she cried, as she ran down the stairs and made for the front door.

Pierre released his grip on the Baron on hearing her voice. He looked around and saw her run out of the house.

Having been freed, the Baron said, "You'll pay for this, you villain! I'll have you arrested and thrown into jail – I have some very influential friends!"

Pierre was ready to run after Mady, but on, hearing the Baron's threat, he turned around, grabbed him by the coat and pinned him hard against the wall. His eyes were like daggers.

"You do that, Monsieur, and you're a dead man. The last thing I wanted you to know is that I am hiding from the Gestapo. To have me arrested will endanger the entire Resistance in this area. They are the ones who are hiding me. It won't be me who will silence you, Monsieur, but every man in the Resistance, and I'll make sure that they have your name and full description. What happened here is a private matter between you and me and will have to wait until this war is over. Do you understand me Monsieur?"

'Yes! Yes!" shouted the Baron, as Pierre pinned him harder against the wall. "I wouldn't do anything to endanger the Belgian Resistance – I'm a good patriot." The Baron looked at him, astonished.

"Good, so be it, but my warning stands."

Pierre released him and his thoughts returned to Mady, who had disappeared. When he stood outside his eyes looked in every direction. Where could she have taken refuge? Then he caught sight of the tall impressive church tower across the road. He began to walk towards it whilst reflecting on what he had done. The violence he had displayed surprised even himself, but the damage done could not be undone. For the first time he understood how easy it was for anyone to commit a blunder through sheer blind hatred.

'Mady, oh Mady! Have I lost your love for ever?' The thought echoed back and forth in his head, and he had to fight against the panic that suddenly overtook him. He entered the church and immediately felt that guilt which he had been experiencing of late, a feeling that he should bow his head and empty the hatred from his heart before entering a church. His eyes came to rest on the altar and beneath it he saw the kneeling figure of Mady deep in prayer. As he came closer he realised that here she was at peace. It gave him a strong feeling that he had lost her, a feeling that this was where she belonged. He had driven her into the arms of the love she knew would never betray her – the love of Jesus.

She remained deep in prayer. He came close and knelt beside her. He lifted his eyes up towards the life-sized crucifix that stood above them, but the hatred which the war years had embedded in his heart remained. Jacques was right when he had said of Pierre: 'It's a great

sacrifice to make for one so young – think of what it will do to him.'
It was this change in him which had made Pierre resort to violence.
He reached out for Mady's hand. At least she would not reject him,
of that he was sure.

She turned her head and sadly looked into his eyes.

"Oh Pierre, I'm so frightened – the war has changed you so.
What can we do? He will never forgive you."

"I'm sorry, Mady. I didn't mean to do it. I don't know what
came over me. He had no right to say those things. I did it without
thinking."

"I know, darling. I watched you from the top of the stairs.
Somehow I could tell that you were being torn apart inside, but you've
made matters worse – he'll never allow me to see you again. What
can I do?"

"I don't care what he says. It's how you feel that matters to me.
I'm truly sorry for what I did. Please forgive me. Tell me that I will
see you again. Tell me that you still love me. You are my only hope.
I wish to know. If you love me tell me so."

"You know I do and shall always try and see you, but I don't
know what will happen now. He's very clever in exercising his
authority over us. I can promise you this: if I can't be with you, I
shall never love anyone else."

They were two young people very much in love. Their hopes and
desires were plain for anyone to see. They wanted to be together, but
one thing stood out clearly. Destiny had mapped out a path for Mady
which was so strong that even Pierre was aware of it. She was a
chosen child for God's purpose. No matter how much they wanted to
be together the call for Mady was there, and Pierre's presence and
actions seemed instrumental to that calling. His destiny in life had yet
to be mapped out. The time they spent together at this very moment
was the only time left to them. Unconsciously he felt it and clung to it
for as long as he could.

The Informer

It was a moonless night in the early spring of 1944. Max and Jean-Paul lay hidden close to the ground in a wooded area a few kilometres from Brussels. They were looking at a track which ran straight through this wooded area. Buried deep down along the track lay the German underground communication cables of which Jacques had spoken, and they were here to sabotage them.

Max and Jean-Paul lay listening quietly. They were very apprehensive. 'Group G' had run into trouble on their first attempt to sabotage the communication line near Charleroi only a week ago. They had been surprised by a German patrol which had just happened to be there. The Germans opened fire, killing one of the men instantly and wounding two more, one of whom died later when they reached the villa.

Max and Jean-Paul viewed this incident with a certain amount of suspicion. To them it seemed more as though the Germans had been there waiting for them. The other two men with the two saboteurs were close behind. The four moved towards the track where they would find a marker, put there earlier by a member of 'Group G' who knew the exact location of the communication cables. They were to dig down and place a charge of explosives timed to go off once they had cleared the area and were well out of any danger of being caught.

Max had very sensitive hearing, and now he was twice as attentive due to his suspicions. They had hardly begun digging when he suddenly heard the faint sound of a twig snapping. No one else heard it.

"The Germans are here," he whispered to the others.

They all listened, straining their ears.

"You're overreacting, Max," said one of the two men in a low voice.

"I tell you they're here. Let's move deeper into the woods." Max's voice sounded almost like an order.

The others followed.

As they moved away, the sound of another twig snapping stopped them. This time they all heard it.

"Oh God, we've been betrayed."

All four took to their heels in the direction from which they had come. Jean's truck was parked at least one kilometre away from their present position. He had done this purposely so as not to attract any attention.

Suddenly all hell broke loose. The Germans, realising that they had given away their presence, opened fire blindly into the darkness of the night. The bullets were heard drilling deep into the trees all around. Max and Jean-Paul were running close behind the other two when, suddenly, Jean-Paul stumbled and fell.

"Come on, get up and run!" shouted Max as he got hold of him and pulled him back to his feet.

Jean-Paul made no sound, but concentrated on putting one foot in front of the other in a deliberate way. Then he stumbled again and fell heavily to the ground. Max picked him up once more, but as he did so he saw that his back was covered in blood. His right shoulder had been shattered by a bullet.

"You've been hit!" cried Max, and he turned round to face the Germans, drew his pistol and began to fire into the darkness as if he intended to make a stand to protect Jean-Paul.

"Come round to the other side of me," said Jean-Paul. "I can still run."

Max put Jean-Paul's other arm over his shoulder and together they ran on. The other two men had already disappeared into the darkness of the wood.

Suddenly the firing stopped, a sign that the Germans were doubling back to pick up their vehicles, but they would soon be in pursuit again. The trees in the wood were set apart in such a way that it was possible for vehicles to move through it. Jean-Paul was now practically being dragged along by Max. His breathing sounded dreadful. The air in his exposed right lung could be heard escaping through his shattered shoulder.

"Max! Stop! I can't go any further. I'm done for."

"Don't talk like that – don't say that. I'll carry you."

"Max, listen, I won't make it." Jean-Paul's breathing was very weak and he could hardly speak.

"You must save yourself. The Germans will be here soon."

"No, don't talk like that! Don't!" Max continued dragging him, but there was no longer any movement in Jean-Paul's legs.

"Listen, for God's sake listen. There's no time to waste. The Germans will be here. I'm done for – can't you see?"

Max was now looking at him, his eyes wide open, listening.

"You remember the promise we made to each other?" Jean-Paul was looking at Max, almost pleading.

"No! No! I won't do it! I can't!"

"You promised! Don't let them take me alive. They will torture me to make me talk and they'll kill me."

He pulled Max's gun clear from his belt and stretched it out to him.

Max was suddenly panic-stricken. He had promised, but he had never thought that it would ever come to this. His eyes looked down at the gun, his hand trembling as he reached for it. Would he find the strength?

Jean-Paul's eyes were fixed on him, pleading.

Slowly Max's hand came up and he pointed the gun at his friend's temple. He pulled the trigger.

Click. The gun was cocked, but no bullet came from it. Again he pulled the trigger. *Click-click*.

Jean-Paul looked up at him, pleading.

"Max!"

"The magazine is empty. I must have fired the last bullet back there," he said.

Jean-Paul's eyes filled with fear. The Germans would find him, torture him and make him talk. Then suddenly, as though possessed by supernatural willpower, he said, "Leave me the empty gun and go! Save yourself! Get the bastard who did this to me! Promise me!!"

His hand grabbed at Max's clothes as if he wanted to drag the promise from him.

"I promise. I'll find him – I'll get him for you."

Then, putting the empty gun near his friend, Max took his hand and said in a grief-stricken voice, "Adieu, Jean-Paul, adieu."

For a while he paused, looking at him. Then he moved away, his eyes everywhere. He didn't hurry; it was more as though he slipped into the darkness of the night and disappeared, determined to stay alive to fulfil that last promise.

The sound of the German vehicles was very close now, their headlights transforming night into day. Jean-Paul lay on the ground fighting to stop himself from fainting. He was too weak to move, but too strong to die. One vehicle came so close that it almost ran over him. It stopped dead as the driver saw him. Out stepped a Gestapo officer, the very same officer who had interrogated Pierre at Wavre.

"Good, he is still alive. Bring him to me," ordered the officer as he leaned over Jean-Paul.

It was the moment the Belgian had dreaded. It was the reason he had fought to stop himself from fainting. His hand pulled away from underneath his body and with outstretched arm he pointed the revolver at the officer as though about to shoot.

"Watch out, he's got a gun!"

Almost simultaneously all the Germans' guns were blazing and Jean-Paul's body twisted in a final convulsion, riddled with bullets. His arm stayed outstretched and his hand stayed wrapped around the pistol, half-pointing it at the officer, as if inviting him to take it from him. For no special reason, except perhaps that the officer was wondering why the young man had not fired his revolver, he took the gun and casually opened the magazine, only to find it empty.

Jean-Paul's face had what could only be described as a triumphant smile on it. The officer paused for a while, looking at that twisted young body. What went through his mind at that very moment no one will ever know, but he raised his hand to his cap and gave the young man a salute. His kind always drew strength from heroism. Then he got back into his vehicle to continue the chase.

Jean and Pierre were waiting by the truck parked on the outskirts of the wood. They heard the sound of gunfire and saw the lights of the German patrol cars moving amongst the trees. Both came to the same conclusion: they had been betrayed. They moved the truck as close as possible to the edge of the wood for a quick getaway. Jean ran deeper into the wood, but did not dare go too far for fear that he might miss the four lads who were being hunted. The patrol was still moving towards him. 'That's a good sign – the lads must still be running in this direction,' he thought, but that last burst of gunfire and the shouting – that wasn't a good omen.

"What's keeping them?" said Jean, talking aloud to himself. He doubled back to the truck and jumped into the driver's seat. He looked at Pierre, who sat in the passenger seat with an unfolded map and a torch, from which the tiniest pinpoint of light was shining.

"Did you hear that last burst of gunfire?"

"Yes, I heard," he answered, but neither made any further comment.

Pierre turned in his seat and looked in the direction of the light moving in the wood.

"There!" He shouted, pointing. "I can see movement."

He couldn't make out exactly how many, but he thought he saw at least two figures running towards them.

"Over here!" shouted both he and Jean as the two figures emerged from the wood.

"Where are Jean-Paul and Max?" asked Jean as he helped the two men into the back of the truck.

Exhausted and breathless, one of them managed to reply, "They must be close behind. One fell, probably hurt his leg, but there was a strange burst of gunfire and shouting after the patrol stopped for a while."

"I don't like it," said Jean, as he turned to Pierre.

"Let's wait two more minutes before we move out," said Pierre. "Then take that path on your left over there – it circles round those trees you can see silhouetted in the distance. We'll be behind the trees by the time that patrol gets here and it will give us cover. The path eventually joins the road leading to Brussels – I studied the map."

"Are you sure that path isn't sealed off at the other end?" queried Jean.

Pierre looked at him. "The alternative is to move out of here as fast as we can. That's a straight road ahead and the truck will stand out against the skyline."

"OK, two more minutes." Jean's eyes lowered as he spoke; he knew there was a suicide pact between the two lads, and he began to wonder.

The seconds were ticking away, but there was still no movement. Pierre then ran close to the edge of the wood. A minute went by. Although the Germans couldn't move fast between the trees, they were getting dangerously close. He stayed as long as he dared, peering into the darkness, then ran back to the truck. The two minutes were up. Jean looked at him when he got back in the truck.

"There's no movement, no noise, no sign of Max or Jean-Paul. If they are between us and that patrol I should have seen or heard something. The trees are set well apart and their bodies would have been silhouetted against those lights." He looked at Jean and waited for his reaction.

"We're moving out. Hold on tight back there." Jean spoke just loud enough for the two men in the back of the truck to hear him. In total darkness he turned on to the path indicated by Pierre. He didn't press down hard on the accelerator because they could not make too much noise, but he had to reach the trees fast. The patrol would be coming out of the woods any moment now. Once he was certain that they were completely shielded by the trees, he pushed down on the accelerator and went as fast as he dared, still in total darkness.

"We'll follow that road you mentioned and circle Brussels from the south. We can pick up the Brussels to Charleroi road near Waterloo."

"Why take the risk of being caught on the roads after curfew?" asked Pierre, surprised. "Why don't we go to our hideout near here as planned?"

"If those two lads are taken alive they will be tortured until they talk. Can't you see? We must warn Van Den Bos and Jacques. None of us is safe at Groenendael until we know for sure what's happened."

Pierre hadn't even given that possibility a thought, but now that Jean mentioned it his thoughts turned to Jeannine and Nadia. It would be certain death if they were caught by the Germans. He kept silent as a sign that he understood.

"I'll stay off the main road," added Jean. "I know this area."

The German patrol giving chase to the saboteurs came to a halt when they reached the edge of the wood. The Gestapo officer jumped out of his vehicle and began looking around for clues.

"These men from the Resistance couldn't just vanish! They must have left some trail. They must have had some sort of transport from here so they're somewhere on the road," he said to the NCO standing next to him.

He looked round by the light of his torch and noticed fresh tyre marks leading to the edge of the wood. He walked back to the road and saw the path on the left where tyre marks were faintly visible.

"That's the path they took," he said to the NCO.

They ran back to their vehicle where he studied the map for a while. When his finger came to rest at the area of the Forêt-de-Soigne in the south-east corner of Brussels, he lifted his head and his eyes lit up.

"It's a natural area for the Resistance to operate from and not far from here," he said aloud.

Through the NCO he ordered the patrol to move to the nearest communication post. There he alerted various posts along the road to Brussels and ordered several patrol units to comb the area of the Forêt-de-Soigne, warning them to be on the look out for a truck which would be in that area in less than an hour or so.

Driving in the dark, with the minimum amount of headlights showing because of the blackout, Jean drove his truck at full speed along the twisting country lanes of Brabandt. Once he reached the main road near Waterloo, he felt safer. Here at least he knew of one or two places which he could drive into to hide the truck, should they meet up with Germans patrolling the roads after curfew. Needless to say, his truck was without number plates. Something of which he was not aware was that the area had extra patrol cars which had been alerted to look out for them. One of these patrol cars lay in wait along the Brussels to Charleroi road. It was parked partly hidden in the darkness by the side of the road near the racecourse at Groenendael, where the Italians had once been billeted.

Jean's truck appeared over the crest of the hill, unaware of what lay ahead. The Germans waited until the truck came close, then the patrol car moved out to the middle of the road with full headlights on.

"What the hell?" shouted Jean, as he slammed on the brakes, but, once he recovered from his initial surprise, he used one of his carefully rehearsed manoeuvres to turn his truck round. In a matter of seconds he had made the full one hundred and eighty degree turn and was facing the direction from which he had just come. It gave him a much needed lead over the Germans. There were two gunshots which passed clear of his truck before the Germans got into their patrol car to give chase.

Jean's aim was to reach the crest of the second hill where, once out of sight, he could turn into a well-concealed entrance which led to a hidden barn a short distance from the road, with its doors wide open. There they would abandon the truck knowing that the farmer would remove it completely out of sight; it was a prearranged emergency plan.

Once inside the barn, Jean took the Bren gun from the side of his seat and shared out the hand grenades. He reached for a torch and passed it to Pierre.

"Lead us through the forest. We must warn the others before it's too late," he said.

Pierre knew the area: this was the land of his boyhood. To reach Le Pitoresque, where the villa was situated, they had to cross the main road – it could not be avoided.

"This way. Follow me," he said.

They were getting close to the main road, to the point where he considered it to be safest to cross, when they heard the engine of the patrol car which had doubled back, having realised that they had been given the slip. From the other side of the road, in the direction of Brussels, they could hear the sound of heavy vehicles approaching.

"Troop reinforcements," whispered Jean. "Get down."

When the vehicles met further along, the sound of the engines stopped. They could hear orders being issued, and then the sound of disembarking soldiers.

"They're going to comb the area – we're trapped," said Jean looking at Pierre. "You're in charge, son. Where do we go from here?"

That was a tall order even for Pierre. They were in a situation from which only a bird could escape. Then he suddenly thought of a way for them to disappear underground:

"The tunnel of ancient times!" he said aloud.

However, the tunnel he knew of on this side of the Château-de-Groenendael was a dangerous one. In several places it had caved in, unlike the one in which he and his school friends had used to play. In one place, where it had caved in, it was very difficult for an adult to get through. It was now more than four years since he last visited it; it could be even more difficult now.

"Which way, Pierre?" whispered Jean with a note of urgency in his voice.

The sound of the soldiers combing the area could be heard. The other two men from 'Group G' kept silent. They had lived all their lives in the city of Brussels and knew very little about the area.

"The tunnel. There's an entrance into the tunnel through one of the air vents not far from here, but it's a long drop down."

"The tunnel? There's no tunnel here. What are you talking about? We're in the middle of the forest."

"Yes there is – follow me."

The four moved deeper into the forest away from the main road, with Pierre leading. After a while he led them to a crater, probably caused by exploding bomb shells during the last war, but this one was slightly deeper. He went down into it, followed by the others. Once at the bottom he pushed aside the dead leaves and uncovered a hole through which a man's body could pass. No one would ever dare crawl into such a hole, except Pierre who knew where it led. He went in feet first, holding his torch.

"Give me a few seconds before you follow then come down feet first – I'm warning you, it's a long drop. Slide down on your stomach – I'll be at the bottom ready to catch you."

Jean waited a few seconds before letting one of the men go down. He watched both of them disappear into the hole, as though the earth itself had swallowed them up.

Pierre wasn't joking when he had said that it was a long way down. When it came to his turn Jean began to think that he would never come to a stop. He was sliding down at a steep angle on his stomach. Suddenly he felt himself being grabbed and he came to a halt.

It took only a few minutes, and they found themselves in a long subterranean tunnel, a place of absolute silence. The change was unbelievable. They were below the Forêt-de-Soigne. They had passed from tumult to silence; the stillness was like that of a tomb. From near peril they were suddenly in absolute safety.

After a few moments, when their eyes became adjusted, Jean said, "I've lived in this area all my life, but I never knew about this tunnel. Who built it?"

"All I know is that the tunnel was excavated centuries ago by the monks of the Château-de-Groenendael, which was then a monastery. They built it to get away from their persecutors, exactly as we're doing now."

"Some things never change, do they? Where does it lead?"

"It comes out close to the Château-de-Groenendael, providing we can get through."

"What do you mean 'providing we can get through'?"

"The tunnel has caved in further along, and last time I was here it was very difficult to get through. That was four years ago. It might be worse now."

"What do we do if we can't get through?"

Pierre turned his eyes to the hole through which Jean had just dropped.

"You're joking! We'll never get back up there!" He looked at the young man, but then realised that Pierre had chosen the lesser of two evils.

"How long is this tunnel?" asked one of the men.

"It's not long, but we'll be well behind the line of Germans combing the area above us towards Waterloo."

"Come on, let's move," ordered Jean.

By the light of Pierre's torch they moved through the tunnel. Once or twice they stopped when some of the dust between the close-fitting stones fell down. The area had not been disturbed for years and it was probably just dust, but it made them wonder whether the tunnel was at all safe. When they reached the place where the roof had caved in, they realised what Pierre had meant when he said that it was a very tight squeeze for anyone to get through. The tunnel, however, had not fallen in any more since the last time he had visited it. Fortunately none of them were heavily-built. Jean presented the only possible problem, but, after months of privation and rationing, even he weighed under 155 pounds.

The largest opening was a space between the wall on the left-hand side and the debris which lay solid in the middle. Apart from that, there was only an opening here and there through which small animals could move.

Pierre was the first to work his way through, followed by one of the two men. Jean was the third.

"I'll never get through this gap!" he cried, but with the help of Pierre and the other man pulling on one side, and the third pushing and guiding his body from the other, they managed to drag him safely through.

"Get me out of here – I can't breathe!" he said once he was on the other side.

"It's only three or four hundred metres more and then we'll be outside in the fresh air." Pierre was using a tone of voice which inspired relief and confidence.

When they reached the outlet of the tunnel, he put up his hand as a sign that they should stop. He alone went to the opening to listen before venturing out. Jean had but one thought: to get out into the fresh air and rid himself of this claustrophobic feeling. When Pierre had satisfied himself that all was clear, he gave a signal. Once outside Jean soon recovered from his unpleasant ordeal.

"Come on, we've lost enough time – let's go and warn the others."

Jacques and M. Van Den Bos sat silently listening to Jean's report. They were devastated to learn about Jean-Paul and Max. This made four men they had lost in just one week. All agreed that none of them was safe at the villa now. Jean was right: the lads could have been taken prisoner in spite of the fact that a suicide pact existed between them. The Gestapo were experts in making the bravest talk. One thing, however, puzzled Jacques. If there was an informer in their midst, then why hadn't the Gestapo been round sooner? It became clear that the incident of last week in Charleroi was no accident either. So why hadn't the Gestapo come to arrest them all here at Groenendael, rather than surprise them on their second raid? The more he thought about it, the more he became convinced that the informer, although he had told the Germans of the raids, hadn't yet told them of the place from where they operated. Significant, he thought, but how was that possible? There was no doubt in his mind that the Gestapo would have wanted to know this, even if they had to torture and kill the informer to get it out of him.

Mme Van Den Bos didn't think it safe for the women to go to her apartment in Brussels. The Gestapo could easily find out that the family had a second home in the city, and they would only be arrested there. So it was decided that they would ask Meterke if they could stay at her cottage, until such time as the truth was known.

In a situation such as this, Meterke showed her true nature: protective towards those whom she loved. Up to now she had insisted that she would have no part in the Resistance, for it was too risky for Jane and her baby girl. But this was different. Those whom she loved were in danger and in need, and that was enough reason for her to open her home to all of them. Her main concern was how to accommodate all her guests in a small cottage.

Jacques Courtoy and M. Van Den Bos, together with the men from 'Group G' and the Légion Nationale, stayed in hiding at the cave where Pierre and Jeannine had spent those two lonely and frightening nights in the autumn of 1940. In all the precautions for the safety of the women, Jacques made one exception, that of allowing Nadia to be included amongst the men. She had become too useful to be left out, especially now that he had lost four of his men.

Once in the cave, Jacques unfolded a coded message which he had received from the Belgian Government in exile. It read: IMPERATIVE YOU CUT GERMAN UNDERGROUND COMMUNICATION LINES AT ALL COSTS. A similar message had been sent to other French, Belgian and Dutch Resistance groups, urging them to do the same in their area. The invasion of France was imminent, and it became vital for the communications lines to be disrupted. The Germans believed their coded radio messages to be safe, but Allied intelligence had succeeded in deciphering the code, and they would be able to gain valuable information as to the movement of German troops.

Van Den Bos and Jacques were now faced with a problem. Within their group there was an informer. They looked at the men around them and could see that they all felt uneasy. Morale was affected and nerves were stretched to near breaking point. An argument broke out amongst them. François and Léon were being questioned. Where had they been the other day when they were missing for several hours? Léon's temper flared up at the thought that he was suspected of being an informer when his only reason for going out to mingle with the villagers of Hoeylaert was to give vent to his caged-up feelings.

François, in his diplomatic way, again came to the rescue and explained why once in a while they found it necessary to mix with the outside world. His explanation was accepted, but the atmosphere remained electrically charged. It didn't alter the fact that there was an informer in their midst.

Jacques's position in view of this was not an easy one. He was about to order them to go out for a third attempt at sabotaging the communication lines. Silently they sat listening to what he was saying. He could see that every man present did his fair share of thinking as he stressed the importance of sabotaging those communication lines and how vital it was that they should try again.

"As soon as we learn that the Germans have repaired them, we strike again," was his last sentence. But there was no feedback from the men, only silence and worried faces all round.

"I suggest we strike tonight at exactly the same place. I don't think that the Germans will expect us to do that, and I can't see how anyone can inform on us in that short space of time. I'll be leading the party myself."

There was not a sound from anyone, so Jacques took their silence as a sign that they were all in agreement.

"Good, that's settled then – tonight. Let's all get some sleep. We'll need it."

Each man, with head lowered, moved to his designated place of rest.

Whilst the accusations and arguments had been going on, the figure of a man had entered the shadows of the cave unobserved. The men were so absorbed in their problems that he remained unseen.

As soon as Jacques finished his speech, the man retreated into the darkness of the tunnel; someone had been listening. Once outside the tunnel he slipped into the forest where he hid, as if waiting for something to happen.

Half an hour or so went by until another figure came out behaving like one who didn't want to be seen. It was 11.45 a.m. and all was quiet in the cave. As soon as the man had cleared the tunnel entrance, he headed in the direction of Boitsfort, cutting through the forest. His behaviour left no doubt that he knew exactly where he was heading by the most direct route. The other man also came out of hiding and, keeping well out of sight, began to follow him. At one point they crossed the main railway line and continued through the forest on the other side. The man ahead was moving at the double, probably wanting to get back before being missed by the others. When they reached the outskirts of Boitsfort, the man stopped a safe distance from the main road, where he hid behind an old chestnut tree which stood out like a landmark amongst the other trees, and waited. At precisely twelve noon the sound of an approaching vehicle was heard. As it came closer, it stopped almost in line with the old tree. It was a German field car, and the tree was undoubtedly the meeting place. A man in civilian clothes wearing a black leather jacket came out and began to walk towards the old tree, but before he was anywhere near it the sound of a twig snapping stopped him in his tracks: they were not alone. Without hesitation the man in the black leather jacket turned round and ran back to the car which was waiting with the engine still running. The meeting had evidently been intended to be a short one, but it never took place. Once the civilian was back in the car, it pulled away at full speed.

The man in pursuit of the one hiding behind the old tree, realising that his presence was uncovered, dashed forward to confront the suspected informer.

"Hilaire!" he shouted, with a voice that boomed out into the stillness of the forest. The tone of his voice was menacing: it left no doubt as to his intentions.

It was Max, his eyes red with fatigue, obsessed with but one thought: revenge. What he had seen left no doubt in his mind as to who the informer was. It was Hilaire, the loner from 'Group G', the one whom Jacques suspected of having a problem, and it was now clear that he had chosen to side with the Germans. Max might have understood his mixed feelings about the rights and wrongs of the war, but the way he had done it – betraying his fellow countrymen – that he could not forgive.

"You've killed Jean-Paul! You bastard! I'll get you for that!"

Like a wild animal he threw himself against Hilaire, lashing out with his fists. Max, however, was no match for Hilaire, a much heavier man who stood six foot tall whereas Max was much smaller and weighed far less. At first the two men seemed almost well matched, but then the heavier man gained the upper hand.

Max's determination unnerved Hilaire and, instead of finishing the fight, he turned and ran in the direction from where they had come. Once Max had recovered sufficiently from his beating, he ran in pursuit. Of the two he was a faster runner. Several times he caught up with Hilaire, but each time the bigger man beat him off and continued to run.

Eventually they crossed the Brussels to Charleroi road near the racecourse at Groenendael. On the other side of the road there ran a spur of the main railway line which led to a loading bay, used by the Germans to load and unload their ammunition, stacked around the entire forest. Both men stood on the platform of the loading bay and confronted each other. Max was too exhausted to continue the fight. At that very moment an ammunition train was slowly pulling out, gathering speed. Hilaire found the strength to jump and cling to one of the carriages, and all Max could do was to watch him get away.

As the train moved into the bend of the railway track further along, the carriages began to shake excessively to and fro. It caused Hilaire to lose his footing and he fell. Max watched him as he disappeared between two carriages and the wall of the platform.

One by one the carriages rolled along, gathering speed. When the last one had passed, Max waited for a while, then he dragged himself to the spot where he had seen Hilaire fall. When he reached the wall, he looked over it and saw Hilaire's body sprawled on the ground with his head and his right hand lying across the line - but all that was left of it was a red pulp, for the wheels of the carriages had rolled over him.

Max's eyes turned to the sky above, and with both hands clenched in a fist which he held above his head, he began to laugh hysterically.

"We did it, Jean-Paul - we did it!"

François lay on the floor of the cave with his blanket wrapped around him. He was tossing and turning. Normally he was a heavy sleeper, but events of late had disturbed him and he couldn't relax. Suddenly he heard what he thought was a noise of movement in the tunnel. He opened his eyes without moving. Was that something or was he imagining it? He listened for a while longer, but heard nothing. He felt tired and wanted to dismiss it from his mind, but he couldn't. Suppose there was someone? Perhaps Germans who had discovered their hiding place? He felt that he had to warn the others. He turned round to where Léon lay fast asleep and, putting his hand over his mouth, in case he made a noise, he woke him up.

"I heard a noise in the tunnel, like someone moving around," he whispered.

"Are you sure?"

"No, I'm not, but I can't just ignore it - not under the circumstances. Let's wake the others - quietly."

When Pierre was awake, he woke Nadia. She was the only one he was sure wouldn't make a sound. He put his hand gently on her shoulder so as not to startle her. Nadia woke up from her deep sleep looking confused.

"François thought he heard a noise in the tunnel. It may be nothing, but we have to move out just in case," he whispered.

She moved her head, and put her arms around him as if asking to be reassured.

"Don't worry. I know another way out of here – whatever it is, they'll never catch us." Pierre smiled at her reassuringly and then, as if he couldn't stop himself, he put his arms around her in a loving embrace.

It confused her, but before he could show Nadia whether his embrace was motivated by brotherly concern for her or something deeper, they heard Jacques call out in a whisper, "Pierre, guide us out of here."

One by one they left the cave, following Pierre, who led them to safety towards another opening of the tunnel. It was at this point that they discovered Hilaire was missing. This could be serious. Jacques needed confirmation of what François thought he'd heard: was there indeed someone in the tunnel? He had to know. Léon and François volunteered to act as the rearguard, and stayed behind hiding in the darkness of the tunnel, Sten gun at the ready. Pierre would return once all the others were safely outside, to guide them out too.

It was not long before they both heard more noise: there was definitely someone moving in the tunnel in complete darkness. There it was again. Whatever or whoever it was didn't seem to care too much about making his presence known. Had Hilaire betrayed them?

Jacques had ordered the candles to be left burning, and the blankets were arranged in such a way that it looked as if they were all still asleep. This left the area of the cave lit up. François and Léon concentrated on the shadows created by this light. Suddenly the figure of a man entered in a deliberate way wanting to be recognised.

"Don't shoot! It's me, Max!" cried the figure which came out of the darkness.

They looked at each other as if they were seeing a ghost. Max was dead, or so they had thought. Léon peered intently at the figure that stood in full light of the candles and recognised him.

"Max!" he shouted. "We thought you were dead!"

He came out of hiding and rushed towards him.

On seeing that he had been recognised, Max practically fell into his arms.

"My God, who did this to you? Was it the Gestapo?"

Max looked completely exhausted and in bad shape as a result of the beating he had taken during his fight with Hilaire. This made

Léon think that he must have received his injuries at the hands of his captors.

François in the meantime called out for the others to come back.

"Jacques!" he shouted and paused for a while to let the echo die away. "It's okay."

"Okayyyyy..." returned the echo at several intervals.

When they were all safely back in the cave, Max, who sat holding a glass containing a generous measure of brandy which he was sipping slowly, began to tell the others what had happened.

"Jean-Paul dead! Hilaire an informer!"

Hilaire's name was on everyone's lips.

"What a horrible way to die," said one man.

"Are you sure he didn't pass on any information to that civilian in the black leather coat before you gave chase?" It was the second time Jacques had put the question: he had to be sure.

"Hilaire was nowhere near the civilian who came out of the car, of that I am sure, Jacques. I want to be there tonight when you blow up the communication lines. I've got to be there for Jean-Paul's sake."

"You shall be there, my boy. But get some sleep first."

"Yes, yes," replied Max, staring straight ahead and slowly sipping his brandy. "I'll sleep now."

His experience over the past forty-eight hours had taken its toll. He was no longer that happy-go-lucky carefree youth he had once been. He lay down and became so still that Léon had to lean over him to listen and make sure he was still breathing.

"He's asleep," Léon said, almost in disbelief.

"Good, let's all do the same. We have work to do."

Jacques was anxious for them all to be fully rested before going out in another attempt at sabotaging the communication lines.

An atmosphere of relief followed. Each man lay down with complete peace of mind, knowing that the informer had been eliminated.

After resting a while longer, Nadia was sent to Meterke's cottage to tell the women that it was now safe for them to return to the villa, and also to inform them that the men, once the job was done, would pass the remaining hours of darkness at their hideout, so as not to be on the roads after curfew, and then they too would return to the villa.

On her way to the cottage, Nadia had noticed one or two checkpoints along the roads, set up by German soldiers. She had not made any notes about this because she didn't attach too much importance to it, and also she didn't want to alarm the others.

It was not until one o'clock in the afternoon of the following day, when Mme Van den Bos became worried, that Nadia wrote the following on her notepad: *I saw two checkpoints on the roads yesterday on my way to the cottage.*

"Oh, that could be the reason why they are late – Jacques is making a detour as a precaution," exclaimed Mme Van Den Bos, and she returned to what she was doing.

It was 1.30 p.m. when they heard the engine of Jean's truck turn into the grounds of the villa. Nadia had the feeling that something was wrong. Everyone agreed that she had the ability of foresight. She couldn't tell the others why or how she felt because of her affliction, but it was something about the sound of the engine. To her there seemed a sense of urgency about it. She hurried outside without looking at anyone.

The truck came to a standstill behind the villa and Nadia saw the men hurrying along. They brought out the body of one of their comrades from inside the truck.

"Call Mme Van Den Bos! Hurry!" shouted Léon, as he caught sight of Nadia.

She stood there with her eyes wide open and both hands touching her mouth, which was also open, but not a sound came from it. The person being carried out of the truck was Pierre, the lower part of his body soaked in blood. Nadia wasn't listening to what Léon was shouting: she stood there as if in shock.

"Hurry Nadia – get Mme Van Den Bos!" he cried.

The urgency in his voice made her jump. She turned round and ran back into the house. Once inside she stopped in front of Mme Van Den Bos and looked at her. There was no need for words. The older woman immediately saw that there was something wrong: the expression in Nadia's eyes said it all.

"Is it bad?" was the first thing she asked.

Nadia shook her head in the negative.

"Who is it?"

The look of fear on Nadia's face answered her.

"Not Pierre?"

Nadia's eyes filled with tears and her breathing became faster. But before the deluge of tears, Mme Van Den Bos issued instructions to get her involved in doing something useful.

"Boil some water, girl – hurry! Pull out the dining room table to its full length and cover it with blankets and rubber sheets!" Then she ran out to see what she could do.

Pierre was being carried along into the villa by four men. His face twisted in pain at each movement of his body. He was shivering violently.

"What happened?" asked Mme Van Den Bos as she walked alongside Jacques.

"We ran into a road block on the way here – it took us by surprise. Jean swung the truck round as fast he could, but one of the soldiers fired a few rounds. A bullet passed through the door of the truck on the passenger side where Pierre was sitting. It hit him in the thigh. I think the bone is broken, and he's got a nasty flesh wound. I did what I could – I applied a tourniquet. He's lost a lot of blood – it was a long time before we could stop. Jean drove through the forest and managed to lose the patrol who were chasing us. We're lucky to be alive."

"How long has the tourniquet been on?"

"Almost fifteen minutes – it needs to be released."

"Take him into the dining room. Nadia is covering the table with sheets and blankets. I'll see to his injuries there."

Pierre was lifted on to the table.

"Cut his trouser leg whilst I give him an injection of morphine." Mme Van Den Bos was giving orders to all who stood near. Shortly after she had given the injection, Pierre began to relax; his body no longer shook violently. She examined his wound. The bullet was lodged inside and the bone was broken.

"He needs hospitalisation," she said. "I can only do so much for him. His leg needs to be put in traction first and then a pin inserted to reset the bone, which means surgery. But what he needs immediately is a blood transfusion."

Nadia stood close to Mme Van Den Bos as she continued to work whilst she spoke. She was no longer frightened. Quietly she worked on, standing next to Mme Van Den Bos, who was telling her what to do.

When she had done all she could for Pierre, she turned to Jacques and looked at him enquiringly.

"Leave it to me," he said. "I know a doctor who might help."

Nadia was in the kitchen whilst Jacques was phoning the doctor he knew in the city. Her eyes brightened as she could hear from the conversation that this one would help. She ran to Mme Van Den Bos and, with a smile that betrayed her relief, gave her a big hug.

"He'll be all right, girl, he's in good hands," Mme Van Den Bos said with a reassuring note.

All that could be done for him had been done and the waiting began. Nadia returned to the kitchen unable to sit still. She was looking for things to do and was trembling all over: the strain of waiting was beginning to tell. It was then that Mme Van Den Bos came looking for her.

"Nadia, Pierre is calling out for you. Go to him – let him know you're near."

Nadia looked at her in confusion, not quite taking in what she was being told, and she drew back as if questioning what she had heard.

"Go to him, girl. It's you he's calling out for, not Mady." Mme Van Den Bos emphasised the name Mady purposely because she could see what was going through Nadia's mind.

Clutching at her breast to keep herself from choking, Nadia, pale and trembling with agitation, looked in the direction of the room where Pierre was lying on the table. Then her face became calm, gentle and happy.

"Go on, girl, what are you waiting for?" Mme Van Den Bos whispered, edging her on with a movement of her hand towards the dining room.

Pierre was not completely at rest: the injection had taken effect, but his head was still rolling from side to side and at times he groaned. Nadia drew close to him and held his hand in hers. She looked puzzled. Could he have forgotten about Mady? she wondered. Was she the one he really wanted near him?

"Nadia... Nadia."

Twice he called out her name: it was so clear. She couldn't stop herself from trembling. 'Oh, if only I could talk!' she thought. 'To tell him that I am here, to give him words of comfort and encouragement.' She felt so grown-up whenever she was near him. 'I've heard of this happiness,' she told herself, 'but it's only now that

I feel such love for him. Dear God, make him get well, make him remember this moment when it was my name he called out.'

All the time she was caressing his hair and forehead whilst her other hand held his pressed against her breast.

Pierre sensed that someone was near. His eyes half-opened as his head turned towards her. A smile appeared on his lips when he saw her, then he sank back into sleep, but he was at peace with Nadia at his side: he no longer tossed his head from side to side. He seemed to know that she was there.

When the time came to move him to the clinic in Brussels, Nadia wanted to go too, but Jacques couldn't take that risk.

"It will be difficult enough to keep him in hiding without having you to worry about," he said. "Don't fret. He won't be gone long, but he needs surgery on his leg. Mme Van den Bos has done all she can for him."

Nadia nodded her head as a sign that she accepted the situation in which they found themselves. Eventually an ambulance arrived and he was given a blood transfusion before being lifted into it. She was at his side until she had to let go.

Four days had passed since Pierre had been taken away. Nadia was in the garden admiring the early spring flowers that were now well in bloom. She looked radiant and very happy. Her golden hair, which she brushed every day with at least one hundred strokes, was soft and shiny. The boys' clothes she wore didn't make her look any the less feminine. On the contrary, they accentuated her shapely figure.

The news she was given about Pierre was good. On arrival at the clinic his leg had been put into traction, and he was no longer in pain. She had no means of telling the time, except by the sun that stood high in the March sky.

'He must be on the operating table by now,' she thought.

Jacques had told her that he would be operated on at eleven o'clock that morning, and that in two days he would probably be brought back to the villa, which was as good a place as any for his recovery. To stay longer at the clinic would only endanger the doctor's position; Mme Van den Bos would look after him. It was already known that both his legs would be in a plaster cast to immobilise him.

'One more day to wait,' she thought. There were still many questions that remained unanswered regarding his feelings towards Mady. Was he still very much in love with her? Would he remember that it was her name, Nadia, that he had called out in his pain? Would he remember that it was she who had stood by his side? If only she could speak to tell him how much love she felt for him.

"Actions speak louder than words," Mme Van Den Bos kept telling her. "Don't worry about your voice – that will come back one day," she added.

It was as Jacques had said. Pierre was brought back to the villa early in the afternoon of the following day. It was too dangerous for him to stay at the clinic. Mme Van Den Bos was given full instructions as to what was required in the way of medication and dressings. It would be three weeks before the plaster cast could be removed.

The days which followed were the happiest for Nadia. She took full charge of looking after Pierre. He did remember that it was she who had stood by his side that day when he was in such pain. Nor did he think it strange that it wasn't Mady for whom he had called out, but what his real feelings were remained uncertain to her, and she couldn't dismiss it from her mind. He didn't talk about it and she was unable to ask him. To deliberately put her fears down on paper concerning such an intimate matter was something she couldn't bring herself to do. All she could hope for was that he had forgotten about Mady, and that he had finally realised how deep the gulf was between them: she the daughter of a Baron, and he the son of a racehorse trainer ruined by the misfortunes of war. 'But what if Mady tries to get in touch with him?' she asked herself. 'What then? Would it bring back all she had meant to him?' Nadia wasn't sure how she would cope if this happened, but she kept her true feelings to herself and made sure that she did not betray them to him. It was for him to decide if it should happen. One thing she had made up her mind about was that she would not settle for second best no matter how much it hurt. She had already experienced the bitter taste of a disappointment in love and she had learned by it.

Pierre confided to her the thoughts which had gone through his mind when he realised that he had been hit by a bullet.

"I have never been so frightened," he began. "I didn't think we were going to make it. Jean kept driving through the forest like a madman, and I couldn't make out where we were. At one stage I thought we were going to crash. That would have been the end," he added. Then he told her that ever since that day when the plane crashed in the forest, he had carried a hand grenade. He had made up his mind that, rather than being caught alive, he would blow himself up.

He could tell by her expression that she was horrified at the very thought that he would ever do such a thing.

"It would be worse if we were taken alive by the Gestapo – they show no mercy to Resistance fighters," he added quickly.

Nadia put her finger across his lips, as if to say, 'You shouldn't think of such things.'

Although she couldn't speak, she had become very clever at expressing herself. Her face, her hands, the movements of her entire body were almost as good as the spoken word. Pierre was getting good at interpreting this body language. The upshot of all this was that he constantly looked at her so as not to miss any movement. He became aware of her graceful movements, the natural flow of her long golden hair and her beautiful feminine figure. She knew that he was looking at her in a way in which only a man looks at a woman and this added sensuality to her every move: she wanted Pierre to notice her. Whenever their eyes met, he tried to pretend that it was only by chance he was looking, but every so often their eyes locked and a smile appeared on their faces. Alas, they were seldom alone. The occasional contact with their eyes was all that had gone on between the two of them so far.

Jacques, who was following Pierre's progress very closely, was hoping that it would not be too long before he was back on his feet. Events were moving fast and he needed his special skills. Pierre had a natural ability and understanding of the terrain in which they had to move, a gift which is vital in guerrilla warfare. In addition to the area in which they lived, he had also studied the topography of other places further afield. Jacques was convinced that he had a photographic memory because he could remember the layout of the land in places he had visited. It was remarkable the way he did it. Places such as Namur, Dinan, Liege, Maastrich, he could describe as though he were actually there. Charleroi, which he had visited with Jean, was another place he knew well. This meant a great deal to Jacques because they were the areas in which they would carry out their acts of sabotage.

The Légion Belge had been reshaped since those early days of the war, when their main concern was to organise the escape of endangered citizens and restore King Léopold of the Belgians to his throne. As early as July 1943 the Belgian Government in exile had taken control and ordered the Légion to form 'une armée sécrète'.

This army now numbered well over fifty thousand men. The mood of the Resistance in France had also changed. Whereas once the members of General de Gaulle's Bureau Central de Renseignements et d'Action (BCRA) were distrusted by their fellow countrymen, a change had taken place ever since the Germans had forcibly recruited Frenchmen to be sent to Germany for work in factories. Since 1942 the young men had taken to the hills in France, especially in the area of the River Rhône known as the scrub Le Maquis.

This was now a formidable army, and the day when they would be called upon was getting close. Early June was the most likely time they would be ordered to go into action.

Jacques was reflecting on all this while he watched Pierre and Nadia. It was not difficult to come to the conclusion that these two young people wanted to be together.

"He's got the best nurse anyone could wish for," he said to himself. "She'll soon get him on his feet."

The Allies

Along the coast of the Netherlands, Belgium and France, the Germans had built the so-called Atlantic Wall consisting of coastal defences buried deep in the sand, their guns pointing out towards the North Sea and the Atlantic Ocean. Behind this wall were ten panzer divisions ready to repulse any attempt at invasion by the Allies. The Germans were on the alert.

Of these ten divisions one was located at Beverloo in Belgium. They were the Liebstandarte Adolf Hitler – one of the best, if not the best. Jacques felt uneasy about that. They would have to be very careful in their sabotage activities. The orders he received from the Belgian Government in exile were very demanding.

The plan adopted was to restrict the enemy's mobility by crippling the French and Belgian railways. The River Meuse and the Albert Canal became the selected waterways on which they were asked to concentrate. These rivers were vital to the supply of the German Fifteenth Army and the crossings over them had to be demolished in order to cripple the supply lines from the east and to halt the German advance lines moving westwards.

The priority of these orders for the Resistance group led by Jacques Courtoy was to cripple the Belgian coal transportation at Charleroi which supplied the French railways.

It was now May 1944. Since March tons of bombs had been dropped all over the Continent, and it became clear that the Allies were reducing the country into a railway desert. The heaviest bombing was reported to be north of Le Havre.

"It looks as though the invasion will be in the Pas-de-Calais," remarked François, standing next to Jacques, who sat at the table with papers and map unfolded in front of him.

"That may be, that may be," he replied looking intently at the map. He was deep in thought and only half-listening to what François was saying. He had received further intelligence about the landings, but was reluctant to volunteer this information to the others. Small crafts from the Royal Navy were seen making reconnaissance trips along the coast of Brittany checking sea currents and beach conditions. But the fewer people who knew about that the better. The excessive bombing in one area could be a decoy to distract from the real landing place.

"What's on your mind? The map in front of you is of the Eastern Front – the Allies won't be landing there."

"I know, that's not what I am concentrating on. It is the Eastern Front that intrigues me."

"How so?"

"I'm almost afraid to make another prediction. So far I have been wrong on all accounts. What seems obvious from a strategic and political point of view is not necessarily the move the Allies make. One has to believe that the Americans see no threat in Communism and Stalinism, otherwise the constant supply of weapons they keep pouring into the Soviet Union doesn't make much sense. The truth is that they are getting too strong and becoming a threat to us all. They have already started their advance into Romania, and have reached Czechoslovakia and forced the Germans to withdraw from the Crimea. They plan to start their summer offensive to coincide with the allied landings along the French coast."

Although the room was now filled with men of the Resistance, everyone was quiet. They were listening to what Jacques was saying, but it was not so much what he said but the way he said it which caused the silence. It was unlike him to be so vague, for he usually made a more positive statement on matters of strategy and politics, so this drew immediate attention.

On the map of the Eastern Front which lay open on the table in front of him, Jacques had drawn a line running from north to south beginning at Leningrad and ending at the Sea of Azov. The line represented the position at which the Russian 1943 autumn offensive had left the two opposing armies.

Léon was now standing beside François and with facial gestures made it obvious that he was trying to attract his attention. It was as though he did not want to speak, but he made it very clear that he was there to represent all the others. They felt uneasy. Moving his lips and expecting François to lip-read, he mouthed, "Ask him what's wrong."

François's eyes moved from Léon to Max, who stood nearby, then to the other faces in the room. 'Perhaps a word from Jacques at this point would be in order,' he thought.

Jacques was still looking at the map with a few notes beside him.

"How bad is it then?" said François, as though the conversation had never been broken off.

It made Jacques look up and he saw everyone looking at him, and he realised that the remarks he had made earlier on had caused his men to react. He cleared his throat once or twice before he began, because he needed a little extra time to sum up the situation and prepare a suitable reply to reduce the tension which his comments had induced.

"Well, if you all come a little closer, perhaps we can follow the Eastern Front together." He stood aside so that every man there would be able to see the map.

"The line I have drawn here is the position where the German and Red Armies stopped fighting after the Soviet autumn offensive. The fighting involved the whole of the Eastern Front. They liberated a lot of territory and their successes were very considerable, but for all that, we know the German Army is still intact."

His remark did not cause any surprise amongst the men, since they all knew exactly how he felt about the total destruction of the German Army, and they agreed with him on that point because it made good sense. With the German Army totally destroyed, nothing could stop Communism from spreading its influence across the whole of Europe. The communist-organised Front de l'Indépendence in Belgium was getting stronger and becoming a real threat to democracy.

"The Russians will start their summer offensive in early June. So will the Allies, with landings along the French coast, probably, as François said, in the Pas-de-Calais area," continued Jacques. "The general plan is to advance on both fronts simultaneously and squeeze Germany in a vice. On the surface it looks as though the Allies are not particularly concerned which of them gets first to the centre of Europe – the Americans, the British or the Soviets. They give the impression that all they want is to terminate the war as quickly as possible and save lives but, as you have heard me say before, the idea of winning battles is so that you yourself are in a favourable strategic position. Nothing has changed: Vienna is still the centre of gravity strategically and politically. To get there first is paramount if you want to be the one exercising the greatest influence after the war is over. If the Americans don't see it, I'm sure Stalin does. But I have a feeling that the American chiefs of staff *are* aware of its importance."

"Surely, if it's known that Stalin sees it, then the Americans must realise it," remarked François.

"No, I disagree with that – we all know that the general public, unless properly informed, is ignorant of what is going on, until such time as the American press informs them. So far the American newspapers are not saying anything against their Soviet allies, which gives the general public the impression that the Soviets are our true allies and that they are a friendly, practically democratic, partner. So to them it doesn't matter that the Soviets will be the dominant power in Europe. The other point we cannot dismiss from our minds is that the Americans are engaged in a war in the Far East, and that most likely every family has at least one member fighting there, which makes it their main concern. But I have a strong feeling the American chiefs of staff are being advised of the European fears by the Allies who see the danger. We know for sure that the prime minister of Spain is trying hard to make them see the threat the Soviets present if allowed to penetrate deep into Germany. We in Europe see things differently. All through our history we've been warned against the danger of Mongol hordes crossing the River Oder in Germany to advance into Europe as far south as Spain. Russia is a country constituted to hide everything from public knowledge, and as far back as Peter the Great their policy has been one of conquest. To allow the Soviets to advance deep into Germany now would be putting ourselves in the position Europe was in during the time of Charlemagne in the eighth century. A Europe dominated by Stalin and his Bolshevik followers would be as bad or even worse than being occupied by Hitler and his Nazism."

"You said that the German Army is still intact along the Eastern Front. Does that mean you're of the opinion that the Allies will be in the centre of Europe first by invading along the French coast, and that they will fight their way across all of Western Europe, and still get there before the Soviets do? I thought that we all agreed the Allies will be lucky if they reach the holiday resorts of the Black Forest before the winter." It was Léon who addressed Jacques thus.

"No, my opinion hasn't changed there. The Allies will find it a long and costly battle through Europe, but in addition to these landings, which are code-named 'Overlord', the Americans are also launching another operation, code-named 'Anvil', and that is in Italy. General Alexander has been nominated to command this campaign. The aim is to carry out amphibious operations along the coast of Italy, in order to reach the River Po valley, here, and the Lublyana gap to cross the mountains, there." Jacques was pointing at these places on his map, so that everyone could follow what he was saying. "From there they will cross into Austria to reach Vienna. Already we've heard they are making good fast progress toward Rome. In my opinion that's the real plan of operation adopted by the Americans. They only agreed to the landings on the French coast in order to keep friendly with Stalin, who insisted on it. He's not stupid – he wants the other Allies to be as far away from Vienna as possible, but keeping the Soviets on our side until Hitlerism has been stamped out is most important. I can see the reasoning behind these landings in France very clearly, even though they can't see that Stalin is being two-faced."

"Do you think the Germans will carry on fighting with such odds against them? Having to fight on all sides and being harassed by the Resistance everywhere?"

It was Max who was talking. He was leaning over to get a good view, but he couldn't make out why the Germans would carry on with the odds stacked against them.

"Men like Hitler can't give up, Max. They have to fight, win or lose. Besides, the Allies don't even talk of peace with him. It's unconditional surrender or nothing."

"Why is this unconditional surrender so important to the Allies? Haven't they learned from history? Don't they realise that demanding such a surrender awakens a strange spirit in men, where they'd rather die than accept it? It's like the words of Macbeth: 'At least we'll die with harness on our back.'"

"There's a lot of truth in what you just said, Max. Even we realise that the Allies are not differentiating between the mass of the Germans who don't want Nazism and those who do – they've all been lumped together. Kill them all and the masses will turn to Hitler as their only hope for the future as a nation. I think we understand this more than anyone else, because we wouldn't stop fighting either if we were ever to fall under Communism, heaven forbid."

"I don't think we'll ever come to the end of this fighting. We'll never get our freedom back again. This war has been going on for five years now, and things are no better now than at the beginning. Even if we do get liberated by the Allies, we'll still be fighting for our freedom, that's what you're saying, isn't it?"

It was one of the 'Group G' men, the same one who had been in the tunnel with Jean and Pierre when they were nearly caught by the patrol combing the forest. He had a desperate look on his face as he spoke. His eyes moved from one member of the Resistance to the other, as if searching to see if any of them felt the same way he did and were prepared to speak out. His fears were genuine. Five years of war, of which four had been spent in hiding, were beginning to take their toll. He was no weakling, but he was young and there had to be some hope for a future.

The point struck home. Several of the other members sided with him and expressed their fears as to the outcome of this struggle; they too saw no end to it. An argument broke out which threatened to split their loyalties.

M. Van Den Bos was quick to see the danger of fear spreading amongst the men. Words like those could easily start panic. He had been sitting in the back listening to what Jacques was saying.

"Now hold on, boys!" he shouted loud and clear. "A Resistance fighter who thinks too far ahead is likely to stumble on a few home truths – but let me remind you that nothing has changed since the beginning of this war. We're fighting for our freedom and that's exactly what we'll keep on doing. The side we're fighting for is the only one that will give us back our freedom – you all know that. The Allies are proposing to free us, and in that they will have our full support. How or when they do it is for them to decide."

The room went quiet then, as every man there turned those words round in his mind. What became clear was that human weakness had set in and from now on any further setbacks could drain their courage to carry on fighting, until the time came when they could once again accept that it was better to go down fighting rather than live under the oppression of an occupying army.

Mady's existence was almost unbearable, living in the house at Menton-Garavan with her stepbrother as head of the family. The rift between them had grown deeper since the day Pierre had attacked him. To make matters worse, he tormented her by making life miserable for her mother and her sister Dédé. He forbade her to ever see Pierre again or mention his name in the house, and made it quite clear that, in this, he would never change his mind until she repented or left the house.

The only news she had received about Pierre had been on two occasions, and that was by word of mouth through a friend of a friend. He wanted her to know that he was thinking of her constantly, that he prayed for her well-being and for the day when they could see each other again. He felt responsible for what had happened to her, and also for bringing the worst out in her stepbrother.

She often tried to get in touch with him, but she had a feeling that her every effort was intercepted by her stepbrother. It seemed that he could find allies everywhere who were only too eager to inform him in order to find favour in his status as the young Baron. She was a prisoner in her own home. This again was instrumental to her destiny of hearing God's call. She was in church more often and constantly prayed, in which she found consolation. She made up her mind that to become a nun was now most important to her, and she wanted it more than anything else on earth. Her father, who might have been able to stop her, was dead, and she had come to realise that the gulf between herself and Pierre had deepened so much that it had become impossible for them ever to be together in this life. She had always said to him that if she couldn't be with him, she would never turn to another man. If she couldn't be with Pierre then there was nothing to stop her from turning to her faith and the Church.

It was not a sudden decision, but one that she had turned over and over in her mind during the time she lived in Menton-Garavan. But, as the desire to follow her destiny grew stronger in her, so did her wish to speak to Pierre face to face to explain to him why she had reached this decision. She knew that it would be difficult for him to accept this and she was frightened of what he might do if he found out through a third person. The war had turned him to violence, and this made it important for her to see him and make him understand just how hopeless their relationship had become. The whole of her family had to be considered.

To see him became an obsession with her, and she was constantly looking for a way to go to the house at Boitsfort where she would be nearer to him. She hoped that by speaking to her stepbrother he might be willing to let her go, especially if she made a promise that it was to tell Pierre she would never see him again, and that this was the wish of her entire family. So far he kept silent but he had not dismissed it from his mind. His dearest wish was that Mady would make a suitable marriage to a rich young man one day, which could be to the advantage of the whole family. She was a beautiful and desirable young woman, and some of his closer well-to-do male friends had already shown an interest. This was important, because the family wealth was draining away fast: he was something of a gambler. If she was to tell Pierre she didn't want to see him again, then that would make life much easier for him. Unlike his father, however, he was not aware of Mady's strong religious tendencies, and it never crossed his mind that one day she could become a nun.

One day early in May, Mady was introduced to a man who had just arrived in Menton. He was, everyone said, a collaborator with the Germans. Ever since the beginning of the war he had been able to get papers to travel throughout Europe and continue with his business, that of making weapons, but to a very few he was known to be a double agent. He was in touch with the young men who had taken to the hills in France in the Rhône Valley, and had connections as far north as the Ardennes and the Black Forest. His contributions to the cause of freedom were invaluable.

Through him Mady learned about Pierre. No personal messages were passed, but she learnt that he had been wounded; how or where was not known. What was known was that he had made a complete recovery thanks to the treatment he had received from a doctor who was practising at the Edith Cavel Clinic in Brussels.

Mady confided to this man her decision to enter a religious order in Brussels, but, before doing so, she told him just how important it was to her to see the Pierre of whom he spoke, to tell him personally of her decision. So convincing was she in her plea that the man took note and more or less agreed to help her reach the house in Boitsfort.

"You've chosen a bad time to go all that way, Mademoiselle," he began. "The Allies are dropping a lot of bombs all over the country right now. Travelling by train is out of the question, but if you can get your brother to give his consent, you can travel with me – I'll be leaving here in two days' time. I must have his consent though – I can't afford to be reported to the authorities for any illegal kidnapping – and I must warn you and your brother that the journey is not going to be an easy one. Most of the time we'll be travelling by truck, but some of the way will be on foot and by horse-drawn cart. You'd better think about it carefully, Mademoiselle."

"I don't mind how hard the journey is. I'll wear proper clothing and won't be a burden to you, if only you will take me with you, Monsieur – please."

"All right, but you'd better have a word with your stepbrother, and I want to hear it from him that he agrees. You have to hurry because I must get all the papers in order to include you."

"Oh thank you, Monsieur! I'll meet you back here with my brother as soon as I can convince him of this."

The young Baron listened very carefully to Mady's request to be allowed to go to the house. The attitude he adopted was that of one who doesn't care all that much, but all the time Mady spoke he was thinking of the gains for himself. If she did renounce this vagabond Pierre it would be a big step towards a suitable marriage for her – he was already thinking of a candidate. Mady was almost on her knees to him, pleading, begging, promising. Finally he gave his consent: her journey to the house was to take place at long last.

It was, as the man had said, a most difficult and dangerous journey. They had to shelter from the worst bombing the country had suffered so far in this war. To make matters worse, the man had to follow a route which took them a long way across France. When they reached Avranches, then Coutances, the bombing increased. From there they were forced to make a detour to avoid being killed before reaching their destination. Scurrying along the streets in Coutances, they moved from building to building up the steep hill and narrowly escaped being killed by falling masonry. From there they travelled on to Alençon, then via Chartres to Paris and so on to Brussels. A frightening journey, one which Mady would not soon forget.

It was around the time when Mady reached the house at Boitsfort that her step-brother learned of her strong religious tendencies and her plans regarding the Church, and that her reason to make the journey to the house was to speak to Pierre personally and explain her decision to become a nun. He was told this by his stepmother at the same time as he told her that he would invite one of his well-to-do friends to the house on Mady's return, the intention being that, if it was agreeable to both of them, he would give him her hand in marriage. The revelation that she wanted to become a nun hit him like a bombshell.

"The lying wench! The deceiving little brat! The..." There was no end to the names by which he called her after realising that he had been tricked into giving his permission to let her undertake the journey. His immediate reaction was to write a message to be sent by whatever means possible to Belgium, and order M. and Mme Gérard, who were the servants living at the house, to keep Mady prisoner. He also ordered them to forbid her to see a young man called Pierre Fenbeau and threatened them with immediate dismissal if his wishes were not obeyed.

On the afternoon of June the 5th Pierre was told by his friend who lived near Mady's house at Boitsfort that she was there especially to see him. He also told him that she was desperate and had to see him urgently. That same day M. and Mme Gérard received a note from the young Baron Declerq to keep Mady a prisoner until further instructions from him. To complicate matters even more, Jacques had been instructed by the Belgian Government in exile to be on standby for immediate orders; this meant an invasion. Pierre, on receiving this news so unexpectedly through his friend, became unreasonable. The first thing he said to Jacques was that he had to leave immediately for Boitsfort. Jacques denied him that request because he was waiting for important instructions from England.

"We need you here, Pierre. We'll be asked at any time to go into action. I think the target will be the bridges in the area of Maastricht and you're the only one who knows that area."

All this time Nadia stood close by, listening to what was going on. She saw the state Pierre was in upon receiving news from Mady. During the whole of his convalescence he had never once spoken of her or said how he felt about her, and she had never had the courage to write to him about it. Now it was plain to see that he had never forgotten Mady and that she was foremost in his mind.

Nadia learned from bitter experience. The day she discovered that Pierre was in love with Mady her world fell apart. Since then she had hardened and told herself that she would never be hurt again, nor would she ever settle for second best. Unnoticed, she turned away from the room to retreat into her own silent world. Jeannine was the only one who saw her move away and understood the agony she was going through, but there was little she could do. Nadia was best left alone at a time like this.

Pierre was still moving around like a caged animal; he kept on hitting everything that stood in his way with his fist. Then suddenly he turned round as though he could stand it no longer and disappeared. He left the villa and ran in the direction of Boitsfort. Breathless, he arrived at the house and stood there for a long time to recuperate from his ordeal. He had not controlled his breathing and felt the worse for it. He rang the bell and waited. From within came voices. One was Mady's; he recognised it. There was a lot of shouting but no one came to open the door.

In the house Mady was locked in her room. As soon as the doorbell rang, M. Gérard had locked her bedroom door for fear that she might run to answer the front door. Their instructions were clear. She was to be kept in the house and was not to see Pierre. To go against the Baron's orders meant that their livelihood was at stake.

"Monsieur Gérard, Monsieur Gérard!" cried Mady from behind her locked door. "Please tell me – is it Pierre at the door? Oh please tell me."

Both M. and Mme Gérard were standing outside her locked door. Mme Gérard had tears running down her cheeks and she was trying hard not to make any noise. She held her hands over her ears to stop herself from hearing the pleas that emanated from within Mady's room. Mady was shaking and rattling the door:

"Please, Mme Gérard, tell me – is it Pierre? Please let me have a word with him! I promise not to run away. I only want to talk with him! Please !"

At that moment they heard glass breaking downstairs. M. Gérard ran down and when he reached the kitchen he saw a young man standing defiantly in front of him.

"Where is she?" yelled Pierre, squaring himself to his full height in front of M. Gérard.

"I beg of you, M. Pierre, don't try to see her or we will all be punished by the young Baron. His instructions are clear. She is not allowed to see you or speak to you. He will turn me and my wife out of our home if he finds out that we allowed you to see her. We have just received this letter written in his own handwriting. Here, read it." With that he pulled the letter from his waistcoat pocket and handed it to Pierre.

He gave a quick glance at it, then asked, "When did you receive it?"

"Early this morning."

"You haven't received this letter yet, do you understand? No one will ever know. All I want is to speak to her – she's made a long and dangerous journey to talk to me. It must be important. I swear, no one will ever know that I was here, and if they do, then we will say that I came here before you received the letter."

M. Gérard stood silently listening to what he was saying. Whilst Pierre was talking they could hear Mady pleading with Mme Gérard to open her bedroom door.

"Give me one moment and I'll speak to my wife."

When he reached the top of the stairs, he looked at his wife and nodded.

"Let him see her. We have found a way out of this – we haven't seen this letter yet – and no one will know."

"Oh Marcel, I don't think I could have stood it much longer anyway." Mme Gérard went to the bedroom door and opened it.

Mady practically fell out of the door straight in the arms of Mme Gérard.

"Thank you, oh thank you," was all she could say.

Pierre had followed M. Gérard up the stairs and stood on the landing waiting. Mme Gérard was holding Mady in her arms. She was so emotional that she found it difficult to speak.

"Forgive us, darling," she pleaded, "but we didn't know what to do. The Baron sent us such a threatening letter. If he finds out that we allowed you to see M. Pierre he'll put us out of the house – we have nowhere else to go. His letter didn't say why, except that we were to keep you in the house and not to let you see this young man. We had no idea. Please don't let him find out, darling – please! Your stepbrother can be so cruel."

" I know, Mme Gérard. Don't worry, he won't find out from me. I won't even tell him that I saw Pierre – but I *must* talk to him."

"All right. M. Pierre, we'll leave you alone to talk, but please promise not to do anything that might hurt us, I beg you," said M. Gérard.

They had every reason to be frightened. Pierre looked as though he was capable of anything. It was something about his eyes: one could see the hatred in them. Mady noticed it even more, because she knew him from before, when his eyes had radiated kindness and were full of a love of being alive. She turned to him cautiously, as though frightened of what he might do.

Pierre sensed something was wrong, but he was unaware that it was he who had changed and not Mady. They entered the bedroom, as they had been invited to do by M. Gérard. Once inside the room, he closed the door and turned to her abruptly,

"There's something wrong, isn't there?" were his first words to her.

He drew her close to him in a forceful way, forgetting that Mady was a gentle and sensitive creature.

"Pierre, don't frighten me like this! You're hurting me."

There was fear in her voice and she backed away. She was frightened that he was going to hurt her further.

It was then that Pierre realised that it was he who had changed. It was he who had turned to violence and he was being cruel to her for no reason.

"Mady, Mady!" he cried. "I'm sorry – I don't know what I'm doing! Please don't say that you're frightened of me – it hurts! It hurts. I know I've changed. I can't help it."

Mady realised for the first time what he had gone through. For over four years his entire world had been disintegrating. He had lost the security of his family, the love of his parents, had had to fend for himself and his sister, had been on the run for fear of being caught by the occupying army, and had lived perpetually in fear of being killed.

Mady looked at Pierre, who had turned his back to her to hide his face, and she suddenly saw that he had almost turned into an animal fighting for survival. Slowly she drew close to him from behind and put her arms tightly around him.

"I didn't know. I didn't understand how lonely you'd been, and what you'd been through. I was so far away."

He turned round to her and said, "I know what you're going to say. I know the reason for your visit. I've known it all the time –

ever since that day when we were in the church at Boitsfort, that day
when I burst into your house uninvited. You've made your choice,
haven't you? Somehow I think I've always known. Don't ask me
how – I just knew. Don't say anything just yet. Let me accept it."

She lowered her eyes when she realised that he had known all
along. They stood silently for a long time rocking slowly to and fro,
as he had done with Auntie Blewett, all those years ago. This time it
was a sign of lost love.

"I must get back to Groenendael," he said after a long silence.
"We're expected to go into action soon. Jacques will be wondering
where I am. I left without saying a word to anyone."

"Take care, Pierre, and thank you for understanding. You don't
know how frightened I was at having to tell you. Will you come to
my initiation if ever I am accepted to take my vows? I expect that's
quite a long way off yet, but will you come?"

"I wouldn't forgive you if you didn't invite me," he said with
glassy eyes. He made an effort to give her a smile, although his heart
was heavy with grief.

Gently he held her in his arms, as if he were saying goodbye to her
for the last time, then left without another word. The last memories
of his childhood which had so far given him the strength to carry on
had now faded away, and it fuelled his hate even more.

It was getting towards 10 p.m. that evening. Jacques was pacing
up and down the room. He was expecting instructions from the
Belgian Government in exile, but all he had learned so far was that the
landings were being delayed, mainly due to bad weather and tidal
conditions along the French coast. In addition Pierre had suddenly left
without saying a word, even after being told to stay put. He would
have liked to have been able to go over the details of the topography
around the River Meuse and the Albert Canal which Pierre so vividly
remembered and also to talk to him to see if he could remember
anything else which would be useful when the time came for them to
go into action. The men from 'Group G' were ready with all the
sophisticated equipment necessary to blow up bridges, but they also
needed as much information as possible about the layout of the
buildings and other obstructions in the area. Pierre had recently taken
a journey with Jean and made some drawings and maps of what he
saw around the bridges. These were to be used by 'Group G' during

their sabotage activities. Jacques would have liked him to brief the men once more and add anything else he could remember. The more information they had the better the chances of success without casualties.

It was just after 10 p.m. when Pierre returned. He looked mortified. On seeing him, Jacques was about to jump down his throat, but then he looked again. He couldn't help noticing that the young man looked completely disorientated. Jacques had always been of the opinion that Pierre was far too young to have been dragged into the Resistance and now he saw it even more. He looked as if he needed help and understanding and someone who could give him advice. What he needed was a father.

Jacques held back on what he was about to do; after all, Pierre had come back on time and it did look as if he had cut short something which must have been very important to him. That in itself proved he felt responsible for his own actions.

"Ah Pierre!" he began, with a tone as if he was pleased to see him. "How do you feel about going over these drawings and maps again, just to make sure that we've got it right? We're all keen to get it absolutely right – and who better than you?"

Pierre suddenly looked more like himself on hearing those words. The reception he received was not the one he had expected and it put a little sparkle back into his eyes. The questions which were then being asked during the briefing forced him to concentrate and to a certain extent made him forget his personal problems. Although he would not be involved in the more dangerous and complex work of dynamiting the bridges, should any of them be left standing or only partly destroyed after the bombing by the Allies, he did feel that he was playing an important role in working out the escape routes. When the job was done getting out was all important. To get back safely counted for a lot to the men of 'Group G', and he would be their guide.

Once or twice, as the conversation changed to other things, he looked around the room to see if Nadia was anywhere near, but she was not to be seen. He left the room and went to look for Jeannine.

"Have you seen Nadia anywhere?" he asked Jeannine, who was in the other room.

"Where have you been all this time? You're a fine one disappearing like that – and then calmly asking where Nadia is! She

was in the room when you got the news that Mady was in town. You
didn't see her, but she saw how you reacted. You never even turned
to her. All you were concerned with was getting to Mady. I saw her
leave after she realised just how much that girl means to you – and
believe me she looked hurt. Did you ever think of telling her how you
feel about Mady? You haven't exactly been fair to her. You made
her feel you loved her – we all saw that. To run off like that without
bothering to explain what it was you felt for Mady, or what it is you
want from her, was not exactly the thing to do – you could have
explained or said something. You let her draw her own conclusions
and that's exactly what she did. There's something you should know
about yourself, Pierre. You don't talk to people about yourself, you
don't tell them how you feel yet you take things for granted, you
expect them to know, but believe me being nice is not enough. You
must talk to people."

Jeannine was not trying to be nasty to him – she only wanted him
to realise what he had done. But he had gone through a difficult time
and he was in a strange frame of mind. Physically he had grown up,
mentally he had not. Where love was concerned he was only just
beginning to learn. What his sister was telling him now made him
suddenly realise. It was as if he was being forced to understand love
in one lesson, not explained through words, but through feelings. He
knew there was love towards people, the love he had for his parents,
for animals, then there was the love he had for Mady, innocent and
pure. But nothing compared with the love he had for Nadia, and what
Jeannine was saying was that it was too late now. He had driven her
away.

He did exactly what Jeannine was accusing him of. Instead of
talking and asking advice or seeing if anything could be worked out,
he remained silent. His face turned grey with guilt, or was it
remorse? It was hard to tell. He turned away from her and headed
for the back door, as though he were going to leave; probably to look
for Nadia.

At that precise moment the telegraphic machine, which was in the
other room, began sending out Morse code messages.

"This is it, lads! It's from headquarters. The orders have arrived
– the invasion is underway! We're being asked to go into battle as
from midnight tonight."

It was Jacques who was calling out loud and clear for all to hear, having been handed the piece of paper with the deciphered message.

"Pierre, don't leave now!" Jacques just caught a glimpse of him going to the back door. He was about to close the door behind him, but stopped. He hesitated for a moment, then came back into the room to join the others.

It took only half an hour to finish preparations and Jean's truck disappeared into the night under the light of a full moon, moving towards the area of the River Meuse and the Albert Canal, with the men from the Légion Nationale and 'Group G' on board. Jean's cover, should they be stopped by the Germans, was that he was on his way to the early market at Namur with a load of vegetables. His papers said he was a market trader, and his truck was loaded carefully so that it looked full of such merchandise.

The morale of the men was getting better. They were hiding in a big farm a few kilometres from Liège, and the news which reached them was that all went well for the Allies. General Montgomery had firmly established his bridgehead.

On June the 13th something strange happened. For over two years they had been listening to rumours of new weapons being developed: pilotless planes carrying enormous warheads; atom bombs that could bring about the end of the planet.

It was in the early hours of the morning when they heard a strange noise in the sky. It didn't sound like a plane, but it came from above. It sounded like consecutive explosions following each other very rapidly and it gave off a rattling noise. They looked up to the sky and saw what looked like a plane, leaving a trail of fire behind its tail as it moved at an unbelievable speed. It was flying in a straight line towards the west.

"What was that, Jacques?" asked the men once they were back inside the farm.

"That was a pilotless jet-propelled plane. We've already been told about these new weapons, but so far they've only been testing these things and failed. This is either another test or it could be the real thing."

"Are they very destructive?" asked Jean.

"Well, they carry a warhead of a thousand kilos. This could change things – we could be entering a completely new type of warfare."

M. Van Den Bos was looking around at the men while Jacques talked. He had been right the other day when he noticed that human weakness had set in. The sudden change in their attitude, as they listened to this bad news, convinced him of it, but since everyone remained silent and quiet he didn't make any comment. During the silence both he and Jacques looked at each other, and seemed to have reached the same conclusion, but it was best left alone for the time being.

It was in the beginning of July that their desperation was brought out into the open. The campaign in Italy under the code name Anvil, where General Alexander was making such good progress towards the centre of Europe, and on which Jacques had pinned great hopes for the Americans to be first in Vienna, was suddenly wrecked. Alexander was ordered to withdraw most of his men for the invasion of southern France and this made it impossible for him to reach Vienna before the Soviets.

The only conclusion which could be drawn from this was that the American chiefs of staff did not understand the importance of reaching Vienna first. In addition the Soviet summer offensive proved devastating to the Germans and their allies. It was worse than anything they had experienced so far and there seemed little doubt now that the Red Army would be entering deep into Europe. The prospect of a Soviet army occupying their country brought on a feeling of fear, but they also felt a rage growing in their hearts.

"What is it we're fighting for?" shouted one of the men of the Légion. He was frightened and confused.

If the campaigns and invasion by the Allies did not bring back their freedom, then why should they fight at all? It was a question asked by all. Would Hitler's new weapons force the Allies to reconsider their demand of unconditional surrender? If that were to happen, would it mean that their future would be one of being governed by the Military Governor Von Stuelphagel or something similar, continuing to live under the oppression of a foreign power? Or if the Soviets were to penetrate as far west as the North Sea and the Atlantic Ocean, how intolerable would that be?

These changes in the continuation of this war provoked strong feelings amongst the members of their small group, who now showed their true fears. It lasted for several hours. Finally the arguments reached a point where M. Van Den Bos could seize the moment he

180

had been waiting for to revive in them the will to fight, to make them see the reality of their position. Was it better to go down fighting or live under an oppressor? That's what it was all about.

"Now listen, all of you," he said, bringing down both his fists hard on the table to make them pay attention, after choosing the exact moment where the point he was about to make would have its full impact. "This war has come to us, my friends. None of us wanted it. We must choose a side. We all know what we had before the war, and we all know what it is like now. We must choose. Some of you have been with us for four years now and I know you all as I know myself, and this is what I say: like our ancestors I prefer death to slavery." He spoke clearly, pausing as he spoke and looking every man straight in the eyes, as though he were trying to reach deep into their souls.

The silence was almost deafening after all the arguments that had gone before. Then, as if with one voice, they shouted:

"We fight!"

This was followed by a series of handshakes, as if to create a new kind of brotherhood.

It was over two months since the men had left Groenendael. So much was happening that they had only been able to make one or two visits back, and then only for a very short time. Nadia had not been included in the latest sabotage activities for they were considered too dangerous. She hadn't seen Pierre since the day he had heard about Mady. She reached the conclusion that he was heartbroken over that girl, and since she avoided him it became a hopeless situation. Pierre was consumed with guilt and remorse and looked as if he had lost all the will to live. François noticed that on several occasions he took unnecessary risks during the fighting. He always took great precautions when leading the group to safety, but it was on those odd occasions where it was not even necessary for him to be around that he took risks. François worried so much that he thought it advisable to speak to Jeannine, to see if she could talk to Pierre and find out what it was that made him behave so unnaturally.

"I'll try talking to him, but he doesn't seem to pay much attention to what I say," she said when he spoke to her about it. "I think I know what the problem is."

"Do you think he's unhappy about being asked to join in this guerrilla warfare?"

"No, it has nothing to do with that. It's the two girls in his life which make him behave like this – he's lost both of them now, and he doesn't know what to do about it. When it comes to opening his heart to anyone he doesn't know how. Just how much it's affecting him is hard to tell, but it must be worse than I thought. There is only one person who could help him, but she has her own problems and can't."

"Do you mean Nadia?"

"Yes. Have you seen the change in her? She has completely withdrawn into herself: she doesn't show any signs that she wants to be approached about Pierre. In fact she too behaves unnaturally. I think it's serious. She suddenly wants to find her family. I know she is seeing M. Pettit, who has been helpful before, and doesn't seem to care about the risk she's taking in doing so. If anyone found out that she is Jewish, she could be picked up and we would never know about it."

"Yes, but she carries forged papers that say differently and they look very convincing."

"I'm still worried, François – anything might happen. Perhaps it would be a good idea to tell her how much Pierre loves her and that his guilt is driving him to near suicide. Perhaps you could speak to her. Being his sister, she might think I am on his side and only protecting him."

"Well, I'll try if you think it would do any good, but you had better tell me the whole story about those two girls in his life, or I won't be able to build up a case for him."

Jeannine then told him from the beginning what Mady meant to Pierre, and how it was that he realised the love he had for Nadia was greater, or at least different, from what he felt for Mady.

"All right, I'll do my best, but heaven knows when I'll next see her. We're moving out again in two hours, and I could be away for some time."

Nadia was taking a risk by going to see M. Petitt without making some enquiries first, and she knew it, but the way Pierre had reacted when he heard about Mady left her very low in spirit. There was no doubt in her mind that he was still very much in love with the girl.

Perhaps she should have made an effort to ask him about it while he was convalescing, but it seemed pointless now: she knew the answer.

Confused and sad, she began to feel lonely and her thoughts turned once again to her lost family: she missed them enormously now. It was this which made her take the risk of seeing M. Petitt, hoping that he might help her to trace them. Luckily for her, he was the kind of man who would help. Already he had assisted Jews in hiding and obtaining news of their loved ones.

Through him she learned of an exceptional case which had remained a mystery ever since it had happened. It was that of a little baby who had been abandoned. It happened about the same time that her family were removed from their home by the Gestapo. The story was that when a truckload of Jews, who had been snatched from their homes, passed through the village of Overijse, a woman had thrown her baby from the truck as it pulled away. The baby was apparently still alive when it was found by one of the villagers, but was never heard of again. It was also said that the baby was a little girl with a birthmark.

On hearing this Nadia became very excited. It seemed too much of a coincidence: the baby girl, the date it happened, the birthmark. Her baby sister had also had a birthmark. Could it have been her mother who had made this desperate choice to throw her baby from the truck, in the hope that she might be saved?

M. Petitt advised her not to attach too much hope to all this hearsay, but he promised that he would make further enquiries as to what became of the baby girl after she was found.

Nadia was overexcited in spite of the warning he gave her. She couldn't help it, she was clutching at the possibility that this little girl could be Julienne. It also took her mind off what had happened between Pierre and herself: it made it more bearable, for he was no longer her sole reason for living.

Weeks passed without much success. M. Petitt had followed up several leads about similar cases of abandoned babies, but they did not help with finding baby Julienne. Nadia had even made several journeys with him.

"It does worry me so the way she follows M. Petitt in this search," said Jeannine to François on one of those rare occasions when he came to the villa for a rest. "I tried to warn her, but she is so determined to find her little sister."

"The baby would be at least six years old now – she was only an infant when Nadia last saw her – so how will she recognise her?" remarked François.

"Julienne had a birthmark – that's bound to help. But the fact that she is letting it be known that she is of Jewish origin worries me most."

"Let's hope the Gestapo are too busy saving themselves rather than looking for more Jews to persecute," was the comment François made.

The Partisans

As was predicted, the Allies found it a long and costly battle through Europe. Eventually on the second of September they crossed the frontier into Belgium. It was the British Second Army which liberated Brussels. Groenendael and the village of Hoeylaert were transformed beyond recognition. During the night the Germans had withdrawn in a great hurry and the whole area was thought to be free of the occupying army. Some of the more prominent citizens were looking at restoring some sort of administration. Pierre, François and Léon went to the village to see for themselves. It looked as though there was total anarchy and the breakdown of everyday life. There was not a single uniformed person to be seen. The area was crowded with self-styled partisans wearing the Tricolour armband. They were executing a kind of justice, but mostly they were using the liberation as an excuse to settle personal scores. Women who were known to have collaborated with German soldiers were dragged from their homes, and their heads were shaved publicly in the village square.

The men who were executing this type of justice, they observed, were those who had joined the Resistance a week or a day before. To them they looked more like a band of gangsters and delinquents, roaming the streets, spreading fear and looking very dangerous.

Food was urgently required and there would be a shortage until the British Army undertook the supply of it.

Around twelve noon shouting was heard coming from the direction of the Chaussée de Bruxelles, made by a group of people moving towards the village square. It drew everyone's attention and the villagers were beginning to gather around.

The commotion was created by three or four young men who were shouting at the top of their voices:

"The Germans are in the forest! They are hiding there. Let's go and flush 'em out. They're the same ones who have occupied our country for all these years. Are you going to let them get away? Let's kill 'em!"

The crowd now gathered in the square began to stir and respond to the hatred being generated by such talk, as if they had become intoxicated by the sudden liberation of their country and wanted to take part in the killing that was going on. Already one civilian who was known to have collaborated with the Germans had been executed, and the way things were going there could be more.

Pierre couldn't believe that they were the same young men with whom they had mingled during the war years. What was it that made them suddenly turn to violence this way? What were they trying to prove? He would never admit, of course, to the change the war years had brought about in himself.

The situation worsened when two trucks appeared in the village square.

"I don't believe it!" said Léon. "One of the trucks is Jean's!"

"No! You've got to be wrong! Jean wouldn't join a mob like this."

"I tell you that's his! Over there, look for yourselves."

"He's right, you know," replied François. "That is his truck."

When they reached the truck it was Jean who saw them first.

"What are you three doing in this crowd?"

"We were just about to ask you the same thing," replied Léon. "We couldn't believe it when we saw your truck."

"I've been pushed into this. The mob were going to confiscate my truck. They say someone saw German soldiers hiding in the forest. I don't see anything unusual about that. When an army retreats in a hurry as the Germans did, some of them are bound to be left stranded. They were getting rough with me because I refused to let them drive my vehicle. I'm not letting any of them drive – there probably wouldn't be anything left of it by the time they had finished: none of them hold a licence! Look at them! They're burning up with a fever to kill. I came along myself, that's why I'm here."

No sooner had he finished his sentence than these self-styled partisans climbed into the trucks.

"Come on, let's go! We've wasted enough time – let's flush 'em out of the forest!" shouted one of them who had taken charge of the mob. He was a rugged-looking type with tanned skin and a gruff voice. At the same time he ordered Jean to get into his cab and drive on. All three of his friends quickly climbed in beside him: they were not going to leave him alone with these men. All were armed with guns and hand grenades left behind by the Germans. The one who had taken charge decided that the best place to start was at the Château Prince Léopold, which the Germans had occupied for such a long time.

Once they entered the forest at the château, they began to shout and scream, hitting the sides of the trucks with their guns. The noise created by the mob was enough to scare anyone, and the idea behind it was to bring out any Germans who were there.

They drove along the path leading to Boitsfort, where Pierre and Mady had walked to see the carpet of bluebells that day when she had felt so frightened at the thought of the coming war. At various points they turned either left or right to comb the more remote parts of the forest, but there was not a soldier to be seen. Eventually they turned back towards the main road.

When they were on the main road they saw a boy of about eleven or twelve years of age, riding his bike for all he was worth. He was coming from the opposite direction to the trucks. When he came close, he shouted, "I've seen German soldiers over there!" and he turned around and pointed in the direction of Groenendael.

"Where exactly were they, boy?" asked one of them.

"Near the Château-de-Groenendael, more to the right in the botanical garden where the Germans had their observation tower."

"You go home now, boy – don't stay in this area. It's too dangerous for you."

The boy stood looking for a while with his feet on the ground, half-sitting on his bicycle with his eyes wide open, as the trucks drove away in the direction he had pointed out.

When they reached the area they started a commotion again, shouting, screaming and banging against the side of the trucks.

François couldn't see the reason for it.

"We know where the Germans are, so why all this racket?"

"I think we've got ourselves a very frightened group of men here. Most of them only put the Tricolour band on yesterday, and we're probably up against trained soldiers."

Jean looked at all three and said, "I'm stopping this truck and taking charge of these partisans. It's obvious they haven't given this situation any thought whatsoever. Are you all with me?"

"Yes, we're with you. They'll only get themselves killed if we don't do something," replied François. "Let me talk to the one who seems to have taken charge – I'll try and talk some sense into him."

Jean stopped, knowing that the truck behind him would have to do the same. François jumped out as quickly as he could.

"Hold on, men, we must talk. We could be up against a German panzer division or just ordinary soldiers left stranded, but until we know for sure you could all get killed – we haven't got a hope against tanks. Let me talk to your leader first and work out some plans. To go straight in without knowing the facts is sheer suicide."

Stopping the trucks so abruptly had put an end to the shouting and banging, and François's warning was heard by most.

"Hey, Alfonse! This guy has a point," shouted one of the partisans, looking round at the man who had taken charge.

"Well if you're so clever, what do you propose we do?"

"I'll tell you what we'll do," came Jean's voice from the other side of the truck. "We send in a scout to see what's what, and if there's a panzer division, we'll high tail out of here, that's what we'll do."

Alfonse had little choice but to listen, because all the men gave a vote of approval to Jean's proposal. It took a while as they all looked at one another to see who would volunteer to go ahead and investigate.

"I'll go," said Pierre. "I know this area like the back of my hand."

Again François noticed Pierre's willingness to take unnecessary risks and put himself in the front line when there was really no need for it. Most of the men were locals, and knew the area as well as he did, but before anyone could say another word he had gone.

Pierre didn't volunteer for any special reason, except that when there was this pause he had already visualised the terrain which lay between them and the observation tower and had worked out a safe way of approaching so that he would have a good view. As Jacques said, when it came to topography, Pierre was a natural.

From the spot he had chosen, he could see the tower and the area around it. He saw the movement of men in grey uniforms; they were Germans, and he was certain that he recognised the uniforms of German NCOs. So far he could only count five men moving around. He waited a while longer to make sure there was no other movement in the area. When he was satisfied that those were the only soldiers there, he returned to the trucks. He walked straight up to Jean to make his report, but Alfonse made sure that he wasn't going to be ignored.

"I'll listen to what you have to say, young man," he said in his gruff voice. He was still moving towards Jean and the rest, but François pulled the other two over towards Alfonse. The last thing they wanted at this time was a clash of personalities and authority; it satisfied Alfonse.

"Five men. I've seen five soldiers, no more. They wear the uniform of NCOs – they must be the engineers in charge of exploding the ammunition stacked in the forest, the explosions we heard throughout the whole of last week. They were probably left behind in the retreat from here last night."

Pierre was precise in his report, and added the conclusion he had reached to explain the reason for the few Germans being there alone.

"Are they armed?" enquired François.

"Didn't see any."

"Come on, men, we've got ourselves an easy catch here. Let's go and get the German bastards!" shouted Alfonse, who already saw himself as the village hero.

"Why don't we wait until they surrender?" interrupted François. "They're in no position to do any harm."

"Wait until they surrender? They'll probably blow up the whole village with all that ammunition lying around in the forest! Come on, men, let's get 'em! Stay with your truck if you haven't the stomach for it."

It was too late for any further reasoning. Urged on by the other four young men who had stirred up the hatred in the village and who were also intent on becoming the toast of the village, they rushed towards the tower. The noise they made was enough to warn anyone a mile off. When they reached the area, there were no German soldiers to be seen. Alfonse gave the signal for everyone to halt and take cover.

"Where were they when you saw them?" he asked, turning to Pierre.

"Over there – eleven o'clock – close to the foot of the tower."

At least one minute passed, during which time all eyes were directed to the tower, then suddenly, much further to the right, there was movement. One soldier holding a pole with a white handkerchief tied to the top came into view from behind a ridge.

"There they are behind the ridge," shouted one of the young men.

"Hold on there! That's the white flag of surrender! You're not just going to ignore it, are you? Uniformed soldiers come under the Geneva Convention," shouted François.

"Geneva Convention! We'll give 'em Geneva Convention the same way they would us if they caught us," shouted another of the young men.

All four then rushed towards the ridge. The soldier, on seeing the aggressive mood these armed young partisans were in, disappeared.

When they were within close enough range, two of them pulled the ring from their hand grenades and simultaneously threw them well behind the ridge. There followed an explosion which surprised most of the partisans.

"My God! What have you done? This is murder!" shouted François as he looked on in disbelief.

He ran forward to see what lay behind the ridge, and reached it just about the same time as the young men. All they saw was the damage done to vegetation, but there were no bodies.

"They were never here in the first place," said one of them.

Several minutes passed and everyone wondered what would happen next. They had all taken cover.

"Over there," whispered one of the partisans, pointing to the foot of the tower where they had first expected to see the soldiers.

Sure enough from underneath the tower came an NCO holding a detonator for all to see. He was the same loud-mouthed NCO who had nearly picked a fight with Léon in the café that day when the Italian soldiers were there. He pointed to the ammunition stacked around them and to the detonator which he now held, with the palm of his right hand on the plunger, as if ready to push.

The whole place went quiet. Not a sound could be heard, except for the wind in the trees. They had walked into a trap. These were professional soldiers they were up against, who had prepared themselves for such a group of partisans who would not behave like soldiers to whom they could surrender as prisoners of war. If they couldn't surrender as soldiers, then it looked as if they were prepared to die at their own hands rather than be slaughtered like animals and take all of their enemies with them. During the seconds that passed, the NCO was joined by the other four. Pierre now recognised another of the soldiers. It was Karl's friend. All five stood waiting for the partisans' next move. Then the loud-mouthed NCO spoke.

"We tried to surrender to you... but you are obviously not in the mood. Too bad. We all die... No use running. See for yourselves... There's enough ammunition here to blow up the entire area... even your village will be damaged by the explosion. We made our choice and now you make yours. Too bad if you don't speak German, because you won't even know what I am talking about."

"I speak German," replied Léon.

"We won't speak to anyone except him," replied the NCO, pointing at François.

He and François looked at one another:

"Do you want me to come with you?"

"No, stay here. We don't want to give them an excuse to press that plunger."

François walked towards the soldiers. His heart was beating fast, but he was trying to stay calm and stop himself from shaking. It wasn't easy. Unlike these men, he was not ready to die. He couldn't help wondering why it was him they wanted to speak to. It was the NCO who spoke first. François recognised him.

"Do you speak German?"

"Yes.

"Where... where have we met before? I recognise you," said the NCO as he looked at him with half-closed eyes.

"In the café near the Château Prince Léopold, you and your friends had a quarrel with Italian soldiers."

"Ah yes, now I remember. You stood up for your friend when I confronted him. Well, here we meet again. We saw what you did earlier on. You don't think like that group of wild animals who wouldn't hesitate to kill us – that's why we want to speak with you. We think you are forced into this situation, the same as we are."

"I have little control over these men, as you saw."

"We understand, but we think there is a way out of this, if you would co-operate."

"Well, tell me about it – how can I help?"

François felt a little calmer upon hearing those words: perhaps they wouldn't die after all. At that point the other, more senior NCO stepped forward: it was Karl's friend.

"Just before you and those men arrived, we saw English soldiers. They stopped at the Château-de-Groenendael. You see, we've been here so many years we know the entire area," he added. "We are soldiers and we will surrender to soldiers as prisoners of war – that way we have a better chance to stay alive. To you we would also surrender, but your friends out there wouldn't let us, of that we are certain. They are not in the mood to take us alive. If you agree to go and speak with the English, to explain to them the situation we find ourselves in, we will surrender to them. You can tell them we will personally defuse the explosive charges placed under the ammunition if we can surrender to them as prisoners of war. The alternative is that we die here as soldiers."

François nodded his head.

"Agreed. I'll go and speak to the British. I will convey to them exactly what you told me."

"Thank you, sir, and goodbye, whether we see each other again or not. Warn those partisans out there to stay put and not make one false move, otherwise we have no alternative but to explode the ammunition."

François turned round and walked back. They were all waiting anxiously, looking frightened and bewildered.

"What did they want?" asked Alfonse.

"They won't surrender to you, that's completely out of the question. You'd better tell everyone not to make one false move. They mean what they say."

He continued to tell them what they wanted him to do, then he added, "If all of you can stay perfectly still until I get back, then there's a chance we can come out of this alive. It's up to you to keep those young idiots under control," he added, turning to Alfonse.

He left immediately once he had made his point, and began the slow descent towards the Château-de-Groenendael.

As the NCOs had told him, the British were there at the bottom of the hill. Once he was on the road he made his way towards the parked vehicles.

"Can I speak to your commanding officer?" he said to a corporal who stood near one of the trucks. "My name is François Charlier and I am from the Belgian Légion Nationale."

"What's it all about, sir?" enquired the corporal. "The CO doesn't come out just for anyone, you know – you must have a good enough reason."

"My men and a group of partisans are trapped on top of that hill – five NCOs from the German Disposal Unit have primed the ammunition stacked around here and it's ready to blow up. All it needs is for them to depress the detonator. They are experts and they are prepared to blow up themselves and the entire area rather than surrender to the partisans who want to kill them. I spoke to them personally, and they mean what they say. They are prepared to surrender to the British, and they will defuse the charges if they can do so as prisoners of war. Believe me, corporal, even you won't be spared down here if all that ammunition blows up."

"Blimey, mate, I'd say that's good enough reason for me to take you myself to see the old man! Follow me on the double. He's over there in that building," replied the corporal, pointing to the château.

The urgent message was passed to a major by the corporal, who went inside to inform the CO. He returned almost immediately with the colonel. It was Major Aue, who had returned, but he was now a colonel.

"What's this I hear about the Germans being ready to explode ammunition?" he said as he walked up to François.

He repeated what he had told the corporal and added, "Those partisans only joined the Resistance a day or two ago. I can't say what they'll do next, but one false move from them and the NCOs will assume the worst."

Colonel Aue said little but he was taking note.

"Up that hill, eh?" he said, as he looked in that direction. "Is that the top of an observation tower I can see above the treetops?"

"Yes it is, sir. That's where the five NCOs are, probably watching me."

"I think we'd better go and talk to these experts, since they seem to have the upper hand. We'll take some of the men." He turned to the corporal and said, "See to it, corporal. Twelve men with rifles and one round of ammunition each."

"Three men will do, Colonel – we don't want them to think we intend to take them by force."

"M. Charlier is right. They wish to surrender as prisoners of war otherwise they would have set off the detonators by now." Then, turning to François he added, "Show us the way, sir. We can't afford to waste too much time – nerves must be stretched to the limit by now."

When they reached the foot of the observation tower, all four NCOs were ready and waiting, one still holding the pole with the white flag attached to it. François did the translating. After a short talk, both parties were in agreement.

Colonel Aue turned to Alfonse who was pointed out to him as the partisan leader and said, "Send your men home, sir. We'll take over from here – we'll stay until all the ammunition has been defused. Please thank your men for a job well done."

Alfonse's attitude changed completely as he listened to the Colonel. He smiled and thanked him. He returned to the men and repeated what the Colonel had said. Most partisans took this with a certain amount of pride, for it was something they could take back to the village and boast about, while others simply removed the Tricolour band from their arms.

The Colonel asked François if he would be prepared to stay a little while longer, at least until the German NCOs had finished defusing the charges, as he would need him as an interpreter. He agreed, so Jean, Léon and Pierre all stayed. Jean wasn't particularly interested in taking back the self-styled partisans anyway. During that time Pierre, who had recognised Colonel Aue, gave him all the news about his family.

"My goodness," said the Colonel, "I would never have recognised you. Pierre, you've grown up fast! Sorry to hear about your grandfather and your parents. I suppose they'll all be returning now. Remember me to your family – tell them I won't have time to visit them, but I daresay I'll be returning to this part of Europe one day."

Pierre then went to the men who were defusing the charges and walked up to Karl's friend. Their eyes met, but he stayed silent. He obviously didn't think it wise to shake Pierre's hand or make any other sign of recognition in case it would incriminate him in any way. It hurt Pierre. For a moment he didn't know whether to walk right up to him or not, then he thought that perhaps Karl's friend was doing the right thing. He smiled when he saw that he still had the same fatherly appearance and his eyes still seemed to be laughing.

In-mid September it was learned that the southern flank of the Germans on the Eastern Front had been changed dramatically by the collapse of Romania and Bulgaria. It was obvious that it would not be long before the Soviets entered Vienna, Prague and Berlin before the rest of the Allies. These events brought a rapid escalation of tension between east and west. It seemed as though suddenly the Allies saw the importance of Vienna as the political centre of the war in Europe. To the Resistance it was no surprise – they had seen it coming for a long time – but all they could do was pray that some kind of military occurrence would prevent the Red Army from occupying the whole of Europe. It was clear to them that at least one third, or perhaps half of Europe would come under Stalin's regime. Poor Europe, doomed to stay divided.

M. Petitt at that time had been able to find out that the little baby abandoned after being thrown out of the truck in Overijse had been taken to Antwerp by the woman who found her, for safety. Her sister had said that she would adopt the baby and bring it up as her own. Her sister and husband were known by the name of Vandervaeren. They lived in Zeil Straat in Antwerp. M. Petitt, accompanied by Nadia, made his way to see them. They were in Antwerp at the time when the fighting there was at its worst. Luckily the British 11th Armoured Division, together with the brilliant effort of the Resistance fighters, was able to take Antwerp and the docks undamaged.

It was on the 8th that he managed to persuade the family to agree to letting Nadia see their little girl. They were unwilling at first because they had always feared that someone would discover the baby had been found and they would have to return it to its rightful family, especially in view of the fact that they hadn't had the opportunity to have the birth registered, in case the baby was suspected of being Jewish and was killed by the Gestapo. M. Petitt promised to assist them in having the birth registered once the country was back to normal, and Nadia would be a vital witness in certifying that the little girl was without family. In addition, he made a further promise that Nadia would never take the little girl from them even if it transpired that she was her baby sister. Only then did they finally agree to let her see the little girl.

It was an emotional moment when they both stood at the door of the house in Zeil Straat. The thought that perhaps she was not the only one of the family who had survived made Nadia weak at the knees, and M. Pettit had to support her. He knocked twice at the door. A woman in her forties, with a beautiful smile and wearing a fashionable dress, answered the door.

M. Petitt, who had already met her, introduced Nadia.

"Mme Vandervaeren. this is the young lady of whom I spoke."

She looked at Nadia as though she almost recognised her. She had to admit to herself that there was a strong family resemblance between this young lady who now stood before her and her little girl.

"Come in, my dear," she said, taking Nadia by the hand. "You have great courage to come at a time like this. It would have been very bad if the Germans had managed to blow up the docks. Thank heaven it didn't happen – I think we can all breathe again. M. Petitt has told me of your affliction. It must have been terrible for you." Mme Vandervaeren spoke nervously.

Nadia smiled at her and entered with a gesture that meant thank you.

"Well, we won't waste any more time now," Mme Vandervaeren said. "She is in this room. We've already told her that a special lady, who has lost her voice, is coming to see if I could help in bringing it back – you see, I'm a nurse. We haven't told her anything else."

Nadia was led into the room where the little girl, now six years of age, was politely sitting on a chair waiting. Nadia didn't need to see the birthmark. Baby Julienne had grown, but her little face was still as she remembered it.

"My name is Yvonne," she said when she saw Nadia look at her. "Mummy told me you have lost your voice and that I mustn't ask any questions. My mummy is very good with sick people – she'll bring back your voice."

Nadia couldn't keep her eyes off her: she wanted to take her in her arms and burst out crying, but she held back. Little Yvonne was embarrassed as she felt herself become the centre of attraction and she became shy to such an extent that she quickly ran to her mother for reassurance.

After a while, when her emotional feelings were overcome, Nadia looked at M. Petitt, which was the signal for him to ask if she could see the birthmark in order to confirm that the little girl, now known as Yvonne, was indeed her baby sister.

He had spoken of this to Mme Vandervaeren, so it was no surprise to her when he said, "Just to confirm beyond any doubt, Madame, can we just see the birthmark?"

She gently pulled back the little girl's garment from her left shoulder, to expose the birthmark.

Nadia turned to M. Pettit with a big smile which said it all. It was her sister Julienne.

Having received reassurance that she would never put in a claim on her sister, Mme Vandervaeren insisted that Nadia stay for as long as she liked, and said that she would eventually tell little Yvonne Nadia was her real sister, but today was too soon.

"It looks as if I adopted another girl," she said, turning to M. Petitt with her beautiful smile.

On September the 14th everything at the house with the stables in Groenendael was in turmoil. News had been received that the Château-de-Dongelber, where Madeleine was held as a prisoner of war, had been liberated. She and all the other women were now free after many years of internment. She was expected to arrive at any time.

A Land-Rover had been laid on by the British soldiers, now billeted at the Château Prince Léopold, who had been invited on several occasions to the villa and were well acquainted with the hardship through which the entire family had gone during the years of occupation.

All the women – Yvonne, Isabel, Jeannine and Mme Van Den Bos – were doing their best to get the place looking respectable for Madeleine's return. None of the furniture in the house was hers, except for what was left behind by the German officers who had used the house as living quarters; some of the furniture was very good.

Isabel was in a terrible state. Although she was pleased that Madeleine was coming home after all these years, she could not forget James. He had not been heard of since the beginning of the war, but she had not stopped hoping that when all the fighting was over somehow he would come back. The British Red Cross were making every effort to find him, or at least to find out what could have happened to him.

Jeannine kept running to the window for every noise she heard made her jump, thinking that it was them. The exact time of their arrival had been left open. Eventually at 3 p.m. the large vehicle turned into the courtyard.

Madeleine came out of the Land-Rove looking bewildered, having been imprisoned for such a long time. Her eyes couldn't take in what was going on around her. The journey itself had been something of an experience. To her the house looked different: it was not the house she had left at the beginning of 1940. She had lost that bubbly enthusiasm which was once so much a part of her personality. Perhaps, given time, it would all come back.

Seeing Jeannine and Pierre so grown up and tall saddened her. It was not the way she had imagined it to be when the time ever came. She had expected them to be more like children.

During the hours that passed, whilst they were talking and reminiscing, she noticed how distant and disturbed they both were, especially Pierre. He seemed to carry a heavy burden, but to ask him now what it was that troubled him would have been wrong. It was far too early for her to resume her role as a mother: that would have to wait. She also felt that Pierre would go his own way to find a new life for himself. There was no one to pick up James's business at the stables where he had left off in 1940. There was no money and there was no way they could keep up the cost of running this big house with stables, short of a miracle. All these problems would have to be faced eventually. It was obvious that Isabel would have to be looked after. Madeleine had not heard from her husband for over a year now. He was known to be in a concentration camp in Eastern Europe, and it would therefore be the Soviets who would liberate his camp. It was said that they demanded full proof of identity before releasing any prisoners of war. They believed that some of the Germans who were guilty of war crimes had taken refuge in such camps, portraying themselves as prisoners of war of the Germans in order to escape punishment. George, although he was British by descent, had a very strong foreign accent when he spoke English and would have to prove his identity. By Eastern European standards that could take a long time.

While everything was going on around her, Madeleine suddenly realised that something was missing. It was Nadia, of whom they had spoken during her children's visit to her prison château, the young

Jewish girl whose family had been violently removed from their home and who had lost her voice through shock.

"Where is Nadia?" It was Pierre she was looking at. She remembered that it was he who was concerned about her. "I hope nothing has happened to her."

Something painful seemed to grip Pierre's heart when she asked the question. She saw it immediately. The whole of his being changed. He replied, but each word, she noticed, caused him pain.

"She's fine. She's in Antwerp. Something wonderful happened to her, but I haven't seen her since then. We're all waiting to hear from her."

Madeleine realised that she had touched on a tender subject. Nadia was the cause of Pierre's being distant and looking so disturbed. She lowered her eyes for a while, trying to work out what would be the best thing to do and how to find the right words. What could she say, now that the moment had come to reach out to him?

Jeannine broke the silence, and saved the awkwardness of the moment.

"Nadia has found her baby sister! She is still alive – that's why she is now in Antwerp," were her first words. Then she told her mother the whole story of Nadia's baby sister, or at least the whole of what she herself had learned. She also told her about Mady.

Pierre in the meantime had left the house – he wanted to be alone. He had lost his zest for life. He walked along the footpath in the forest which had always given him such pleasure in the past, but he no longer recognised the natural beauty it once held. The gentle valley with its lakes looked unfamiliar. He looked around as if he had been put on a planet without life.

Both Léon and François were back in Antwerp, their home town, and were reunited with their parents. They had both taken part in the fighting to save the docks from being blown up by the retreating Germans, and were proud of the fact that they had assisted in saving their town. The port of Antwerp was an important one capable of handling large merchant vessels. Very soon it would be open and then could cope with ten to twelve thousand tons of supplies a week.

Through one of the British soldiers who made the journey from Groenendael to Antwerp, François received a letter from Jeannine giving him the latest news about the family, but in particular it was to ask him if he could look up Nadia, who was staying for a while in Zeil Straat with her baby sister. She told him of her anxiety for Pierre. He stayed away from home for long periods and his behaviour gave everyone cause for concern. She was still convinced that the only person who could help was Nadia, and since he was aware of the love he had for her perhaps he could intervene and persuade her to go and find Pierre before it became too serious.

François hadn't forgotten the promise he had made to speak to Nadia, it was only that he hadn't seen her since Jeannine and he spoke of it. Zeil Straat was not too far away and he decided to go there without delay. He too had seen a great change in Pierre. He knew that he still carried the hand grenade which seemed to have become part of him, and it worried him.

It was M. Vandervaeren who opened the door. François introduced himself as one of the Resistance members of Groenendael, where Nadia had been in hiding. M. Vandervaeren knew about him because Nadia, unable to talk, had made a list of all the people who were with her throughout the war years, and she had also written a few lines about all of them.

"Ah, François the diplomat," was the way M. Vandervaeren greeted him with a smile. "Nadia doesn't talk but she writes about you. She's very clever that way."

François was in for a surprise when he entered the room where Nadia, her baby sister and Mme Vandervaeren were sitting. She no longer wore the boys' clothes which had become so much part of her. In fact he had never seen her wearing a dress. The one she was wearing now had been hand-picked by Mme Vandervaeren, and that, coupled with her long golden hair, made him look twice.

"You look stunning in that dress," he complimented, looking at her.

Nadia lowered her eyes. Then she made a little turn to show him the whole dress with a look indicating, 'Do you like me in this?'

François turned the conversation to the reason for his visit. When he mentioned the name Pierre, M. and Mme Vandervaeren sensed that there was something special about this person. Nadia had written very little about him, but the way she reacted now could only mean one thing at her age – love.

"Why don't you two move into the other room?" suggested Mme Vandervaeren. "You can talk more freely there."

François thanked her for her understanding, and they both went into the room.

Nadia had been looking at him ever since he mentioned Pierre's name. She was expecting the worst. 'What could be the reason for his visit? Has something happened to Pierre?' she kept thinking to herself.

François pointed to a seat for her and sat beside her.

"I came especially to speak to you about Pierre," he began. "Jeannine sent me a letter. She's very worried about him and asked me to come and see you. She believes that you are the only person who can help. I know about the problem through her, that's why she asked me to speak to you." François paused for a while then continued, "Pierre and Mady grew up together and believed themselves to be in love, as children do, but before they had a chance to find out whether theirs was true love, they were parted by the war. Pierre relived their relationship by remembering how it had been when they were young, so he never stopped thinking of her in any other way. They were children, in love with the idea of love. Since then he has made one or two big mistakes by being violent, which is how he has become due to the war. Her family would never accept him now. Mady came up especially to tell him of her decision to become a nun. It is what she really wants. It did not come totally as a surprise to him, but nevertheless it gave him a terrible shock. In the meantime he noticed you. I don't think he knew what love was until then. Now he does."

Nadia closed her eyes for a while. Was he going to say what deep in her heart she longed to hear?

François continued, "It's you he loves, Nadia. He hasn't been able to see you. He was taken away to Maastricht, and each time he returned home you were not there. He's come to the conclusion that it is too late now. He believes that you've been hurt too much and that he's lost you. Go to him if you love him – he needs you."

Nadia's heart was racing: she couldn't believe what he was saying. She picked up her pad and quickly wrote: *Take me to Groenendael.*

"He is not at home. Do you know where he could be?"

Nadia nodded her head eagerly in the affirmative.

"Come on then. The soldier is still in Antwerp – he'll drive you there."

For the first time Pierre saw himself as he really was: a cold. solitary young man. His life, which consisted of memories that he constantly relived, was pale. He had no education, not the education which has a basically sound purpose, education which is stern and profoundly conservative. He was a young man seen to attempt innovations; he had grown up with different ideas. He did not fit in with those who maintain that the fate of the nation depends on the education of youths. They don't accept an adult unless he is acquainted with the education of which they approve. Pierre's ideas would be considered revolutionary, and he would be seen as one who tended to anarchy.

Most of his dreams now lay shattered around him. Mady was no longer his, yet the more obvious it became to him that he would never see her again, the more radiant did the memory of her become. It was a strange feeling he could not explain, but Nadia was the cause of his depression. She was his weakness. He saw her as a woman – desirable, lovely – with whom he could face life. She could be his strength and drive. The war could last for a hundred years, and yet he would take on the struggle for no other reason than that she was by his side.

Carelessly, he let his head hang low. He could not find the will to run away and he could not find the strength to rise above it. The silence around him was absolute, as if a cloud of his own making was muffling humanity. He sat alone out there in the forest, an area of natural beauty, listening and thinking for hours. The memories of his childhood, which he tried to bring back, were now in fact a last glimpse of his past, and he was not sure that he would survive the tidal wave which came over him. He wanted to destroy himself.

The wind moaned through the trees. A storm was in the offing. Pierre wrapped his jacket tightly around him against the growing cold of the night. For a while his thoughts went to Mme Bronowska and her family. He had often heard her say 'You'll always find an open door amongst us – our custom is to treat everyone as a brother, if he respects our ways.' The thought comforted him. He smiled, then his smile became a chuckle.

It was an hour before dawn and the storm had passed, but Pierre was still in the forest. The first lights of a new day were breaking the darkness of the night, but by the time the sky lightened he had left his resting place and began to walk without knowing where to go – he just had to walk. He had always had a devotion to the dawn, but did not know why. It was a strange feeling that everything was at its best. He saw it as an uplifting of beauty, something the day that followed had yet to spoil. This feeling was not in his heart today as he walked. It seemed as though the awe inspired by the miracle of life had left him.

The day remained cloudy after the storm. He walked for some time then came to a halt. He sat down on the wet ground. Carelessly he unhooked the hand grenade which he still carried with him attached to his belt and began to play with it, letting it slip from one hand into the other.

"Here is the means to end it all," he said aloud.

At that same moment he looked up and was surprised to find himself sitting beneath the walls of the little chapel of Our Lady of the Lovely Scent. He had not realised that he had walked in this direction. An inner voice then spoke to him accusingly: 'The deed that you harbour deep in your heart cannot be committed here. This is a place where prayers are offered in the hope to receive life, not destroy it.' It pulled him out of this suicidal mood and it all suddenly became clear to him. What he should do was to stay alive, without expectation of reward or punishment. He began to talk to himself.

'I should be looking for happiness which is not the reward of virtue, but virtue itself. I won't find it with sorrow and sighing. This mood I am in is preventing me from acting. I want to find happiness, and I want to do the right thing. I... I... I... Oh please, Lady of the Lovely Scent, help me.'

Pierre was on his knees now, with the hand grenade slowly rolling away. Suddenly a noise from behind the chapel startled him. Someone was there, and he heard it just as he found the way to lift up his spirit. The noise came from behind the tall tree that stood nearest to the little chapel. It was someone about to say something, but unable to do so.

"P... P... Pi... Pi..."

He slowly walked towards the sound. He couldn't make out what it could be, except that it was made by a human being – of that he was sure.

As he came closer he was able to see more of what lay behind the tree, which at first was completely hidden from his view, and there he saw a young woman on her knees leaning against the tree.

It was Nadia, her eyes frightened and bewildered, looking up at him.

"Pi... Pi... Pierre!" She was trying to speak.

The sound suddenly escaped from her lips. It was not very clear, but she had unmistakably called out his name.

In no time he was there beside her holding her face in both hands, looking into those frightened eyes.

"P... Pierre, don't k... kill yourself." She fell against him, almost lifeless through the effort of speaking. Then she began to weep, but even the sound of her weeping came feebly from her lips.

Pierre could hardly believe what he heard: her voice was coming back. It was he who could not find the words to speak. All he could think of was the suffering he had caused her and now he was frightened that she might go into shock.

"Don't... Don't... I love you," she whispered, the sound of her voice becoming stronger, although it was still very faint. "I love you," she repeated.

Pierre was holding her close in his arms. He remembered Jeannine's words and her accusation that he did not speak to people. This time it would not be so.

"Nadia, everything today has turned out so wonderfully, so sweet. Let me talk and you listen. You tremble, you weep – I can feel it throughout your body. I love you. Never in my sweetest dreams had I foreseen this moment. I feel I must live – I feel my soul rising to the sky. How could I not have spoken of this to you before? I can tell you that I have always noticed you. Last month you changed your hairstyle. Your hair dazzles like a bright flame when the sun catches it. What words can I find at a moment like this? Please forgive me all this emotion but it is this sweet new sensation. I can be myself – it's quite wonderful. Nadia, Nadia, you have found your voice again. It's wonderful! Let us stay near and listen to the sounds of the forest without talking. You must not talk too much yet, but the sound of your voice is like music to my ears."

"Pierre, I love you. I'm stifling – my heart cries out your name. I've loved you more with every passing day."

A gentle breeze was moving the branches of the nearby trees and a lovely scent enveloped them, but they had hardly noticed. Their love made them feel wonderful. Somehow they sensed that everything would come out right in the end.